PRA

Salvaged

"*Salvaged* scared the hell out of me, and I write horror for a living! Madeleine Roux conjures real darkness with a brilliant novel that any fan of *Alien* will simply devour. Brava!"

> —Jonathan Maberry, *New York Times* bestselling author of *V-Wars* and *Ink*

"Elegant and inevitable, this is the prose equivalent of playing a survival horror game. Each piece feeds perfectly into the next. Beautifully written."

> —Seanan McGuire, *New York Times* bestselling author of *Angel of the Overpass*

"Madeleine Roux's *Salvaged* is a breathless, claustrophobic twist on the SF thriller, full of deep space dread, conspiracies and malevolent alien spores, with a woman at the center whose courage was forged in all-too-human trauma. This is the *Alien* we need right now."

> —Christopher Golden, *New York Times* bestselling author of *The Pandora Room* and *Red Hands*

"*Salvaged* is riveting and brutal, a study in scars. The masterful writing and bittersweet beauty of these characters will haunt you long after you finish reading."

> —Ann Aguirre, *New York Times* bestselling author of the Razorland trilogy

"*Alien* meets *The Expanse* in this nonstop thrill ride. Rosalyn is a reluctant heroine on the run from her past . . . her resourcefulness and courage lend this unconventional space opera depth and heart."

> —Michelle Gagnon, author of *Unearthly Things*

"Madeleine Roux's *Salvaged* is the fantastic sci-fi 'Beauty and the Beast' story you've always needed in your life."

> —Peter Clines, author of *Paradox Bound*

"Roux's *Salvaged* is a tale of creeping horror and daring love, heavy with the weight of loss and trauma. Spooky fungus in space, devastatingly intimate hive minds, terrifying resource management and shockingly sweet romance combine in this love letter to redemption and recovery (and mushrooms)."

—Caitlin Starling, author of *Yellow Jessamine*

"Roux delivers a feminist sci-fi with plot twists, gut punches and a female lead with the strength of resilience."

—Mindy McGinnis, Edgar® Award–winning author of *The Initial Insult*

"Part science fiction, part horror, part suspense, *Salvaged* is all awesome."

—Geeks of Doom

"The rich description dumps you right into the world of *Salvaged* and won't let you go. Roux engages all senses; this is sometimes a good thing, sometimes bad, always brilliant. . . . I loved it!"

—Mur Lafferty, award-winning author of *Six Wakes*

"From the first searingly brutal line Madeleine Roux seizes the reader by their space helmet and drags them screaming and flailing up into the air ducts of this deeply engaging story of deep space horror. . . . Truly remarkable and unsettling in the best of ways."

—Jordan Shiveley, cohost of the podcast *Caring into the Void*

"This entertaining, deeply disturbing and clever story hits all the right notes for those who like a little horror with their SF."

—*Publishers Weekly* (starred review)

"[A] solid piece of survival horror in space. The tension and desperation of the situation meshes perfectly with the characters' development as they struggle to stay themselves and survive." —*Booklist*

"*Salvaged* is entertaining, funny and frightening as we begin to care for the characters and despair for their chances of survival."

—*The Oklahoman*

Also by Madeleine Roux

SALVAGED

RECLAIMED

MADELEINE ROUX

ACE
New York

ACE
Published by Berkley
An imprint of Penguin Random House LLC
penguinrandomhouse.com

Library of Congress Cataloging-in-Publication Data

Names: Roux, Madeleine, 1985– author.
Title: Reclaimed / Madeleine Roux.
Description: First Edition. | New York : Ace, 2021.
Identifiers: LCCN 2021001469 (print) | LCCN 2021001470 (ebook) |
ISBN 9780451491855 (trade paperback) | ISBN 9780451491862 (ebook)
Classification: LCC PS3618.O87235 R43 2021 (print) |
LCC PS3618.O87235 (ebook) | DDC 813/.6—dc23
LC record available at https://lccn.loc.gov/2021001469
LC ebook record available at https://lccn.loc.gov/2021001470

First Edition: August 2021

Printed in the United States of America
1st Printing

Book design by Alison Cnockaert
Title page art: Abstract wave by s_maria/Shutterstock.

For Zeva, Jeremy and Christi,
who pulled me from the quicksand

We must come to grief and regret anyway—
and I for one would rather regret the reality
than its phantasm, knowledge than hope, the
deed than the hesitation, true life and not
mere sickly potentialities.

—A. S. Byatt, *Possession*

1

More than anything else Senna remembered the bitter silence. At some point during the night, everyone around her on the ship stopped breathing. The soft, human sounds of sleep had mixed with the reverberation of space outside the passenger craft, a lullaby of organic white noise that helped her drift to sleep, but once it was gone, the absence was far louder. Unmistakable.

It was like how she imagined the dead of winter, still and adrift, though Senna had never experienced a true winter herself. Her entire life had been lived in outer space and, more than that, in almost total confinement.

She had taken a pill and gone to sleep surrounded by life, then woke among the dead. Senna had rolled over, tossing restlessly, and felt her hand brush something cold and almost rubbery on the sleeping mat next to hers. Startled by the sensation, she jerked awake, and under the reddish glow of the emergency lights above, she found herself staring down into the open, glazed eyes of her best friend, Mina. The blood trickling from between Mina's full lips was as crimson as the emergency lights blinking overhead.

Senna gasped, and it was the only sound in the entire ship.

Oh my God. They're all dead.

"You can't leave me," she whispered to Mina. The fear made her tremble; the shock made her grab Mina by the shoulders and shake. Her bones were thin and birdlike, and her head swiveled back and forth as Senna tried to rouse her. Nothing.

A door opened across the room, and Senna whirled to face it, torn between the sudden knowledge that she was alone and now the worse fear that she wasn't, that whoever was responsible for all this death was still alive and with her. That she was next.

"Senna," she heard him say. "I didn't know you were awake."

Why was she the only one left alive? And why wasn't he surprised by it? She didn't know what to say. What *could* she say?

They're all dead, every last one of them, except for you and me.

"Hello? Lady? Earth to blondie."

She blinked, hard, gazing around not at the interior of a doomed passenger craft, but at an impatient barista glaring down into her face. Grabbing her chest, Senna nodded and waved at him, but the memory took its time fading away. One year ago. It still felt like she was living inside that moment, crushed on all sides by it.

I didn't know you were awake, Preece had said. To her, it still felt like she was deep, deep asleep. Dragged under.

"S-Sorry," Senna stammered. She hadn't been outside Marin's apartment in weeks. The neon haze of Tokyo Bliss Station hurt her eyes. A halo lingered around the barista's head, the self-driving coffee cart lit with an amber glow. "How much is it?"

"Ten for the drink," the barista replied. He was tall and thin, tattooed from the collar of his shirt and apron to his mouth. A series of scrollwork arrows pointed to the ring glinting in his lip. "Three for the cup."

Senna frowned up at him. "Three? Really?"

Rolling his eyes, he shrugged and handed her the mottled brown cup, frothy yellow liquid steaming inside. "Fine, no charge for the cup. Bring something reusable next time, okay? Anything else I can get you?"

Senna stared down into the drink, the familiar color and smell threatening to bring another wave of painful nostalgia.

Anything else, she mused. A new brain? A tranquilizer?

"No," Senna told the young man. "No, I'm . . . That's all."

"Just remember the cup thing," he muttered, tapping the scanner on the coffee cart counter, waiting for Senna to hold up her wrist and flash the VIT monitor that ought to be there. But Senna still didn't have one. The barista noticed, the specter of his shaved-off brows looming low over his eyes.

"She will." Marin to the rescue. "She'll remember for next time. And I'll take a sweet drip."

The barista sighed. "Line jumpers pay double for their cups."

"Fine."

Marin, petite and dressed in pristine white patent leather, with a glossy black curtain of hair, leaned across Senna and swiped her own wrist monitor across the scanner. The machine dinged cheerfully, transaction complete. She glared at the thing toiling away behind the barista. AI Servitors, working husks of robots skinned with a kind of human latex mask over a carbon skeleton, were ubiquitous laborers across the stations, on the colonies and on science vessels.

"You know SecDiv is going to roll out lifelike versions of those things soon? With human fucking faces and skin and everything? I guess the regular peacekeeping bots aren't intimidating enough or something," said Marin in a disgusted undertone. She shuddered. "So creepy."

"Will we be able to tell the difference?" Senna asked, more amazed than afraid.

"I've seen this dystopian vid, and the answer is no."

As soon as the coffee arrived, Marin tugged Senna away from the cart quickly, back toward the carbon-black folding chairs and tables clustered on the promenade. The glitzier upper levels of the station rotated above them, rings that rose to impossible heights—financial districts and fashion houses, arcade blocks, cosmetic surgery clinics, augmented-reality parlors and universities . . . Down on their level, close to the bottom of the station and Hydroponica, nothing could be done to control the heat. The food and water operations needed the cooling systems, not the impoverished districts hovering just above them.

So Senna drank her haldi ka doodh in the swelter, accustomed to it. The hot turmeric milk almost scorched her mouth as she took a sip.

"I don't know how you can drink that stuff," Marin murmured.

"It's good," said Senna, shrugging.

"Blegh. Anyway, sorry I'm late."

Senna sat across from her at one of the empty tables. The lunch rush crowd swarmed around them in the plaza, drawn to the coffee cart for their midday blast of caffeine. Behind them, six lanes of self-driving cars and a passenger tram funneled workers back toward the main bank of elevators at the center of the district, elevators that ran the full height of the station.

"Don't worry about it," Senna said, waving off her apology while swatting at the vapor rising from her milk. She liked the slightly grassy taste of the drink. It made her wonder if it was the kind of earthy smell one experienced during a real Earth summer.

"I do worry," Marin replied, drinking her coffee. Her nose wrinkled. "Shit. They forgot my Zucros."

"I can wait."

"No, I shouldn't leave you alone again."

Senna ran her thumb lightly around the softening edge of her disposable cup. She felt stupid and small and unmanageable when Marin said things like that. But Senna also knew she had earned being babied.

"I shouldn't have been late. It's too dangerous for you out here. Anyone could . . . well." Marin trailed off and glanced around in every direction, which, Senna didn't point out, only made them look more conspicuous.

"Anyone could recognize me, yeah." Senna nodded. She wasn't stupid, whatever anyone thought. With a tired smirk, she gestured back toward the coffee cart, the Servitor, and the tat-tooed, eyebrow-less man inside it. "It already happened, Marin. Why do you think he refused to charge me for the cup?"

"Then maybe I should get you back to the apartment." Marin tucked one strand of silky black hair behind her ear, chewing her lower lip. "This was a dumb idea anyway."

"No." Senna clutched her cup and took another sip, even if it burned. "I've locked myself up in your place for a year. I told you—today I'm going to do one normal person thing. And this is it. So we're staying and we're going to do it."

Marin sat very still, probably shocked to hear a single word of dissent from the usually pliable Senna.

"God, that sounded ungrateful," Senna hurried on. "I don't mean to be like that. You've done so much for me. Without the apartment, without you . . . Thank you, Marin. I mean it, thank you. And thank you for meeting me here. It's nice! You know, being out."

She almost smiled, but then Marin looked at her VIT monitor. Everyone—on Earth and in space—owned one. *Craved* one. They were ubiquitous, holding a person's bank access, entertainment, contacts, maps, everything. Most people couldn't remember their own middle names without one, not just convenient tech but a lifeline. The small, flat screen wasn't just hooked up to the wireless but to the owner themselves, jacked into the small implant at the base of the skull; it fed users augmented-reality advertisements curated by their interests, displaying emojis and images that danced in front of stores, enticing passersby to enter. In fact, Marin could probably see any number of specials and sales promoted by the coffee cart spinning around her head just then.

Crime on the station continued to be almost nonexistent—hard to commit a crime when your own convenient method of finding out, well, anything and everything would also show exactly where you were at all times. It controlled where citizens could go on the station, what levels they could access. It managed a person completely. The station's security even monitored bio data, predicting a stroke or a heart attack before anyone even called for help.

Sometimes Senna longed for the convenience of it all, but she had been controlled by outside forces for most of her life. It was time to make her own decisions. She had never gotten the implant. Nobody in the compound had, or if they came there with one, Preece removed it. She glanced up from her drink, realizing Marin had gone silent for too long. And she wasn't lost in thought, but staring at her VIT, scrolling fast.

"Is something wrong?" Senna asked softly. Her pulse started to race. Managing anxiety wasn't exactly her strong suit. That was why Marin's apartment felt so soothing, so safe. Nothing surprising ever happened there.

"Just Jonathan, he's always in a shit mood lately." Marin's eyes flashed back and forth as she responded to her boyfriend's messages, the VIT reading her ocular input through the implant. "Hours slashed again. His division at MSC is a mess. I'll be shocked if they don't sack him before the end of this quarter. Then his mood will really be something." She took a quick, sloppy sip from her cup, spilling coffee down her pristine white blazer. "Goddamn it."

"I'll get something for that," Senna offered, jumping up.

"Forget it. Shit." Marin wiped blindly at the stain, still trying to message Jonathan. She only managed to rub the dark smudge deeper into the fabric. "I swear to God, between the two of you, sometimes I feel like a babysitter . . ."

Senna went still, the tea souring in her stomach.

Finally, Marin glanced up, wincing. "That was harsh, Senn. Jonathan will not get off my ass about everything. His job, his mother, his goddamn squash tournament, you . . . It's just a lot some days, you know? Everything is so much."

Senna wanted to say, *I understand*, but she didn't, because she couldn't. Nobody asked her about anything, not while she was in hiding. While she lived with Marin and Jonathan, she kept to herself, trying to be the smallest possible nuisance. Not small enough, apparently. Her eyes drifted to the holographic screen suspended above the plaza. It wrapped all the way around like a digital ribbon, news chyrons and station alerts adding noise to the already vividly noisy lights and sounds of Tokyo Bliss. Sector 7, where they had met for coffee, was particularly packed, food cart on top of food cart, plazas encroaching on one another, the swarm of commuters breaking for lunch filling the sector with a constant hum of conversation, laughter, shouting . . .

A daily talk show broadcast flickered across the plaza screen. *Daily Bliss.* Senna knew the show well, watched it almost every day. It was just the kind of predictable, cheerful pap that helped her zone out. The hosts, perpetually elated, wore pastel suits and sat between leafy fake ferns, interviewing chefs, writers, actors and the occasional palatable station politician. The hosts, Hali Teng and Zaid Forrester, sat on identical stools, clown-big smiles at the ready, their skin glowing with makeup. That day, a striking woman preened between them, her black skin perfect and lustrous, and seemingly makeup-free. Hali and Zaid chatted and giggled, the barista behind them screamed something at a woman on her VIT, the lunch crowd peaked, bodies crushing against their table while Senna clung to her teacup.

It was so much to take in, she hadn't even noticed Marin was still talking.

". . . It's become this whole thing. I wouldn't even bring it up to you, you know I said you can stay as long as you want. That stands, Senn, I want you to know that. I would never kick you out."

Senna inserted the silent *but*, and she was right.

"Jonathan wants a baby. You'd think he was the one with the uterus the way he won't shut up about it. Baby fever. I told him: Let's just get a puppy first, I don't even know if there's a maternal cell in my body! But of course he's allergic to everything . . ."

She found herself nodding along, half listening, but more intent on the *Daily Bliss* broadcast. The model's name rolled across the bottom of the screen. Just one word, no surname. Zurri. She was there to advertise a new skin cream, one she almost certainly didn't need. Her big, wide eyes were so dark, almost black, impossible to look away from. The beautiful nakedness of her skin and simple, chic slip dress only made Hali and Zaid look more ridiculous—too airbrushed, too injected, too bleached.

"Isn't she gorgeous?" Zaid fawned, flashing his boxy teeth. "Just perfection."

Perfection. Senna put down her cup, realizing her hands were hurting from the heat radiating through it. Someone bumped into her chair without apologizing. Her heart raced faster. She was trapped. Crushed. Just breathe slowly, in through the nose, out through the mouth.

"And even fish are stupidly expensive now. He doesn't want to pay the bio tax, which is understandable, but it will be a lot higher for an actual human child. He doesn't want to hear it." Marin finished, following Senna's line of sight toward the broadcast. "Ugh. Zurri. I would kill for her skin. Jonathan says her new line is too pricey, but whatever, if we can afford a fucking baby, we can afford some moisturizer."

"She's perfect," Senna agreed. And speaking of . . . She didn't know if she had the strength to bring it up, but she had to try. Closing her eyes, she pictured the monitor open on the guest room table. Then she remembered the message, the header in bold and black, unforgettable.

IMAGINE THE WORST DAY OF YOUR LIFE. NOW IMAGINE IT NEVER HAPPENED AT ALL.

Just thinking about those words stole her breath away again.

"Maybe this is the right time for me to go," Senna heard herself say. She hadn't even opened her eyes yet.

Somehow, she expected Marin to at least mildly protest, but she didn't. Instead she tossed her head side to side lightly, saying, "You know, Senn, my shrink says I'm re-creating a toxic cycle with you, that I'm fixing you instead of fixing myself, because it's easier to take on your damage than to deal with my own."

I'm not broken, she wanted to say, but she couldn't. She didn't know if she was broken or not, and if she was, if it was fixable.

The cracks splintering through her heart were so wide, the gulfs there so deep, they felt permanent. Impassable.

"Do you agree?" Senna asked.

"Shit, I don't know. He's right a lot but he's wrong plenty, too."

When Marin didn't offer more, Senna took a deep breath, realizing it was her opening. "There's this study that reached out to me. They want me to apply, and if I got in, then I would need to move out anyway. Maybe it's time."

Marin's black, thin brows rose to her hairline. "What kind of study? Are you sure it's not a scam? If they want you to buy something to start, then it's a scam."

"I would hope it's not a scam," she said with a dry laugh. "Paxton Dunn is running it."

Her eyebrows somehow went higher. "No shit?"

They were never allowed to swear on the compound. "They want applicants who have experienced serious trauma, they want to safely erase the bad memories. I've overstayed my welcome, Marin, I know I have, and if this program could help me, then I think I need to jump on it. This could . . . this could really change everything for me. It could free me."

Marin's shoulders slumped. Her VIT buzzed with more messages, undoubtedly Jonathan, but she ignored it. "This is serious stuff. Serious medical stuff. Are you sure you want to take the risk? What about Dr. Fentner?"

"I like him fine, but it's not enough, Marin." She didn't know if anything would ever be enough. "I need more than therapy. I need a fresh start. And it sounds like you guys need one, too. You need your space. And your baby."

"*Jonathan's* baby." Marin smirked. "But I hear you. You know you're still welcome to stay, Senn. I would never kick you out.

Mina would . . . well, she would want me to take care of you. You can take some time to think this over."

"No, I've thought it over," Senna said. *Just now.* Her heart grew heavier at even the mention of Mina. "And I want to apply."

She could leave the station, escape the noise and lights, go somewhere peaceful and isolated, and come back someone brand new. Someone who wouldn't start to gasp and drown in a crowd, someone who wouldn't wake every three hours from nightmares, someone who could receive a hug or a touch without wanting to crawl out of her skin.

Someone whole.

Marin had gone silent, responding to Jonathan, probably giving him the good news. And Senna looked back up at the holographic screen, seeking out the numbing softness of *Daily Bliss*, the rhythm of something she knew and liked, safe sights and sounds that washed over her like a cool fan gust.

But Hali and Zaid weren't smiling anymore from their little stools. The model, Zurri, was on her feet, trembling. The whole plaza turned to look at the feed while the studio fell into chaos on camera. Someone had burst onto the set, an older man with a bushy gray beard and thinning hair. He was soaking wet. With his back to the camera, Senna couldn't tell what he was saying, but the model was crumpling on her feet, her hands out in front of her defensively. Security rushed toward him, but he had already flicked something in his hand. Then he ignited, nothing but a ball of fire that lurched toward the hosts and the model, slowly falling to his knees.

The plaza had gone silent. On-screen, the man screamed.

2

Someone would put him out. Someone had to put him out. Zurri shrank away from the blast of heat and the smell. Oh God, the smell.

She was already a vegan, but the burnt pig stench would have put her off meat forever.

She knew the man in flames. Tony. He had been Tony. Security rushed onto the set, sleek, silver fire extinguishers held at the ready. White smoke filled the air, a hiss of liquid fat and a strangled moan came after, then the sound of Tony's body, what was left of him, hitting the floor. Next to her, Hali Teng had not stopped screaming, her hands covering her eyes. On her left, Zaid WhateverWhatever vomited onto his six-hundred-dollar loafers.

More security guards in all-black jumpsuits arrived, circling the charred, twitching body. One of them held up his VIT monitor, mumbling something about paramedics.

"Zurri . . . Zurri . . ."

"H–He's alive!" Zaid shook his head, wiping his mouth, a smear of greasepaint makeup coming off on his white sleeve.

Zurri would never forget the sound of her name coming out that way, like a thick, wet bubble bursting out of Tony's mouth. It almost didn't sound like her name, just a death wheeze, the last rattle of breath before the end.

"Get me out of here, I have to get out of here!" Hali Teng leapt to her feet, losing a heel, and raced off the set, shrieking.

Zurri couldn't move. Every muscle in her body refused to cooperate. She couldn't look away from the security guards and Tony. White motes danced around them like snow, but everything felt blistering hot under the studio lights. Winter in the desert.

Her eyes drifted upward, to the little red light blinking over the shoulder of one of the security guards. The camera. Zurri finally found her strength again, wobbling off the floor and storming past the guards and Tony.

"Cut the feed!" she screamed.

The drone cameras buzzed softly in the chaos, hovering at different levels to capture every possible angle, every reaction, every nuance. The little red light didn't go out, so Zurri grabbed the drone with both hands, tearing it out of the air and slamming it onto the ground.

"I said cut the feed! What the hell is wrong with you people?"

The station's first aid personnel scrambled past her, a stretcher hovering after them. Their orange-and-yellow jackets were bright even through the haze of powder from the extinguishers.

"Jesus, Tony, what were you thinking?" Zurri muttered, kicking the drone into the shadows, hoping it broke when it hit the wall.

13

One of the security guards spun to face her. The others parted for the stretcher. Zurri couldn't look—Tony had to be too frail to transport anywhere. She imagined him snapping like a burnt twig, scattering to ash. Her mouth tasted like a campfire. Tony went on moaning. From the darkness surrounding the too-bright studio, Zurri's assistant, Bev, emerged, dressed in a formfitting red suit, her white hair shellacked like a helmet to her head. Tears had carved white paths through Bev's makeup. She couldn't get a single word out, just shook her head and stared in horrified awe.

"You know him?" the security guard asked. The thin silver holographic badge on his chest read: DAVIES.

"Yeah," Zurri said, pulling Bev into a limp hug. Where was the person to hold her? Not there, she thought. Maybe not anywhere. "Yeah, I know him. He's my stalker."

Zurri's knee bounced as she slipped the wafer-thin tab of Rapture under her tongue. She had to crank down her VIT AR settings even before leaving the studio with Bev—the flashing, the blinking, the explosions of advertisements in 3D neon color were too much. On the set, she had been frozen, but now she couldn't keep still.

Below her, Tokyo Bliss Station unfurled like a sci-fi cocaine dream, seen from the top, a bottomless well of possibility, depravity, commerce, research and life. Heady, filthy life, so many people and animals packed into one orbiting meat grinder of humanity. When she was younger it was intoxicating. Now she wished desperately to escape it.

Zurri paced back and forth on the carbon-black balcony, the plaza one level down filled with nosy paparazzi and newscasters with telephoto lenses and camera drones angling for a single picture of her. The invisible holographic wrap around her balcony would make that impossible, distorting any images they managed to capture, standard-issue stuff for celebrity living. Some even went so far as to have the tech installed into their VIT monitors, leaving them a hazy ghost wherever they went. But normally, Zurri liked to be seen. Lived to be seen.

If only she could disappear.

Through the plexiglass separating her from the interior of the house, Zurri watched Bev frantically flipping through different feeds on the vid wall, cycling through the coverage of Tony's self-immolation. Bev was probably on six different calls, juggling their response, spinning and spinning, downplaying the relationship between Zurri, Tokyo Bliss's celebrity darling, and Tony.

Tony.

Zurri shivered, a tremor passing through her leg again. The Rapture was beginning to kick in, but not fast enough. She needed to smooth everything out, polish down all the sharp edges in her brain that threatened to slice and slice deep. Sometimes she took three or four tabs to relax before bed. Her doctor said it was risky, but Zurri couldn't give a shit, not when insomnia was the alternative.

The holographic balcony wrap and beefed-up security measures had gone into place after the break-in. Zurri had woken up with a chill, nausea pulling her out of sleep. Some deep, unseen part of her knew she was being watched, and when she snapped her eyes open, Tony was standing there, looming over the bed. Watching her.

He was doing something else, too, but Zurri wouldn't let herself think about that. They had been close once, as close as two working people could be. He was her first manager, the man who had gotten her her first gig, some small-time modeling for an online shopping bazaar. Things went quickly after that, her upward trajectory as sure and quick as the elevators rocketing up and down the center of the station.

"I'm good at this," Tony had told her at an after-party a year ago. "Because the only thing I care about is you. I don't think about myself. Fuck, at this point, I'm not sure I have a self."

He did. And he had taken that self and used it to break into her condo and violate what little privacy she had left. She had been meaning to schedule a work-life balance talk with him, because she could sense something had changed. But she never scheduled that talk, and Tony took things into his own hands . . .

God. Zurri shook her head violently, trying to dislodge the memory like it was a physical magnet stuck to the inside of her skull. She took another tab of Rapture, and inside, Bev just became a red blur pinging back and forth like a child's ball across the living room floor.

Zurri's whole body went numb, and then her VIT vibrated, and she gasped, startled, nearly falling over. She caught herself on the balcony railing, her head stuffed with the drug's velvet-soft effect. Nothing seemed bad for a second, Tony's flaming torso as inconsequential as a red lipstick smudge on a white dress.

"No interviews," she muttered. All her calls were supposed to be diverting to poor Bev, Bev whom she always kept at arm's length now. She had learned the hard way not to trust her staff. Work-life balance. "What the hell . . ."

Somehow, a call had gotten through. Strange. The caller ID simply read LENG. Swaying a little, Zurri rolled her eyes—even that took immense effort while this high—and tapped the screen on her wrist, the sound of a pleasant bell chime singing up from her hand.

Then a man's voice, nasally, British, began speaking. No

video feed accompanied the call, just a disembodied voice speaking to her disembodied consciousness.

"Hello, Zurri. This is Zurri I'm speaking to, yes?"

She licked her lips, the drug dehydrating. "How did you get through?"

"Ha. I can do that. This is Paxton Dunn."

Frowning, Zurri leaned her full weight against the balcony railing, the Rapture making the world spin slightly. "Is that supposed to mean something to me?"

On the other end, the man cleared his throat. "Christ. I'm sure you've at least heard of Merchantia Solutions."

"Sure," she said. They sponsored half the sporting events on the station, even had an avenue down on the tech level named after them. At one point they had probably paid for one of the fashion runways she walked down. "I'm gonna ask you again, how did you get through to my VIT?"

"The usual way. Beverly assured me you would want to hear what I have to say."

"Fucking Bev." Zurri glared at the fuzzy red-and-white blur that Bev had become, still taking call after call inside the condo. "Fine. You have me for twenty seconds. What do you want?"

"Nasty bit of business today on the *Daily Bliss*," the man said, clucking his tongue.

"On second thought? Zero seconds. Goodbye."

"Wait. Don't do that, Zurri. I want to help you. I can help you."

She turned away from the windows and watched the massive column of elevator banks to the east. The cars glowed for the different level destinations, now green, now pink, now blue . . . Watching them made her head spin a little less.

"Help me with what?" she asked, letting the rhythm of the

lights going up and down soothe her. Help. She doubted it. Nobody got help in her industry. Not really. Not lasting help. It was just a revolving door of surgeries, drugs, rehabs, even more extreme cosmetic surgeries, laser face resurfacing, new drugs, new rehabs, rinse, repeat, then look in the mirror one day and find a stranger. When she next looked in the mirror, Zurri wondered if she would see her own reflection burst into flames.

That's the drug talking.

"What you experienced was harrowing," Paxton Dunn told her. She snorted. "Hell, it was harrowing just watching it from my office. But if I never wanted to think about it again, I could do that. Just—" She heard him snap his fingers softly. "And it would all go away. No more assistant à la flambé."

The elevator cars bled together into one pulsing light. "What do you mean?"

"I just sent Beverly all the information," he said. She could hear the smile in his voice. "There's a satellite office on the station, but the real magic is happening on Ganymede. We're looking for people like you, Zurri, people with memories they want gone, traumas they need erased."

"Traumas!" she scoffed. "That's giving Tony a little too much credit."

"Oh," Paxton murmured. He was quiet for a beat. "I see. My mistake, then."

"Yeah, your mistake."

She heard him shuffling something on his desk, not papers but a keyboard maybe. Why was she still listening to him? Whatever he had to say wasn't relevant, obviously, but for some reason she just stayed on the line. Part of her worried what would happen when his voice was gone. She would be alone again with her thoughts, with the vast, dark city in space glowing all around her, hundreds of thousands of souls all suspended there among the stars with her. Even knowing Bev was there, and the paparazzi below, the whole station felt suddenly empty, and the loneliness in the darkness grew eyes, hundreds of thousands of lights all turned toward her, watching. Waiting . . .

Tony wasn't a trauma. Tony was . . . Zurri swallowed hard. Tony was a cold sweat that never quite left. He was the vague shape that startled her awake every night, a prowling shadow in the corner of her eye, a threat that abated sometimes but never truly left. He was an almost friend turned almost killer.

"What is this?" she heard herself ask. "Like, therapy?"

The shuffling stopped. She could feel, even though he was on a moon far, far away, his attention snap back to her full force. "It's not therapy, no. It's technology. We can zap a scar or a tattoo off your skin, right? And now I can zap a scar off your mind, too. Your worst day, not just forgotten but gone."

Zurri tried to imagine it: Tony's face lingering over her bed just gone. The smell of his burning flesh just gone.

"Sounds too good to be true," she said, rubbing her eye with the heel of her hand. She could already tell the comedown from this dose of Rapture would be brutal. A dance with oblivion never ended quietly.

"Well, it was," Paxton Dunn said simply. "But not anymore. Stop by the office on the station sometime, I think what you see there will really change your mind. I have a feeling I'll be seeing you on Ganymede soon, Zurri. We'll be in touch."

The call dropped. Zurri jerked her wrist up, staring at nothing. He had hung up on her. *He* had hung up on *her*. Smirking, she decided to let Bev keep her job for one more day, then she zigzagged to the window and tapped her knuckle on it. Bev needed to get her an appointment at this office of Dunn's, and she needed to do it right then, wake up whatever receptionist she had to, pull whatever string was required.

They would accommodate her, they had to. After all, she was Zurri.

3

Han couldn't wait to lose his memories.

Not all of them, of course, just one in particular. Or rather, one part of one. It was complicated. Because it was complicated, Han was beginning to worry Paxton Dunn wouldn't be able to do it.

People got rid of all sorts of things—moles, stained teeth, crooked noses, acne. That was modern life. If you didn't like something about yourself, then you found a way to remove it; why did a memory have to be any different than a wart? The difference was just opinion, he decided. Stubborn people being stubborn, a preciousness about the mind. Blah, blah, blah, holy or sacred or whatever. Boring. Small-minded. Eight hundred years ago having a wart in the wrong place made you a witch, and then anyone zealous enough could light you on fire. If the meaning of a wart could change, then the meaning of a memory could, too.

Everyone kept telling him he lived in the future, so it might as well feel like he was, too.

He kicked his legs back and forth under the chair while he waited. Frowning, Han reminded himself that Paxton Dunn could do almost anything. He had been Han's hero for years, his inspirational quotes and speeches the glowing background on each of his devices. Dunn's work and famously enigmatic personality won him the feature story on the VIT mag *TechPulse* three times, and each time they had to just use a silhouette of a man for the image. Nobody knew what he looked like, just that he was this era's promised one, filling the void other disappointing tech giants had left behind, stepping into impossibly huge shoes and tap-dancing away with everyone's imagination.

Especially Han's.

Han paved the pathways of his life with Dunn's words and creed. When Han's family members tried to entice him out of the condo more, to experience life rather than an isolated, virtual simulacra of one via his console, Han would reference Paxton Dunn's July 2267 interview, in which he said, "Life in outer space has forced us to embrace the collective and to forget the individual. Only through isolation and self-reflection can we learn to dream again, to listen to our own inner voice that longs for pure creation. The will of the masses is regurgitation, the will of the individual's soul is innovation."

Dunn lived in extreme solitude, chosen exile, or so went the prevailing story. He made it his business to remain an enigma, building a simplified mythology of one man up against the universe's mysteries. His legacy was hard to argue with—the Dunn family's Merchantia Solutions Corporation led the way in exploration, spacecraft refinement and deep space travel innovations.

Han would tell his family he needed the time alone in his

room to think, to dream, because as Dunn said, "The better we know the mind, the better we can use to it to know the universe."

Mostly, this won him a lot of blank stares and rolled eyes, but ultimately more time alone on his computer.

When he found out about the LENG program, he initially thought he was in trouble. He hated appointments—dentist, doctor, therapist, psychologist—they were all either painful, stupid, a waste of time or all three. His legs stilled under the chair when a door to his right opened and closed. This office was like nothing he had seen before. It was how he had pictured VR parlors looking when he first got to go, but they were mostly dark and dirty, and smelled like stale, flavored popcorn and fog machine chemicals. The young man who stepped through the door matched the office—dressed in a crisp white jumpsuit, with a clear vinyl overlay that skimmed the jumpsuit fabric and crinkled quietly when he walked. His blunt bowl cut was dyed the same color blue as the pale LED lights recessed in the ceiling. The whole place glowed and pulsed like the inside of Han's refrigerated drawer.

Relief. He was glad it was a real-life person and not an AI Servitor; he always felt uneasy around new automated voices. It was impossible to guess what voice profile they would use, if it would be *that* one.

Han stared at the man. A name tag reading *Kris* was affixed over his heart. He sat down behind the shiny white desk positioned between the door to the rest of the office and the other door, which led out into the first lobby. Han's Servitor nanny was out there somewhere; not even the AI was allowed back into this special area.

The white desk was shaped like a slice of melon.

"Can I get you anything?" Kris asked, not looking up from his holo-display. The Merchantia Solutions logo had been embossed on the wall behind him.

"How much longer?" Han felt itchy all over. Ready. Impatient. "Is Mr. Dunn here?"

"Mr. Dunn does not leave the facility on Ganymede," Kris told him mildly. "But if everything goes smoothly today, then you'll get to meet him soon."

"Really?"

Kris smirked. "Really." The door to the first lobby chimed softly. A water feature running the length of the wall behind Han and the bank of waiting chairs kept out the noise from the rest of the station. The tech sector level on Tokyo Bliss Station was relatively quiet, but not even the roar of the lunchtime rush could be heard in the office, just the soothing trickle of constantly running water.

A woman with hair as blunt as Kris's but longer and blond came in, carefully, peering around as if she didn't belong. But Kris stood, smiled and gestured for her to join Han in the waiting area.

"Ms. Slate?" Kris's smile didn't make his eyes crinkle. Han knew from his therapist that only genuine smiles did that.

"I'm early," she said with a shivery shrug. "Sorry."

"That's just fine. Have a seat."

"I didn't think anyone else would be here," she said, glancing at Han with her huge brown eyes.

"I'm sorry about that, we're just a little behind schedule," Kris sighed. "Are you comfortable waiting here?"

"Sure," she murmured. "Yeah, I'm sure it's fine."

She was wearing tans and mauves, a shapeless, boxy linen shirt and loose trousers that almost looked like pajamas. None of her clothes seemed to fit right; even her shoes looked big. She reminded him of one of his au pairs, Molly, the one who had lasted the longest. After Molly quit, his older brother gave up and hired the AI Servitor to watch him instead.

At first he hated it, but he adapted quickly; unlike the au pairs, the Servitor could be hacked and made to do whatever he wanted.

"Hi," the woman greeted him, staring at his feet while she huddled down into a chair across from him.

"Hey."

He wasn't allowed to use his VIT to access the network while he was inside the office. Security measures. It all felt top secret, and that made Han's leg start to bounce again. Top secret meant Dunn might really be able to take his bad memories away.

Without a game on his VIT to hold his attention, Han observed the woman across from him instead. Her face, like a word on the tip of his tongue, was maddeningly familiar but just out of reach. Where had he seen her before? Her haircut was unusual, way out of style, and she didn't wear much makeup. Also unfashionable. He only knew that because his favorite station pop groups spread wet silver glitter across their eyes and drew tiny hearts and stars on their cheeks like freckles.

She must have noticed him staring, and pulled her feet up onto the chair, trying to make herself as small as possible. Her wide brown eyes flicked up toward him, and that was when it hit him.

His stomach twisted. An ugly urge to lunge for her rose in him like the need to vomit. Glaring, he whispered, "You're the cult lady."

She winced and shook her head, hiding behind her blond curtain of hair. "I . . . I don't . . ."

"No, you are!" He shook his head and pointed, frantically, as if she might try to get up and run away. It was definitely her. What were the odds? Could it be a coincidence? "It's not fair. You shouldn't be here . . ."

Kris popped up out of his chair like he had been ejected. "Han? They're ready for you."

"Oh my God," he heard the woman groan, covering her face with both hands.

"Right now," Kris said to him behind a tight, fake smile. Han began to shake, but Kris carefully took him by the arm and began to lead him away. "As you can imagine, we're screening quite a few candidates. Your time slots were not scheduled to overlap . . ."

He could hear the note of frustration in Kris's voice, and the muttered curse that came after, out of place, like a splash of blood on the walls of that pristine lobby.

"Yeah," Han muttered, to both the woman and Kris. "I'll bet."

For a while he couldn't escape this woman's face on the news vids. He turned away every time it happened, every time she appeared, because hers wasn't a face anyone should care about.

"So sad, so sad," his AI Servitor nanny had clucked once, the news rolling by while Han pretended to do his Spanish homework. "It breaks your heart."

"You don't have a heart," Han had reminded the nanny AI. *And sometimes I'm not sure I can feel mine anymore, either.*

The Servitor's smooth, pale dome of a head had turned slightly toward him. "Even I can recognize human tragedy."

Hearing it say that had been particularly enraging. The next day, he dialed back the Servitor's emotional parameters, unwilling to be shamed by a stupid robot.

He walked by the woman from the news vids, the face of the Incident, and she was still trying to disappear behind her knees.

When he was at the door with Kris, he heard the cult lady heave a sigh of relief.

He wouldn't be shamed by that, either. He didn't get a sigh of relief, he only got angrier.

"If Mr. Dunn isn't here, then what are we doing?" Han asked, impatient. He didn't bother asking why that woman was there in the lobby, he could already guess. The corridor was quiet, dark, the walls thrumming softly with energy as if hidden engines waited behind them. "I already filled out your survey online. It took forever."

"We're only taking the perfect candidates to Ganymede," Kris told him, walking ahead. He had a stiff gait, like someone who had worked out a lot. Han's brother walked like that the mornings after he went to play squash. "The selection process takes time, Han. But this is the last step. You're almost there."

"If I get picked," Han muttered.

Kris raised his left wrist, a holo-display rising from the VIT monitor there. A bright blue interface appeared with what looked like a dossier, including a 3D image of Han's face, rotating.

"You have a unique case," Kris said. "It's just the sort of thing Mr. Dunn is interested in. He really wants to test the capabilities of this technology before going public with it."

"Are you saying I'm getting in?"

Kris stopped outside a recessed door. It opened automatically at their approach with a quiet hiss. Then he gestured Han inside with a cool smile. "I'm not saying anything. Step inside."

Usually, Han wasn't any good at following directions. His mother had almost never said a cold word to him, but the few times she had raised her voice were burned deep into his mind. Just thinking about it made his palms clammy.

"Han, just stop. Just stop!" she had screamed, after he reprogrammed the condo's internal alarm systems. He had messed up and the clocks were off, making her late for her flight off station. "I don't care what you think! You are *not* always the smartest person in the room!"

But even if her words hurt—stung—he hadn't really believed her. More often than not, he really was the smartest person in the room. Brushing by Kris and into a claustrophobic white box of an office, Han wondered if that was true currently. Was he smarter than Kris? Probably. But if he went to Ganymede, if he met Paxton Dunn, at last he could understand what it felt like to feel in awe, and small. Just another reason to get there—he wanted this memory gone, but he also wanted more than anything to meet the most brilliant man working in the universe.

"Is that woman out in the lobby getting picked?" Han asked. Her name escaped him; he had tried hard to forget all the news coverage. One of his many therapists suggested that the trauma had indeed blocked out certain things.

But not enough.

"I don't know," Kris told him. "And if I did, it wouldn't be my place to share it with you."

"She shouldn't get picked," Han muttered, and he saw Kris's head turn, perhaps in curiosity. "She doesn't deserve it."

"Okay," Kris said, obviously eager to be moving on. "Just have a seat there."

He gestured Han toward the only chair in the room. A panel on the wall to the left was obviously another recessed door, and beside that was a panel, glass. Two-way mirror, Han thought. The chair for him was long and low, like a dentist's, with a very small rectangular feature sticking out of the headrest, just about where his neck would go. A pair of thick, padded headphones sat on a silver dish next to the table. A now familiar blue glow suffused the room, and relaxing, nondescript music played just above that strange hum that came from the walls.

Han forced himself not to hesitate. He was so close to getting chosen . . . couldn't screw it up now.

"We're just going to map this memory," Kris explained. The holographic display hovering above his VIT vanished, and he waited by the two-way panel. "You can lie down and get comfortable, and put those headphones on. In a moment, you'll hear instructions. Shouldn't be anything too tough for a smart kid like you."

Han smirked. Smart. Sure. Try genius. He wanted to know more. So much more. What was the little square on the headrest? Some kind of reader, he hypothesized, that would tap into the implant at the base of his neck. That implant allowed him to seamlessly interface with his VIT monitor, and served other purposes on the station, too. Tokyo Bliss Station was considered a crimeless, peaceful utopia by many, but it came with its own set of drawbacks. The system that tracked citizens through their VIT implants was mandatory. Of course crime was low when the station PaxDiv knew your whereabouts, blood pressures and temperature at all times.

Even while going to the chair, lying down and putting on the headphones, Han's mind raced. Kris had mentioned mapping. What kind of mapping? Maybe some version of neural imaging that could be used to precisely pinpoint the physical location of the unwanted memory in the brain. This was supposed to be surgical, scalpel-level stuff, not the clumsy obliteration of memory that came from age or disease or substance abuse, but an incision into his very subconscious.

Han really didn't think it could be done, but that didn't mean he wasn't curious.

The simple chair and headset didn't give many clues as to how Dunn was pulling this all off. The key, he knew, had to be in whatever technology was hidden under the chair's soft, white leather exterior. His fingertips burned, and his ears felt hot. In time, he reminded himself, he could grill Paxton Dunn on how it all worked. First, he had to get to Ganymede, so he played the dutiful patient while on the inside he felt almost enraged with curiosity. Han was only fourteen; thinking of someone like Dunn as competition was ridiculous, maybe, but he couldn't help seeing it that way. It was like looking into his future. Destiny. He didn't want to be just like Paxton Dunn, he wanted to *be* him. One day it would be Han's face featured on *TechPulse*.

It was all deceptively simple. A single chair. A pair of headphones. Simple.

Han drew in a deep breath and tried to get comfortable on the chair, which wasn't hard, given how nicely padded and upholstered it was. Then came the headphones, also expensive and comfortable, noise canceling, fluffy as new pillows pressed to his ears.

It wasn't Kris that greeted him through the headphones but a calm, smooth, disembodied voice, androgynous and soothing. A little quizzical, like they had a secret.

Good afternoon, Han Jun, the voice said. Just as he suspected, Dunn's technology interfaced with Han's implant. He remembered skimming the permissions for that in the complex NDA. Similar to the augmented-reality advertisements that bombarded him on the station promenades, this program could appear right before his eyes, a slim, angular figure projected there for him. Like the voice, they were genderless and pleasant, dressed in a formfitting white smock and leggings, their head bald, the features of their face large, exaggerated and almost alien.

Your intake forms indicate that you prefer to be called Han, is that correct?

Yes.

Han had only to think his responses. This thing was jacked directly into his head, interfacing with his VIT implant, and after all, he didn't want to make things too easy. But as expected, the projection—the program—heard him loud and clear.

You can call me Patron, Han. This is a preliminary mapping exercise, to find the parameters and boundaries of your unwanted memories. No adjustments to your memories will be made today, and no changes will ever be made without your consent.

You're the technology?

Patron smiled, but with their almost plastic face it didn't touch or wrinkle their big, black eyes. *I am merely a program speaking to you through your VIT-compatible implant. An avatar, if you will, of the neural-mapping system developed by Merchantia Solutions Corporation in partnership with Belrose Industries, a proprietary program operated by Paxton Dunn. You see, the LENG program cannot be run here, as the necessary hardware is on Ganymede. If you are chosen for the test, then you will experience the real technology there.*

Got it.

The smile on their face faded, and Patron folded their hands placidly in front of their waist. *I need you to think about your mother, Han.* The avatar's eyes seemed to grow larger, blacker, enticing in a way he couldn't quite describe, as if they could physically draw the memory of his mother out of him, whether he wanted to or not. *I would like you to remember her voice.*

Han winced. Her voice, his greatest weakness.

Straight to business, then, he thought.

Would you like for there to be pleasantries?

I guess not.

That same wide, strange smile appeared on Patron's egg-like face. *Our time together is short and precious, Han. Please cooperate, unless you would like to terminate this exercise and forfeit your application for testing.*

It's just hard. He squirmed in the chair. His hands throbbed, and he noticed that the room felt abruptly hot, suffocating. Patron took a small step toward his chair. *I don't like thinking about her. I've tried . . . I've tried and tried to forget.*

But you can't forget, Patron said with a sigh. *And that's why you're here. And why we're here—to help you. I know it's uncomfortable, but I need you to concentrate. I need you to focus on what hurts the most. Show us where it is, show us what it is, help us help you, Han.*

His thoughts drifted at once to the woman with the shiny hair out in the lobby. Did the technology know? Something must have worked, because Patron nodded.

Pathways engaged. Strong activity in the amygdala. Elevated heart rate. Please continue, Han. But as I instructed, focus. Be specific.

Han closed his eyes and licked his lips. This was Paxton Dunn's technology, his baby. His hero's baby. He had to trust it. More than anything, and maybe foolishly, he just wanted it to work.

The morning of. His mother was running late for her flight. Work trip. She had recorded all the guided tour audio for a Merchantia Solutions research campus on Mars. There was only one flight that day leaving from Tokyo Bliss Station to Nolan-Beale Base in Chryse Bay, and she had to be on it. Bored, insomniac from staring at his computer all day, he had spent the night messing with the automated systems in the condo, trying to make the chime say, "Han is king!" whenever someone triggered the motion sensor on the door to his room. Usually that required permissions only his mom had in the system, but he found a way in. A forced factory reset did the trick, but it also erased Mom's morning alarm.

I don't care what you think! You are not always the smartest person in the room!

Her face looked like it was cooking while she screamed at him from his bedroom doorway. She had gotten dressed in such a hurry that the buttons on her jacket weren't done up correctly, and when he pointed it out, sitting cross-legged on his bed, still wide awake at five a.m., she grabbed her bag and stormed away. The swing of her purse caught the door sensor.

"Han is king!"

His mother had let out a roar at that, and then she was gone. She made her flight, informing him of as much in a clipped text. He had saved it, of course, and she was still a contact in his VIT. There were still nights he dreamed that his VIT monitor buzzed on the bedside table, and when he scrambled for it in the dark, his mother's face beamed back at him. Even in the dream, there was a strange hollowness to her eyes, as if even his subconscious knew that this was perilously wishful thinking.

Patron was saying something, but he couldn't follow. That day—those memories—were a riptide, and once he went under, there was no clawing his way back. Everything around him faded, and there was only the dark fog that filled his brain. The only way through was to follow a single light, tempting and bright, but like fabled lights in stories of dark forests, it only led to despair.

And loss.

The day of her trip to Mars, his VIT really had received a call from her, but unlike in his dream, he didn't wake up to receive it. After the insomniac adventures of the night before, he crashed and crashed hard. Crashed. Han licked his lips again, faster, flattening his palms against his thighs as he trembled on the chair.

I want it out. Get it out. Get it out of me! I can't hear her say it one more time . . .

Breathe. Patron's voice hovered on the edges of his hearing. *Breathe, Han. Take me to the hurt.*

The next morning he woke to a voice message from his mother. Her face greeted him around noon on his monitor as he reached for it after rolling out of a fitful doze. Probably just a quick word to say she had landed safely. The expected stuff.

"Sweetie? Are you there? Pick up! Han? Oh, Han, wake up, please just wake up! Oh my God. Something has breached the atmosphere. All the alarms . . . all the alarms here are going. They won't tell me what it means, God, they won't tell us anything—"

Alarms screamed. Humans screamed. Someone not his mother could faintly be heard saying, "We need to move. Now."

Later, when the message cut and he realized that he would never see his mother again, he felt cold and damp all over, and discovered that he had gone numb and wet the bed. Green text had flashed over his mother's face on his VIT, an incoming call from his brother. Through the gray frosted glass of his door, he had noticed his Servitor nanny hovering, waiting to come in. Maybe it really did have a heart, and that was why it hesitated. Then the door had hissed open and the AI nanny toddled through.

"*Han is king!*" the chime had sounded.

"Get it out!" Han sat up in the chair, and the projection of Patron wavered for a moment, distorting. It snapped back to a crisp image, and Patron came forward, hands folded as if in prayer.

Breathe in through your nose and out through your mouth. Yes, like that. The pathways are clear, Han, the pathways are strong, they said, then gesturing up with their hands, toward the nose, then pushing outward as if exhaling.

Han did as they said, glancing down, sure he had soiled himself. No. He was all right. His hands had taken big bunched fistfuls of his pants, and when he let go, there were sweat marks and wrinkles.

"W-What does that mean?" he asked, blinking rapidly as if the room were very bright. It wasn't, but Patron gleamed, perfectly smooth, reflective as a polished agate.

It means we can help you, Patron told him, offering what smile they could, given their strange, alien face. *It means the technology can take it all away.*

4

"Do you think you got it?"

Senna hadn't even had time to flick her shoes off next to the door before Marin's voice rang out from the kitchen. The condo, small, cool, and tidy, wasn't situated on the more sought-after upper levels of the station, but Senna had put up with far more meager conditions. Marin made a decent living in IT but the hours were hellish; she was constantly on-call in case anything went wrong with the servers controlling the station's Servitor-based security force, PaxDiv. There were times Senna watched her fly out the door in the middle of a meal, or after an alert roused her before dawn.

"I'm not sure," Senna called back. Her brown shoes looked misshapen next to Marin's pumps, two perfect, sleek black heels lined up neatly to the right of the door, not a mark on them. Her voice shook as she added, "It was . . . it wasn't what I expected."

"What did you expect?"

Senna hunted for her voice, leaving behind the cramped foyer and passing under a square opening into the open-plan living space. A tinted window to her right offered one of the only outward views of the station itself. Most of the windows were fake, with simulated vistas. Jonathan preferred beaches, pre-cataclysm Bali specifically.

A few white patent leather sofas and a vid projector were clustered to the right, and to the left, a recessed kitchen went deeper into the condo. Behind the tall bar counter that separated the kitchen from the living area, Marin was dumping ice into a cocktail shaker, her black hair pinned tidily behind her ears. It was a good thing she didn't look too much like her sister, or the shock of seeing her every day would've become too much. Mina had been smaller, almost fragile, with mousy brown hair and gentler eyes. Once, on the compound, Mina had told her that she looked just like her father, and Marin took after their mother.

The sisters shared the same lips, so Senna always stared at Mina's eyes when she talked.

"I don't know," Senna admitted with a shrug. The whole thing had been so bizarre, she hardly knew where to begin. Paxton Dunn's people had arranged a transport for her back to the apartment so she didn't have to take the public elevators or light rail. The receptionist, Kris, had noticed that Senna didn't have a VIT, and made all the arrangements quickly and silently, without asking. The driver hadn't spoken a word to her the entire time. The interior of the transport smelled overwhelmingly—chemically—of spearmint. Senna's mind kept wandering back to the boy she had seen in the lobby. Tall, thin, Asian, with intensely accusatory eyes. Bloodshot eyes, in fact, and he had the paper-thin, acne-spotted skin of the insomniac. She knew the look well.

There was so much rage in his eyes . . . the way he talked to her, like they were acquainted, like he had every reason in the world to hate her . . .

Senna sighed and leaned against the counter, listening to the rhythmic *shurk-shurk-shurk* of Marin mixing a drink.

"I thought you and Jonathan—" But she stopped herself. It was none of her business.

Marin smirked and shrugged. She was wearing a prim and tailored red suit, a gold necklace fastened tight around her neck, close enough to leave a little sub-necklace of welts. "Yeah, not exactly my prenatals. Whatever. I'm not pregnant yet. At least I don't think so, and after the day I've had . . ." Marin winked one of her long, false lashes and dumped the cocktail shaker contents into a glass that could've been mistaken for a pitcher. The liquid was electric blue.

"Who cares about my shitty day," Marin added, cozying up to the bar. "I want to hear more about this Dunn guy's office. Jonathan thinks he's not even real."

Senna frowned, the scent of blueberries wafting strongly from the drink. Behind Marin, the kitchen had been neglected, clean and dirty dishes piled high next to the washer, cartons of takeout food stacked beside that. Someone needed to make a garbage disposal run, but the station charged for every use, and Jonathan liked to push it until things started to smell.

"How could he not be real?" Senna asked. "He invited me to do this experimental therapy, right? People must know what he looks like."

"I know, I know, it's fucking stupid. Whenever he's interviewed it's just a silhouette. Adds to his mystique, I suppose." Already half done with her drink, Marin was eyeing the cocktail shaker again. "Sometimes I ask Jonathan if he loves those idiot conspiracy theories because our life is too boring, but he says that's not it. I don't know, I don't get it, he's a smart guy! Well, real or not, do you think you passed the test or whatever? Is that what it was?" She smiled and her teeth were lightly stained blue. "A test?"

"It was more like a clinical exam," Senna admitted. Marin pointed to the shaker and lifted a brow, but Senna shook her head. There was no drinking in the compound, and the last time Marin had tried to get her to drink, Senna had wound up sick and dizzy the next day. Preece was wrong about a lot of things, but maybe not about alcohol. "They wanted to do some neural imaging, figure out if they could really delete my memories."

Marin shuddered and pretended to gag, the sight made all the more ghoulish by her stained teeth. "Delete your memories. It sounds so fucking intense when you put it like that."

"It's intense no matter how you put it," Senna replied. "I had to . . . They made me think about the crash. I had to go over all of it. It felt like walking them through a dream, but it must have worked. They didn't tell me much, just that the data collection was successful."

"That must have been hard," Marin said softly, no longer as interested in her cocktail. "You okay?"

"I should probably sit down." Light-headed. Tired. For a year, Senna had lived in the fog of despair, basic things like showering or getting up to have breakfast seemingly monumental. It was like living under a great, looming shadow, an avalanche of pain waiting to crush her the second her mind strayed to the wrong thing. She crossed to one of the sofas and dropped down, holding her face in her hands, elbows propped on her knees.

Painting had been her light and joy in the compound, but she

couldn't even do that anymore. All her supplies had been inciner-
ated. Once the area was no longer considered a crime scene, station authorities probably wiped out all her murals.

"Let me get you some ice water," Marin muttered.

"I'm fine, really." Adrenal fatigue, that was what one of Senna's many doctors told her had happened. Too much stress, too
much grief, too many changes all at once. Her body had shut
down, but Senna was still waiting for it to open up again.

"Shut up." Marin came to the sofa with the water, and of
course she was right. As soon as Senna's hands closed around the
cold, smooth cup, she felt a little better, and the tide of nausea
rising in her stomach ebbed. With a little shudder of relief, Marin
pulled off the sleek black style she wore as a wig and tossed it
across the room. She scratched at her scalp, and at the thinning
hair there. Senna looked away, feeling as if she were staring at
something private.

"These new anxiety drips are amazing," Marin murmured,
seemingly unbothered by the clump of hair that came away in
her hand. "Guess I was lucky enough to get one of the rarer side
effects. Oh well. Wigs are expensive, but peace of mind is priceless." She relaxed back against the sofa, glancing at her VIT, and
then her eyes popped open wider. "When you're feeling steadier,
there's something I need to give you."

Senna lifted her head, moving the hair out of her eyes. "What
is it?"

"Station Affairs sent it over," Marin said, laughing at Senna's
groan. "They're not going to stop bothering us. You know that,
right?"

"I do." It was part of why Senna felt it was her time to leave.
She couldn't be held liable for what happened on the *Dohring-
Waugh*. The crash wasn't her fault, but she was the sole survivor.

All the questions, all the investigations, led back to her. After she was recovered from the evac pod, SA had taken her into custody. It was the first night she spent alone in a little room all by herself, and the isolation was devastating.

"Here."

Senna hadn't even noticed the small package that had been sitting on the coffee table. It was only just larger than a man's fist, wrapped in nondescript black plastic.

"If it's a bomb," Marin joked, placing the package next to Senna on the sofa, "I'm going to haunt you forever."

"It wouldn't be," Senna replied with a thin smile. "Station Affairs has their hands full with me already. They wouldn't add another problem to their list."

"True!"

Senna peeled off the black plastic, and inside she found a new model VIT, the latest version. On the image of the VIT monitor itself, the agent assigned to her case had written, *Just wear it. Please?*

"Will you?" Marin asked, pointing to the inscription.

"Agent Tiwari has been pretty patient with me," Senna sighed. "So I owe him."

Marin put her hand on Senna's shoulder and squeezed. "You didn't do anything wrong, Senna. You don't owe him anything."

Senna didn't know if that was true. People wanted answers. Justice. Blood. Even the laws had changed after the crash. Now every citizen applying for resident status on Tokyo Bliss Station had to opt in to being traced through their implant. Preece had claimed religious exemption for the compound; that was how they all managed to go about their lives without implants or VITs. Every week or so, another message arrived from Agent Tiwari, reminding Senna that she wasn't exempt either, that she was also subject to the law. Senna just kept putting it off.

Of all the cruel things Preece Ives had done to her, maybe the cruelest was not killing her like he had done the others. After that much death and tragedy, everyone on Earth and the stations and the colonies wanted a scapegoat.

They got Senna.

"He's not all bad," Senna whispered. She sensed, in fact, that Agent Tiwari had a soft spot for her, that he could tell she was brittle, and that one question too far, one step over the line, and she would crack and break. Maybe for good.

She opened the package and wrapped the monitor around her wrist. Even lightweight and cushioned, it felt odd on her wrist, more like a shackle than a fashion and technology accessory. Agent Tiwari had chosen the popular rose-gold model.

"Damn. That's nice, my model isn't nearly as flash," Marin said.

"You can have it."

"And get tracked by SA for the rest of my life? No thanks."

Senna smirked. "I think that ship has sailed."

"Maybe, but this will all blow over eventually," Marin told her, squeezing her shoulder again. "You and I won't forget, but everyone else will move on. I guarantee it, you'll be shocked how fast people stop caring."

The flat front surface of the VIT resting on top of her wrist lit up as soon as it touched the warmth of her skin. A greeting in twelve languages appeared in white text on a black background, then dissolved to let her know that no unlinked AR implants were detected in the vicinity, asking if she would like to proceed with setup manually.

"Maybe this is a good thing," Senna said with a shrug. "If I get into Paxton Dunn's program, I'll be on Ganymede, and I'll miss you. At least I can use this for messaging, since I don't have my own terminal."

Marin grinned with her blue teeth and raised her cup. "That's the first silver lining you've found in a while."

The VIT, as it turned out, was already registered to her, and it only took a few quick password inputs tapped out by hand to link the tech to the messaging address Marin had helped her create. New emails were waiting, blinking, a faint, happy chime indicating as much.

"Another alert from Tiwari," Senna snorted. "They're never going to let the implant thing drop, and they're going to start fining me if I don't comply." Fining her money she didn't have. Her eyes roamed the short distance to the other unread message, and her heart felt like it was expanding in her chest. No. It wasn't possible. Already? "But maybe I can outrun them . . ."

Marin scooted closer, trying to crane her neck and see the little interface on Senna's VIT. She smelled like blueberries and hairspray. "What do you mean?"

"There's an alert from Dunn's office," Senna whispered, hardly believing it herself. "They've already approved me for the experiment. I'm going to Ganymede, Marin. They want me to leave this week."

5

Zurri had sent the rider ahead with what she required on Ganymede, now all that remained to be seen was if playboy hermit extraordinaire himself Paxton Dunn had listened.

Lying on the reclining seat in her private cabin, Zurri began to have her doubts. She had dealt with his kind before. Whatever Dunn's definition of luxury was, he would assume Zurri shared it. Typical billionaire, typical male. If there was someone out there with higher standards than hers, she had yet to meet them. His being absurdly rich didn't mean anything. Plenty of wealthy recluses lived in performative squalor, choosing to stay on Earth in the flood or desolation zones, acting like their "modest" homes weren't, in fact, state-of-the-art bunkers with emergency protocols for immediate airlift in case anything really went wrong. They liked to act out the rugged fantasy, and to her it seemed gaudier than just showing their privilege plainly.

So far, Dunn hadn't disappointed. It was obvious he wanted her in the program, and badly. His invitation to join the experiment in earnest on Ganymede had come through less than two hours after her initial consultation at the little office on Tokyo Bliss. They had cleared out everyone except for one receptionist for her visit. The cruiser he (or more likely, his people) had arranged for her transfer from the station to the Ganymede satellite had been adequate—the temperature controls fixed at a languid twenty-five degrees Celsius, a cashmere robe and fluffy slippers made available, and her private cabin came stocked with more actual champagne, green tea, activated nuts, and frozen cacao-and-spinach-smoothie pucks than she could possibly consume over the length of the flight.

A refreshing detox IV and meditation tracks kept her company for the launch, a technician—provided gratis by Dunn—joining her in the dark, warm room to provide a microneedling treatment of her own plasma, a light dermal infusion, and then a chilled antibacterial mask to help with the swelling. She would arrive on Ganymede fresher than a hydroponic daisy. When her facial was done, the technician strapped Zurri in for the more jarring, dangerous FTL portion of the trip, and left to buckle up elsewhere.

While Zurri drifted to sleep to the sound of gongs and fingertips whispering musically across copper water bowls, she wondered if the other program participants were on her same transfer. She wouldn't see them, of course—Bev had made it abundantly clear that Zurri was not to be transported, treated or housed with the other patients, the trade-off for Zurri signing what Bev described as "an NDA that made a noncompete modeling contract feel like a breezy beach read."

Zurri had promised to skim the NDA herself, and meant to on the trip before she fell asleep, but the gongs were so soothing and she was exhausted, so the NDA would have to wait until she arrived on-site. Of course, Bev had warned that if anything wasn't up to Zurri's standards once she reached the Ganymede facility, it might be too late to pull out of the experiment. The NDA and contracts had included information about the frequent, turbulent storms on Ganymede. Flights in and out, even just shuttle drop-offs, were tightly regulated and subject to last-minute cancellation if weather shifted.

With one foot inside the private ramp to the shuttle, Bev had apologized until she went hoarse. "I'm awful, Zurri, the worst. I should be going with you," Bev had said, wiping mascara tracks off her cheeks. "I know you won't admit it, but you're fragile right now. You shouldn't be alone. You need someone."

"You let his call through," Zurri had pointed out, adjusting her oversized sunglasses and pivoting toward the ship. They were beginning to call general boarding, and as a policy, Zurri wanted to be settled before the corridors were flooded. A fan could be in the crowd, and she didn't need that. "You let his call through and now I'm supposed to have second thoughts? What do I pay you to do exactly, Bev? Change your mind? Inconvenience me?"

"You're right. Of course you're right. I just thought Dunn would let me come with you is all." Bev sniffled and fanned at her own tearstained face, and Zurri was struck by the possibility that Bev was crying because she, too, wanted the exclusive experience of meeting Dunn face-to-face. Her tears were for lost opportunities, not Zurri's fragility. Bev hurried on. "But you're not fragile, are you? You're strong. I know you're strong. And this is good, right? It's like a retreat. I would leak it but Dunn would sue me into the next galaxy."

"Let me work on him," Zurri told her with an easy smile, swinging her bag onto her shoulder. She only carried a single, shell-shaped handbag. Her larger bags had already been brought aboard by a porter. "A little press for him, a little press for me. Everyone wins." She softened, because in the end, Bev wasn't terrible, and if Dunn really could change Zurri's memories, then this was more than just a win, it was possibly a new lease on life. "Stop crying, Bev. It will be fine. I'll contact you when I'm at the facility, all right? And I'll make sure to take plenty of pics. You never know, something might leak."

She winked at her assistant, and Bev gave a squawk of a laugh. Then it was time to go, quickly, while things felt easier and Bev had managed to smile through the ghoulish black-and-tan streaks of her eye makeup and foundation.

Lying on the transport, Zurri blinked up into the darkness. Maybe she ought to glance at that NDA. It was lights-out in the cabin, but an encrypted copy of the NDA and contract had been downloaded to her VIT. Bad on the eyes, she thought, to read in the dark. Did she really want to be confronted with the 187 unread emails lurking in her inbox? If she spotted something annoying in the NDA, it would just make her more anxious, but maybe she ought to be informed, that was the adult way to approach it . . . And then the hard, heavy kick of the FTL came and the whole ship thrummed with gathering energy and Zurri lost the urge to look. After all, they had launched, the time to change her mind had come and gone. The flight accommodations were nice enough, and more than that, she wanted to go.

What she hadn't told Bev was that Dunn could be housing them in a tin shack on the moon to run this little experiment and she probably would have said yes. Tokyo Bliss Station felt claustrophobic. She was done with her same condo and her same life, and her same routine and her same ass-kissing staff, and her same nightmares and the same constant, low hum of anxiety that only drugs like Rapture and U4ya could obliterate. Sometimes, she remembered that her life was only real to herself. Nobody else on station levels one through ten could even imagine it. Their dreams could extend far, she thought, but not that far. Doors were open to her that simply did not exist to others. A cyber-utopia level in one of the AR domes was the closest they could come, but even the programmers designing those things didn't know what she had access to—food, clothes, drinks, drugs, condos, vacations, flights, cosmetic procedures that were too expensive for anyone, but free for her. She had worked so, so hard to be able to afford anything, but now, at the tippy top, she didn't have to pay for any of it.

Pure accumulation. A numbing drag. But Tony . . . Tony had made the numbness go away, punched a hole right through it. She was shockingly alive again and feeling things, and she knew she couldn't go back to the numbness, but the new world of constant pain was impossible, too.

There had to be a middle—had to be—a place to exist between nothingness and too muchness.

What she didn't tell Bev or her therapist or her friends was that when she had walked onto the set of *Daily Bliss* to record her segment, she had noticed things tearing at the edges. It was like a bad trip. She could see the film of excitement and worship and fame peeling away at the corners. It was like a veneer, a sticker, and it could come away from where it stuck to reality and trap her beneath, vacuum sealing her inside, all of it suffocating and isolating.

Zurri told herself to go to sleep. Commanded it. She hated being awake for FTL travel, but her mind wouldn't stay quiet. Her anxiety spun up, jumping from thought to thought, memory to memory. In the early days of her modeling career, a start-up on the station had offered her the chance to experience their new full-body laser resurfacing treatment. Ordinarily, it would've cost way more than she could afford at the time, but they just wanted an endorsement in exchange for the service. Zurri had found herself lying down in what felt like a sandwich press, like the old-time suntanning beds from the 1990s Earth vids. The treatment itself wasn't wholly unpleasant, but she hated the sensation of being trapped in there, and after forty-five minutes the timer never chimed, so she pushed on the edges of the lid and it wouldn't budge. Nobody heard her screaming and struggling for fifteen minutes while the laser kept firing against her skin and the panic rose, a pulsing, living thing in her throat that threatened to grow until she choked. Buried alive. Burned to cinders. She was going to die. What would it feel like to die by a million fine lasers? Would it smell? Would it be like roasting in an oven?

Finally, when the staff let her out, she had cried on the floor in between bouts of screaming at them. After her skin healed, her manager at the time told her to give the endorsement anyway. She did.

Maybe, she thought, Paxton Dunn could snip that memory out of there, too, while he was poking around in her brain. She closed her eyes, hoping to sleep. Halos of fire burst around the edges of the darkness, and she smelled burning flesh.

Zurri groped for the ATTENDANT ASSISTANCE button hidden on the underside of her armrest. The technician from before came running back into her cabin, but Zurri could just barely make her out in the darkness. Everything on the ship trembled, and she saw the woman struggle to keep upright. She wasn't even supposed to be out of her seat and unharnessed, but she broke the rules because it was Zurri.

"Get me something that will put me to sleep," Zurri muttered, feeling her jaw clench. Just like the gift Paxton Dunn promised, this would be a quick taking away. "Something strong," she added. "Now."

6

As was too often the case, Senna heard Preece's words in her head, narrating her present with whispers from the past.

"Every single day," he liked to tell her, "you're taking one more step toward a column of fire. Death is the fire. Every act of selflessness, every moment of service, is how you forge the armor you will need. Give enough, do enough, be enough, and by the time you're inside that fire, you won't feel a thing."

She saw him everywhere, and nowhere. He wasn't a ghost haunting her so much as a gray wash painted across her life. Everything came to her through the filter of his influence. She saw him then as the drop shuttle approached Ganymede, detaching from the satellite in orbit and plunging her at heart-stopping speed toward the surface of the swirling, grayish marble below. His hair had been that color, once vibrantly blond but gone gray early, his beard the same dull and wispy shade.

As the drop ship neared the surface, her stomach twisted. Any space travel made her nervous—the last time she had been in a ship, it was hurtling toward annihilation. Alone in her assigned cubicle, Senna squeezed her hands into fists and told herself the shaking and rocking of the transport was normal. Storms on the surface. Ice and wind. The transfer from Tokyo Bliss Station to the Ganymede satellite had been comfortable enough. Senna forced herself to stay awake, staring around at the other passengers wedged into coach alongside her—if she didn't fall asleep, then she couldn't wake to a shuttle full of dead bodies.

She was the only passenger to stop off at the Ganymede satellite. Not a popular destination, it seemed, and she couldn't help but wonder if that meant she was the only person so far admitted to the experimental program there. For some reason, she had expected there to be a few other passengers on her flight joining the experiment, but she had been told repeatedly that it was an exclusive opportunity, maybe the other candidates hadn't done well during the mapping phase.

Senna shook out her wrist, still adjusting to the idea of the VIT gleaming there. For her entire life, she had been told that such things were evil, not to be trusted. Phones and tablets and computers and VITs were a distraction, isolating humans from one another, taking up all their time and focus when they could be helping one another. It was a big fat joke, Preece told them in the compound, conveniences meant to connect us, but in the end it only drove us further apart.

Believing it was easy when they ventured outside the compound on the station, and she watched pedestrians either squint down at their wrists or blink off into the distance, past one another, their eyes focused on the hundreds of neon augmented-reality advertisements vying for their attention.

"Security bioscan complete. Passenger identity verified, guest protocols engaged. Welcome, Senna Slate, you are now entering the Nysa Shelf, destined for Merchantia Solutions Corporation testing facility Altus Quasar-1277, classification alpha, common name the Dome," a pleasant, automated voice informed her. "Arrival is imminent; do not tamper with your safety harness until we have reached the moon's surface. We are one hundred and twelve hours into the Ganymede time cycle, DT or Dome time sixteen twenty-six. Please enjoy your stay."

Senna had read about timekeeping on the moon during her flight from the station. A typical day cycle on Ganymede took just over seven Earth days to complete, but inside Paxton Dunn's dome complex, normal day-night cycles were observed, the environment artificially simulated morning, afternoon and evening sun, going so far as to shorten or elongate them for seasons, with added variation for cloudy and sunny days. A similar system could be found on Tokyo Bliss Station and any well-established colonies. That was a relief. She couldn't imagine having to endure a single day that took an entire week.

The shuttle itself was small, very small, hardly larger than the evac pod she had used to survive the *Dohring-Waugh* crash. It seated a dozen passengers in individual, upright, closet-like cubicles. Strapped in at an angle, one could choose from a few programs about their destination, or the news in several languages, or animated soap operas. Senna had chosen silence, obsessively listening for any sign of distress, any hint that they were going down . . . A small, circular window to her left gave her a view of Ganymede speeding up toward them. The craft rattled mercilessly, making her teeth clatter, but no alarms sounded, and the shuttle rapidly decelerated, almost floating with momentary, balletic grace before rocking against the ground.

A field of pure, silvery white greeted her, mist swirling against the window. For a moment, it looked as if they had touched down in a bowl of steam, with no hint of civilization for miles and miles . . . But then she noticed the fog dissipating, blasted away from a single, perfect dome structure across the open space of the landing zone. It glowed, clear and bright, like a bead of water clinging to the edge of a silver ornament. Whenever the skirt of mist gathered too close to the Dome, some propulsion system dispersed it again, revealing the structure defiantly, as if it were in constant conflict with the icy winds threatening to swallow it up.

She watched a sturdy, squat, self-driving rover trundle across the LZ, extending a tunnel to the shuttle, bumping it gently when the walkway sealed to the door and pressurized. Her ears popped, and the harness snug against her chest went slack. This was it. She was about to step out of the shuttle and into that rover, and then that rover would take her to the complex. Even with the Dome right there, with evidence of Ganymede being somewhat settled, she felt like an explorer embarking on a grand and terrifying adventure. She felt groundless, and terrified, and alive.

The VIT on her arm, though almost weightless, felt like a hindrance. *Okay, prove Preece wrong. Prove you're useful and desirable, and not a tool of evil.*

Senna waited for directions, and lifted her VIT up, finding the message from Paxton Dunn she had saved. He had reached out personally to send the NDA and contracts, but also to invite her officially to the program. That was a huge deal, Marin said. *The* Paxton Dunn. She even showed the message to Jonathan, proof that the man was real.

"Anybody could have written that," Jonathan had responded, flippant, possibly offended. "It doesn't prove anything."

But Senna chose to believe a real human being had sent the

message. She liked it, and reading it over again calmed some of the roiling in her midsection. The shuttle rocked from side to side again, and at any moment she would need to board the rover. She didn't know if it was time to crap her pants or vomit.

Ms. Slate:

It's my absolute pleasure to tell you that your neural-mapping exercise was a success. I think you're the perfect candidate for this experiment, really I do. Just fantastic. Obviously, the final decision is up to you, but I think we could help you out. From what Kris tells me, you're carrying around a terrible burden. We can lighten the load for you, and I hope you'll let us.

We've put together a special team on Ganymede, the best of the best. We're dealing with your memories here, and those are precious, so I personally ensure that the staff here are trained, discreet and dedicated. This isn't something I say lightly, Ms. Slate—we're going to change the world with our work here, and I'd love for you to change it with us.

Between you and me? It's honestly just cool as hell. Come check it out.

Awaiting your response,
Paxton

Senna couldn't put her finger quite on why, but she already liked him. Just an acceptance letter to the program written by Kris or anyone at the company would have been fine, but a busy, sought-after, famous billionaire scientist was personally inviting her to do something incredible. If he succeeded, if he could carefully excise the memories that paralyzed people, that drove them to self-harm and suicide and addiction, then he was right, he really could change the world. The universe.

What kind of person would she be, she mused, watching the automated door to her cubicle slide open, without so much pain? Would she get up earlier? Attack the day with more energy? Would she take up a sport or start painting again? Maybe she would find love, or forgiveness, or even just the bravery to leave Marin's apartment and explore the station. There were museums and arcades, places to shop, people to meet, things to smell and taste and buy. Maybe she would actually get to Earth, think about tracking down her ancestors . . .

One step at a time, Senn, you're not even off the shuttle yet.

She stood and collected her nylon cross-body bag from the locked compartment under the window. There wasn't much for her to bring. Preece had insisted they incinerate most of their possessions before they boarded their doomed flight, and Senna only had a few lipsticks and a hairbrush that Marin had gifted her, along with a single packed bag of clothes, also hand-me-downs from a local thrift place on the station. Senna didn't know anything about fashion or makeup; none of it had mattered on the compound.

The tunnel leading to the rover was wobbly, shivering from the constant, oppressing winds. She hurried and all but hurled herself into the little car, landing on a hard plastic seat with a belt sized for someone much tinier. Senna just gripped the handrails molded into the plastic and waited, then yelped softly as the tunnel detached from the cylindrical shuttle, and the rover began its gradual, bumpy drive back across the landing zone to the complex.

A gray, mottled marble up in space and the same down on the

surface . . . *Here I am*, Senna mused, *on a moon a lifetime away from the station. All of this is technology's doing. What would Preece say if he could see me now?*

Ugly things, she knew. Confining things. The same kinds of pronouncements that had kept her in a cage of thoughts for twenty-odd years. Preece Ives was a doctor and a scholar, a natural leader, a tall, erect man with the booming voice and commanding presence that made people stop and look when he entered a room. He had seen the devastation of Earth and then had gone to space, and up on the station he had witnessed a different kind of devastation.

"You cannot build a paradise on God's Earth or in God's heavens" was part of his favorite speech, the one he gave to recruit. "Everything humans build is just a monument to greed and hubris."

Senna thought of them all as a family, but she knew what it really was: a cult. When the articles and blogs and takes started rolling out after the crash, Senna read them all. She couldn't help it. She slurped them down like bitter medicine. Cult, cult, cult. Everyone said it, and it had to be true, even if the word always made her flinch. Preece started gathering the family to him when he still had the position and power of a pediatrician, and when he officially broke away from the hospital it took a long time for anyone to realize what he was really doing.

"A monument to greed and hubris," Senna murmured, staring out at the swirling silver mists. "That's what you were building. A monument to yourself."

The Dome rose up out of the fog like a shining city, futuristic and unreal, something straight out of the vids or the arcades. It generated its own pretty light, glowing from within, like a little kid with a secret, like a promise poised just behind loose lips.

The rover slowed down. They were approaching the pressurized doors. Unexpectedly, Senna could see dozens of exotic, leafy plants clustered on the other side of the barrier, the glass filmed with dense humidity,

What would Preece say if he could see me now?

Senna unbuckled her seat belt and told herself she didn't care.

7

The portal to the Dome sealed shut behind her with a loud, pneumatic hiss, the light blasting from farther down the tunnel-like walkway making her pupils flare huge. A long, clear tube led into the Dome proper, and now, inside, she watched the icy mists breathe against the edge of the barrier separating her from the unbreathable atmosphere. She felt on the cusp and took tiny steps, clinging to her meager bag of personal belongings. Light at the end of the tunnel, she thought. What a cliché! But maybe she could've come empty-handed, because each small step felt like it was bringing her toward an unknown as final and strange as death.

The tunnel rattled, hard, chips of silicate and ice peppering the barrier to her right. The storms. The information she had read on the flight over had mentioned the changing weather patterns on Ganymede repeatedly—raging gusts along the Nysa Shelf made travel to and from the campus dangerous, sometimes leaving Paxton Dunn and the Dome staff effectively stranded. So this was to be expected, Senna told herself. And then the sirens began.

The tunnel went dark. True, cold fear swept over her, and Senna hugged her bag and herself tightly, hunching over as a strip of bright red LEDs crackled to life along the edges of the tunnel floor.

"Please remain calm," a disembodied male voice told her. "The facility is detecting extreme wind activity. Please remain calm and follow instructions."

Massive, curved shutters rose up around the tunnel, snapping together at the top and plunging her into deeper darkness. Senna winced from the nearness and strength of the sirens, the high *wooooop-wip-wooooop* sending shock waves from her ears to the back of her neck. She decided it was safer to get away from the doors, even if they were sealed, and shuffled clumsily down the tube toward the Dome's interior, the red strips of light on the floor leaving smudges behind her eyelids when she blinked.

Even as the voice implored her, she didn't feel at all calm. Larger chunks of ice slammed into the tunnel, the impact loud enough to rise even above the deafening sirens. She hurried on, and looked into the thick shadows ahead, wishing the little crimson strips on her left and right would illuminate anything at all. Instead, she stared into a yawning chasm. The way ahead smelled lush and wet, heady like the hydroponic vegetable fields on the station. More slabs of ice pelted the tunnel, driving her under the final archway and into a larger area. She sensed the walls and ceiling falling away, and when the emergency lights on the ground pulsed, she saw fragments of what lay all around her—plants and statues, things that might be pleasant enough in the daylight but that made twisted, untrustworthy shadows in the dark.

Senna stopped, afraid to walk farther and trip over something. The automated voice hadn't given her further instructions, and so she shivered, and winced, and waited. A shape up ahead became more real, a silhouette firming up, like a shadow detaching from the rest and giving itself sentience and form. It came toward her, vaguely human-shaped, hunched and moving quickly, with rapid, stuttering steps and then leaps. Senna began to back away, but then it was right in front of her, and it stole her breath away. The sirens. The red glow. It was happening again all around her—the death, the crash, the end of her own life as she knew it.

What is this? What are you?

This was a terrible, twisted thing, and not like any of the nightmares or traumas or human beings that had given her fear before. This came from somewhere else, a place without a name or a culture or an origin. *I'm on a distant moon, far away from home, and a thing of no origin has found me.*

She opened her mouth to scream. Whatever it was, she wanted to be away from it. Every knowing sinew in her body told her to run. But where? Where could she go?

A hand closed around her wrist and squeezed, and then Senna really did shriek.

"Hey! It's all right. Hey, hey, don't panic! I'm here, I'm here . . ."

It was a different male voice, lightly accented, warm and friendly. British maybe. He said those words, *I'm here, I'm here,* as if that would soothe her and have meaning. His hand was gentle and his skin humid. A light rose from his wrist, a flash from his VIT monitor showing his face. Utterly human and mostly unremarkable, not a thing of no origin at all, just a man with thick black glasses and wavy dark hair.

"Jesus! Not the sort of welcome I had planned," the man said, offering her an apologetic smile and ducking his head. "But that's how it is here on Ganymede, yeah? Unpredictable."

Then he touched something on his VIT, and bright white light filtered through the space around them, illuminating what felt like a snow globe full of leaves and stardust. Senna was still shaking, ricocheting from terror to awe in an instant.

"Paxton Dunn," he said, extending his hand.

It took Senna a moment to come back to herself. She flexed her jaw, slowly lowering her bag and staring at his hand, the hand that had touched her a second earlier. "I thought I saw something in the darkness . . ."

"Just me, I'm afraid," he said with a chuckle. Finally, she took his hand. "I'm sorry you had to get a scare like that right off the jump. The windstorms have been getting worse lately. We shored up the safety shutters before you all arrived, so there's nothing to worry about. The alerts can be jarring, though, and for that I apologize."

Senna had liked his kind message inviting her to join the experiment, but now that Paxton Dunn was in front of her, she wasn't sure she liked him. The man. It was a mean instinct, but her initial thought of him was that nobody really liked him. When he let go of her hand and smiled again, it never touched the corners of his eyes. His teeth were flat white and too even to be real. His heathered gray shirt had been tucked in all the way around except for one tiny corner that still bore a thumbprint in the fabric.

"I'm Senna," she murmured, tucking a strand of hair nervously behind her ear. "But you know that. I'm sure you know everything about me."

"Not everything," he said, laughing again. "But quite a lot, yes. I hope that's not creepy?"

It is now that you said it that way.

"No, no," she said, still shaken. "I just . . . I need a moment, sorry. I don't do well with the lights and the sirens."

"Jesus, of course you don't. Of course! Anju!" he suddenly barked, making her jump. "Anju! Can I get some water for Ms. Slate? Where is that . . ." Paxton Dunn trailed off, turning a tight circle, putting both fists into his hair. He turned back to Senna, biting his lip with concentrated fury. "This is such a bad first impression. Mortifying. Jesus, mortifying."

The *click-clack* of high heels echoed throughout the expansive dome-like structure, tall and airy as a cathedral. Senna took a few gulping breaths, noticing that the tall, prehistoric plants and statues around her weren't so menacing in the glaring light of a fully lit afternoon. Birdsong began to filter quietly and cheerfully through the space. The floor beneath her feet was tiled a turquoise blue and white, like something from a fancy vacation. A woman came flying around one of the bobbling, moistened plants, a slim cylinder of water in one hand, a tablet in the other. She had the perfectly coiffed and made-up precision of a highly organized person, like Marin but with more expensive shoes. Wearing a tight white two-piece suit, she had to take dainty, zigzagging steps in her pencil skirt.

"There!" Paxton snatched the water out of the woman's hand as if he had been waiting for six hours and not six minutes. The woman didn't react, apparently accustomed to this sort of behavior. She waited patiently a step behind him, her huge, tawny eyes fixed on Paxton's back, just below his shoulder blade.

"Do you need to sit? We can take you somewhere to sit," Paxton said, offering her the water.

Senna looped her bag over one elbow and took the glass with both hands, watching it tremble in her grasp.

"You're overwhelming her," the woman, Anju, remarked mildly. "Is he overwhelming you?"

Nodding, Senna glanced away from Paxton, feeling somehow

ungracious. He couldn't control the weather. The storm hitting and triggering the alert system was just bad timing, and Senna felt suddenly sheepish for overreacting.

"I'm not always this jumpy," she promised softly, sipping the water. It helped.

"It's okay if you are," Anju assured her, coming forward, dodging around Paxton and taking Senna by the elbow. Steering her through the wandering maze of tiles in the foyer, or lobby, or courtyard, she took Senna to a low slab bench between two free-form nude sculptures. A suspended walkway hung above them, seemingly floating there like magic.

Senna collapsed, grateful to be off her feet.

"He's a genius," Anju told her with a pinched smirk. "But not always the best with people."

"What was that?" Paxton had joined them, and rested his hands on his waist, gazing down at Senna with the same laser-focused energy as Anju. Senna couldn't help it, she kept looking at the obvious place he had tugged on his shirt to make it look rumpled and messy by design.

"Just girl talk," Anju replied breezily, tipping back her chin. She was shorter than Paxton in her heels by about an inch. Her hair, a slightly deeper brown than her skin, was braided in an intricate design across the top of her head, not a flyaway or bit of frizz in sight. She looked at home in the killer heels, well-developed calves keeping her balanced on the stilts.

If Paxton was messy by design, Anju, by contrast, could have been immaculate by design.

"Anju is our staff coordinator," Paxton explained, giving her a cool smile. There was an odd tension between them, as if Anju's kindness to Senna had annoyed him. Maybe he just liked being the hero. "We keep a limited number of MSC employees on campus. Need to know. Need to operate. That kind of thing. Only staff with my absolute trust are allowed to stay on."

"Picky," Anju added with another smirk. "Or maybe we're the best of the best."

"Not just the best," said Paxton. "Perfect."

Another gust of wind rattled the Dome. The lights had come back on and the sirens had cut out, but the blast shield remained in place, surrounding the otherwise transparent dome in a black shell. Senna shivered and glanced toward the ceiling.

"How are the other guests taking the alert?" Paxton asked.

Consulting the holographic display tablet in her hand, Anju grimaced. "You're about to find out. Zurri is headed this way."

"Zurri?" Senna felt herself perk up. "As in the model?"

Paxton shot her another sheepish grin. She couldn't imagine he actually needed the glasses he wore, since a man of his wealth could afford the nicest vision-correction surgery on the market. Were they functional, some kind of new, strange tech, or were they just an aesthetic choice? "If you've seen the news lately, then you can guess why she's here."

"I did see," Senna said softly. "It was awful. She must have been so frightened."

Just as Anju predicted, the statuesque model appeared, dressed in a melon-orange wrap dress and wedge sandals with clear straps. And as she came closer, Senna saw that Zurri was not happy. She rolled in like a storm cloud, lip quivering, eyes snapping to Paxton with a speed that made Senna shrink, and she wasn't even the target.

"This is bullshit."

"Zurri!" Paxton leapt to his feet, opening his arms as if to greet an old friend. The model froze, staring lasers. "You'll have to excuse us," he went on, shrugging. "The storms conspired against us. It wasn't safe to construct a private wing for your stay. I'm afraid you'll have to rough it with the likes of us."

Swiveling at the hip, he gave Senna a pursed little smile, bringing her in on the joke. Senna wasn't interested. She had seen Zurri in ads even while cloistered on the compound. Paxton Dunn was a household name on the station. Suddenly, she was acutely aware that the only thing she had in common with these people was that they were all carbon-based life-forms.

Zurri propped the heels of her hands on her hips, then jutted those to one side. "I think my demands were clear, Dunn. Crystal. This?" She nodded vaguely to the ethereal, plant-filled dome glittering with moisture and artificial light around them, a technological and horticultural marvel plonked down on a far-distant moon, and said, "Total bullshit. When is the next shuttle back to the satellite? I'll be on it."

"Missed the red lights and the sirens, did you?" His tone had taken a turn, the humorous smirk vanishing. Senna noticed a muscle jumping in his neck. "The rover is magnetically anchored to the ground outside right now. If it weren't, it would be in about a million pieces, scattered across the ice fields of Ganymede. Would you like to be scattered in a million pieces?"

Zurri snorted, but Senna shivered. The way he said it, viciously, like he had imagined it, made her squirm.

"Well then." Zurri sighed. "Have one of your fembots here consult the stars or the charts or whatever it is they do and let me know when I can depart. We had a deal, Dunn. I'm Zurri. I do not compromise. I don't need to."

Paxton took off his thick black spectacles and rubbed at his eyes, then replaced them and gestured for Anju to come closer. "Can you get something to put our guest here at ease, please? You're a vodka woman, right?"

Flicking her eyes skyward, Zurri gave a single, furious nod.

"Great. Beautiful. Vodka, neat, on the rocks for Zurri, and Ms. Slate here will be sticking with water."

"Miss?" Anju prompted the model politely, in a mollifying tone that told Senna it wasn't her first time dealing with temperamental diva types. "There's a bar this way."

Zurri made sure to pin Paxton Dunn with one more enraged glance before falling into stride with Anju and disappearing around one of the nude statues. Her eyes had lingered on Senna briefly, too, a squint indicating that some memory had been triggered. Senna got that a lot. Everyone tended to recognize her. Judge her. She wilted, wishing she had been the only civilian there for the experiment. If they took her memories of the crash away, would the hot, shameful flutter in her chest that came every time she was recognized vanish, too?

Around them, the Dome gradually returned to normal. The blast shields remained in place, but the light twinkled down around them now with a slightly amber twinge, as if afternoon were waning. Somehow, he had managed to simulate the flow of time so seamlessly that the oncoming threat of twilight and darkness felt real, too, the birdsongs emanating from the plants shifting almost imperceptibly.

"How are you feeling?" Paxton asked, gazing down at her.

Senna sipped her water and shook her head. "Better, I think. Maybe starstruck?"

"Ha." His smile returned. "You're a star, too."

"Not for the right reasons."

"You should never back down from the spotlight," Paxton told her. "You should run toward it."

Senna knew that would never be her. She gulped down more

water, hoping it would give her time to think of something witty to say. "But you live in isolation."

His smile was electric. "Yes, but I had the spotlight first, and now it follows me. You need power to do good. To do the most good you need the most power."

That almost sounded like something Preece would say, but Senna didn't mention that.

"Here, let me send you a packet," he said, crouching and bringing his left hand close to hers. His VIT was a design she had never seen before, extremely low profile and sleek, steel gray. "You'll want a map of the Dome, and your treatment schedule, of course."

"I don't really know how to use it yet," Senna admitted. "I've only set up the mail feature. It's . . . it's not something I grew up with, and I never got the implant. We weren't allowed."

Paxton didn't seem surprised at that. "Ah, our Luddite."

"Not for the right reasons," Senna repeated, blushing. "Anyway, it's beautiful and interesting here, right? Why would I want to stare at my wrist all day?"

"You know, that's the first complimentary thing I've heard from any of you," he replied, clucking his tongue. "I'll send the data packet anyway. I want you to have the map, and it will give you a gentle buzz when our third guest is near. You may want to avoid him if you can, at least until he's had a few rounds of the treatment."

Senna frowned, watching her VIT screen light up as Paxton sent the data across to her device. "Why would I do that?"

Without a hitch, he settled into a deeper crouch and found her gaze, holding it for a moment long enough to make her start shifting around on the bench again. "The *Dohring-Waugh*? The ship your people hijacked?"

Senna swallowed noisily and nodded, feeling her hands go numb.

"His mother was on Mars when it hit, she was at the impact zone," he said, venting a quiet, sad sigh. "The *Dohring-Waugh* crash obliterated her."

8

Han was buzzing. This was it. The Dome. *The* Dome.

He paced back and forth in front of the window in his assigned room. On the station, those views were always phony, but Paxton Dunn let them choose whether they wanted a more calming, simulated window vista or the real deal. Han let the swirling silver plains of Ganymede glow bright, hot white against him while he composed a message on his VIT.

> i'll never forget this, lucas. thank you, thank you, thank you thank you

When Han tried to hit **send**, nothing happened. An instant later, a three-dimensional, augmented-reality exclamation point shot up from the VIT screen. Storm activity meant there was no connectivity to anything but the interior Dome Wi-Fi, his message to his brother would be saved for later, apparently, held on the server and then released once the connection was solid once more.

He just hoped Lucas got it, because he meant every word of it. His older brother could be a completely boring loser, but he finally caved and signed the consent forms. As Han's legal guardian, he needed to give the program his blessing. Lucas was old enough that he had met their father, Shui, before their parents split. Typhoons were ravaging their home, but Shui refused to go. Lucas only ever described him as short, bullheaded and loud.

"When he laughed," Lucas would tell him, "it was like someone was clapping in your face."

Han managed to secure Lucas's permission after assuring him about fifty times that he wasn't going to Ganymede to forget their mother, only to delete the memory of her voice message, and her last, ragged words to him. The goodbye he had missed because he refused to pick up . . .

"It's like hypnosis," Han had assured his brother. "Or therapy."

"You've tried therapy," Lucas had reminded him, annoyingly. "You hate it and it doesn't work."

"This is different. This is Paxton Dunn's therapy, bro. He can do anything."

More and more, Han was truly believing that. The Dome was a marvel, more than Han could've even imagined. It was simple, clean, elegant, not an over-the-top bachelor pad like the gossip podcasts on the station liked to claim. They were obviously jealous, Han thought, just haters.

He was buzzing. He was giddy. The Willy Wonka virtual reality experience at the arcade on the station had been the highlight of his birthday the year before, but this was like that cranked up to one hundred.

You've won the golden ticket. Now what?

Antsy, he kept pacing. Now what? Obviously, he wanted to meet Paxton Dunn, get the grand tour, but first . . .

"Starving," Han muttered, leaving the window and going back toward the front door to his quarters. He had been given spacious accommodations, a nicer, more stylish apartment than what he lived in with his brother and his Servitor nannies. Occasionally, their father back on Earth shelled out some cash to keep them going, and their mother's life insurance policy hadn't been much, so Lucas put in nonstop hours in the Merchantia legal department. His division was still fighting some big case after the Foxfire incident the previous year, so he glimpsed Lucas for breakfast twice a week and heard him come home or leave or turn on a vid in the living room. Less of a brother and more of a familiar haunting.

But this? This was nice. Roomie. A big, wide hall that led onto an open-plan kitchen, with a circular dining table. Then came the living room where Han had been pacing, with a flash vid console setup and a huge, squishy couch. He had dropped off his bag on the bed through the door next to the vid monitor, and let his hand sink down into the cloud-soft mattress. The walls were tiled with programmable slats, currently cycling through a series of russet and purple shades. Han would tinker with that later through his VIT and program the tiles for soothing morning, day and night colors. In fact, after meeting Paxton Dunn, his next goal was to dive into the controls he could find through his VIT. The facility was obviously heavily automated, and he was curious if he could find his way into the guts of the system. What would the smartest man in the galaxy's programming look like?

Artistic, he hoped, like when his mother took him to see an actual Monet at the university. He hadn't given a rat's ass about the painting, but everyone oohed and aahed over it, and that?

That's how he would feel finally getting to see Dunn's mind at work.

"What do you have for me?" he wondered aloud, crossing into the kitchen and pulling open the refrigerated drawer beneath the smooth, white countertop.

"Hi," a friendly male voice said. Han turned. On the circular kitchen table, he saw a stack of rings light up, pulsing in a rhythmic sequence. He hadn't given the thing much thought before, assuming it was just a lamp. When it spoke again, the lights grew brighter, following the cadence of the voice. "It sounds like you might need assistance. How can I help?"

Han frowned, leaning over the refrigerator door but looking at the glowing device. More than hating unknown automated voices, he hated being surprised by one. *At least it isn't hers.* "You're the facility AI?"

"The facility designated Altus Quasar-1277 also known as the Dome is outfitted with the GENIE in-home operating system, version oh-point-seven," the voice told him.

"You're a GENIE?" Han almost forgot all about his hunger and irritation, straightening up. "Those are still in beta . . ."

"Correct." The voice sounded like it might be gently laughing at him. The intonations were so lifelike it sounded like he was speaking with a man hidden beneath the table. "You can call me Genie. Do you have questions about the food options available to you?"

Han smirked. "Yeah. Sure. What do you got?"

There was the briefest pause, as if the system were searching some database. "All right, here's what I got: Your recent search terms and station delivery choices indicate a strong bias for Mrs. Bao's Slurp Shack, Fish Delish, Chicken A-Go-Go and Centauri

Snacks. Accordingly, this unit has been stocked with a number of hot and cold noodle options, vegetarian sushi rolls, snack cakes, chicken nuggets in pleasing shapes, carbonated beverages, and sugar-free energy syrups. Further options are available at the dining hall in Zone Seven, approximately a five-minute walk from your current location. Can I help you with anything else, Han?"

Han glanced back at the drawer and then reached in, fishing out a packet of his favorite white chocolate and hazelnut snack cakes. Tearing open the biodegradable packet with his teeth, he chuckled. "What does GENIE stand for?"

The pile of rings lit up again, this time pale blue. "General Intelligence Entity."

"What temperature is it?"

"The current exterior temperature of this facility is one hundred and sixty degrees Kelvin, or one hundred and thirteen degrees below zero Celsius. The current interior temperature of this unit is twenty-three degrees Celsius," Genie replied.

After a few bites of sweets, Han spun around looking for the recycling bin.

"The receptacle you require is in the drawer two spaces to the left of the refrigerated box."

Han snorted and checked Genie's directions before swearing under his breath. "How did you do that?"

"Audible crinkling and your hesitation indicates an empty wrapper. This is your first time entering the kitchen in this unit. The conclusion was obvious."

"You're spying on me?" Han tossed his wrapper.

"My intervention and observation settings can be adjusted if you are dissatisfied with current methods of assistance," Genie replied, this time sounding serious. Maybe even offended.

Han glanced around, finding no visible cameras or recording devices hidden along the edges of the cabinets. Still, he felt naked. Watched. "Are you recording us?"

"For your privacy, there are no security camera devices in this unit," Genie said. "The corridors, medical quadrants, dining hall, Dome courtyard and offices are monitored continuously. Would you like to adjust your privacy settings now, Han?"

"No," he said, walking by the light-up GENIE unit but keeping his eye on it as he passed. "Not yet. Genie?"

"Yes, Han."

"Where is Paxton Dunn?" he asked.

The system hesitated. Was it pinging Dunn himself and asking for permission? Han held his breath.

"Paxton Dunn is currently in Zone One, Dome courtyard. Would you like directions?"

"No," Han replied, hurrying toward the door. "I'll find my own way."

9

So. She was trapped in an overdesigned crystal ball with the weird Kool-Aid cult chick from the news and a guy who looked like an accountant going through his second midlife crisis. Incredible. Zurri would have to kill Paxton Dunn, and then Bev, and then herself. It was a disaster. Worst of all, there was nothing harder than vodka on the entire premises.

At least according to the resident fembot.

She glared at the Anju woman in icy bewilderment. "No Rikter? No Rapture or Kill Switch or coke? Not even synthetic CB-fucking-D?"

Anju handed her a squat glass with the vodka and ice. No cubes here but perfect circles, twee little mimics of the Dome. "There are medical sedatives and several neuroleptics developed for emergency responses to our proprietary treatment but that's all," Anju assured her, sounding more bemused than cross. "And you really don't want to try the antipsychotics for recreational purposes. Trust me."

"Just level with me: How long until the next shuttle?" Zurri pressed, knocking back the drink and handing the cold glass back to Anju for more. She was surprised there wasn't some splashy Servitor bartender. Instead, it was just a simple, recessed set of shelves behind a motion-sensored barrier. When Anju's hand came close to the plexiglass, it flinched away, a cool blast of air rolling over them.

"Even the most advanced MSC algorithms can't predict weather windows with perfect accuracy," Anju said. "A windstorm can last for sixteen minutes or sixteen hours, so some patience will be required."

Anju was pretty enough to land a modeling contract back on Tokyo Bliss. Even Zurri had to admit her dark brown skin was flawless, borderline enviable. She would be in the background of a campaign, sure, but Zurri couldn't imagine what Anju was doing rotting on a moon of Jupiter being some jerk-off's assistant. Or if he was anything like the other men Zurri knew, some jerk-off's babysitter.

"Huh. What are you for?" Zurri asked, tearing the second glass of vodka out of the girl's hand.

She was met with a prim, frozen smile. "Excuse me?"

"What do you do here, sweetheart? Besides serve cocktails, I mean."

"I'm the staff coordinator," Anju replied, with the steady roteness of someone who had endured a bad attitude millions of times. She had an even, robotic manner about her that grated on Zurri. People like that always had a button, and Zurri would find it, and push it, because that was how you got what you wanted.

"What staff?" Zurri laughed. "I've seen exactly two of you plus the cult chick. This place is empty."

"Brea and Dr. Colbie will be at the reception dinner this evening, you may see a few unskinned Servitors around, too, as they perform maintenance functions for us," Anju told her, collected. "I'm sure Paxton made it clear in his pre-arrival materials that there is a limited on-site staff for security and privacy reasons. The facility is outfitted for independence and convenience. It's not a smart home, it's a genius one."

Zurri wouldn't be called stupid, implied or otherwise. She would find that damned button. Tapping her middle finger on the glass anxiously, she slowly looked Anju up and down. "Paxton, mm?"

"Yes," Anju replied. "What about him?"

"First-name basis with the boss? Come on, you're fucking him, aren't you?"

Anju had to be made of steel. Her lip didn't even twitch. Not a dent to be seen. That placid, calm demeanor didn't waver as she tilted her head to the side and reached for the vodka bottle to refill Zurri's emptying glass. "I'm not, no, though we do subscribe to a more casual work environment philosophy here. Anyway, I believe he's unattached, but you're not his type."

She poured exactly a shot as Zurri waited, and wondered, and calculated. "Uppity?" she asked.

"No." Anju put the bottle back in the chiller, then began to walk away. "Unhappy."

"You're both so perfect for the program," Paxton Dunn was saying, while Senna tried not to hyperventilate. "It's taken me years to find just the right people. I didn't want to turn either of you down. This kid . . . I mean, this kid really wants to be here."

So do I. Or I did.

"I saw him," Senna murmured. They had left behind her water glass, the bench and the two artsy nudes, Paxton leading her through the deepening golden light to a walkway suspended over the Dome entryway. It went high, high up, so delicate and fragile it looked like it was floating, every cable, screw and panel of it a strong, clear substance, so strong it didn't even sway under their weight. Senna leaned against the waist-high, solid railing. "When I came in for my neural mapping on the station . . . I saw him there. He looked at me with so much anger, I don't think it's a good idea if I stay. When Zurri goes, I'll take the shuttle with her."

"Number one," Paxton sighed, ruffling his dark hair, "that would leave me with exactly one participant. Number two, Zurri won't share anything with anyone. Most importantly, number three—I'll handle it."

Senna flushed and began to shake her head, but Paxton reached over and closed his big, warm hand over her forearm.

"I want you here, Senna. It'll be handled, okay?" He laughed breathily and took his hand back. "I know how this is going to make me sound, but the kid idolizes me. He's . . . well, he's a big fan. I'll bring him around."

Her brows drew down in frustration. "His mother died. He doesn't need to be brought around to anything. I'm just a reminder of what he's lost, and he has every right to be furious. I would hate me, too."

"You don't know everything about the situation, you don't . . . ," Paxton replied, trailing off. He looked at her for a long, long moment, and Senna felt the impulse to turn away. "It's going to get handled. He's here to forget that night, same as you."

"That's private," Senna muttered. "You shouldn't have told me that."

The gray VIT on his wrist buzzed, and he pushed away from the railing and away from her. "Senna? I want you here, okay? Stay."

She knew then what his VIT had been telling him. Her device vibrated, too. The kid—Han was his name—was getting closer, and now they had been warned of his proximity. Senna clenched her jaw and watched Paxton Dunn saunter away. A strange shape enveloped him, outlining him like there was a shadow clinging to his back, radiating off him in a black surge. It reminded her of what she had seen coming out of the darkness when the facility sirens had blared, and she felt her hand tuck up under her chin. A reflex. The shadow made her want to curl up and become smaller, and hide.

I don't care what she says, when Zurri gets on that shuttle, I should be on it, too.

"Dinner in an hour!" Paxton called over his shoulder, nearly to the delicate, invisible stairs. "It's your favorite, aloo gobi. That *is* your favorite, right?"

He didn't wait to hear her response.

Preece liked to do the same thing. He had the most incredible face for listening, grandfatherly and wise, old but somehow unlined, a welcoming, knowing, caring face. But after almost fifteen years of his constant company, of thinking he was listening when Senna told him her secrets or her fears, she started to see the hollowness behind his pale eyes. She started to test him, subtly. Their compound on the station took up the most unwanted real estate in the sector, placed right above the sweltering heat vents of Hydroponica. Creating enough clean water and fresh food for the station required an immense amount of energy, and it had to go somewhere. It went right into the ground beneath their feet, made them sweat day and night, filled the atmosphere above them with a slightly rotten-smelling vapor.

They had a distinct smell, their group, because the perspiration was constant. Health and virus checks were mandatory, monthly affairs for everyone living on Tokyo Bliss Station. A single undetected outbreak could wipe out the entire population in a matter of weeks if allowed to proliferate. Senna remembered the station health workers twitching behind their face shields and masks, eyes watering from the odor as they took cheek and nasal swabs. They had to swab about three dozen people in the compound, and she could see them fumbling, hurrying to get it done and get out. After the crash, when Senna was the only one left alive, Marin had to explain how the shower controls worked, and the difference between shampoo and conditioner. On the station, there was none of that, just barrels of water, rationed with extreme care for personal cleaning, and a wash rag. Preece made them exercise relentlessly, which didn't help matters.

Preece was a doctor, so of course he tried his best to convince the station workers that the smell was not a sign that they were unhygienic on the compound. They ate a vegetarian diet, he would shout at the bored workers swabbing away, no caffeine on the premises, no alcohol, no unnatural sugars, no drug use. Daily vigorous calisthenics. Healthiest citizens on Tokyo Bliss. The disease checks remained mandatory, and so did his exasperation.

When the younger members complained about the heat, Preece would remind them that they were lucky to be warm, that the cold vacuum of space was just on the other side of the station walls. After the disaster, they would come to be known as the Dohring-Waugh cult, named after the ship Preece had hijacked for his suicide mission. On the station, Senna learned they were mostly referred to as Compound Kids, since Dr. Preece Ives pulled most of them in young, straight out of the bloated station foster and adoption system. Internally, Preece called them his brood.

He was father and mother, and they were all his little chicks, hatched out of desperation but taken under his wing. Cared for. Warm. See? The Hydroponica vents were just simulating their little nest, hugging them with the heat of a round bird belly, holding them down, protecting them.

Senna stood very still and watched twilight fall in the Dome. Everything she knew about light and dark was simulated. Tokyo Bliss Station did the same thing—tricking them all into thinking they were experiencing a normal cycle, a cycle like earthlings, but in the end, it was all just pretend. It probably comforted the people who had actually been born on Earth and moved to the station for a job or to outrun the flooding.

The scent of flowers filled the air around her, delicate and plush, not so different from the orchid and hyacinth perfume Marin wore. Life on the station, on the compound, smelled like sweat, like the coarse natural soap they used to scrub at their clothes and their own stench. Now the Dome felt and smelled like what she imagined a far-off glade on Earth to be. Incredible, that it could seem so real and put her at ease. Was that coded into her somehow? Did that live in her DNA?

Maybe she ought to know, intrinsically, what June smelled like. What did the sun feel like when it began to burn the skin? How did the air and the wind change when summer withered into autumn? She had seen pictures, watched vids, absorbed what she could from stories and poems, but she had never felt it herself. All her life had been spent in space, on a station built by humans but mostly by machines. Even if humanity had built the station, and even if humans inhabited it, she couldn't help but wonder if she was something other than human. A new thing, and almost alien.

With his teachings, with his rules, with his enforcements, Preece had tried to keep his brood human, to connect them to one another because they couldn't be connected to Earth. It didn't work. Whatever he had inflicted upon Senna, it only made her feel disconnected from everyone around her. They all stared. They all knew. She was something else, almost alien.

A new thing.

She heard Paxton's footsteps growing fainter as he descended the stairs. Taking a few steps after him, she called out, "I don't want that, actually. I want meat tonight, um, chicken."

Was that too much to ask? Too rude? Too much of an imposition? Senna shrank back against the railing and hoped he hadn't heard her.

"A new carnivore in our midst!" She heard him give a full-bodied laugh. "How intriguing."

10

"There he is! Han. Han, the man of the hour! Just what the doctor ordered."

Han spun around, buzzing harder. *Man of the hour, is this for real?* It was for real. Paxton Dunn emerged from behind an imposing wall of broad-leafed plants. The Dome courtyard felt more like a greenhouse or arboretum—a suspended walkway above them, simulated birdsong and suffused, thoughtful lighting creating the sense that one had stepped into another world, a new biome, an oasis in the middle of an ever-seething icy desert. Fairy lights twinkled faintly with video game surrealism, long bird calls beginning to echo through the expansive anteroom, simulated holographic dew shimmering on the leaves that bobbed out of Paxton's way as he approached.

Years. He had waited years for this moment, anticipating how slick his palms would be, how he would hold his head high and take on a serious aspect, and try to greet the man voted smartest, no contest, with confidence. But he crumpled, letting out a snorting, goofy laugh, feeling borderline hysterical as his idol strode across the Mediterranean tiles and presented his broad, flat hand.

Han reached for it, shaking, but Paxton slapped it with a laugh of his own. "Now, this is the energy our experiment needed. Masculine energy."

Reading Paxton's articles and biography, Han had never expected him to have a British accent. It only made him sound more sophisticated, more impossibly out of reach. Accents on the station tended to blend together unless someone lived in one of the ethnic districts and kept speaking Spanish, or Japanese, or Korean fluently. Han didn't think he had ever met a British person before, and certainly not one with an actual accent.

"H–Hi." *Idiot.* Han tucked his hands into the back pockets of his jeans nervously. He was already bungling this. "It's . . . Wow. It's so crazy to meet you."

"Smart kid like you? Bound to happen. I don't take interns, but you never know. If this project wraps up nicely, maybe I'll need some new blood around here . . ." Paxton clapped him on the shoulder and Han felt his knees wobble. This couldn't be real. He was dreaming. He had to be dreaming. "I wanted to have a one-on-one before everyone sits down to eat. That okay with you?"

"Yeah. Yeah, obviously. Of course."

"Fantastic. Jesus, it's getting dark," Paxton said, glancing up. "We better hurry. Come on. How much have you seen? Not much, right? What am I saying? You got here an hour ago, of course you haven't seen much. How are you settling in? Oh, hey, there's Brea. Have you met her? Come meet her."

He talked quickly, but precisely, and with the kind of force that told Han he wasn't necessarily meant to answer all the rapid-fire questions. With a hand still on Han's shoulder, Paxton steered him around toward two gigantic bay doors that could be slid open to reveal a gallery, wide and airy, with a museum-like quality. An olive-skinned woman with thick, bunchy black curls clicked toward them with her right palm open and skyward. A small black cube sat on her hand, a red light flickering at its center.

"Smile!" Brea wrinkled her nose. As she came closer, Han noticed freckles dotted all over her face. She was just as pretty if not prettier than the woman who had greeted him when he arrived, Anju. And just like meeting Anju, he felt paralyzed. Han had two online girlfriends for a while, but they were just for gaming with and sometimes he would ask for raunchy pictures. The ones they sent? He knew they were just fakes pulled off the web. It didn't bother him much, he knew they would never meet in person, and so he would never have to be disappointed that they didn't match the photos.

"Just some arrival captures," Brea added, closing her hand around the cube and covering the flashing light. "It's so nice to meet you, Han."

"Thanks," he muttered. Everyone was so nice. Maybe it was easy to be nice in paradise. "It's nice to meet you, too."

He glanced up curiously at Paxton. The man. The legend. Of course he lived in isolation with a bunch of astoundingly beautiful woman. Why would he choose to do anything else?

"Brea will be handling all of our PR for the project," Paxton explained. She wore a similar outfit to Anju's, but Earth-sky blue, tailored, trim, a tight skirt and fitted suit jacket with no lapels. "I never allow press here, but you're going to be one of my success stories. Everyone on Earth, on all the stations, they're going to want to know about what we accomplish here."

Han was already beginning to feel a little tired. He would push through it, and the snack cake had helped, but he never interfaced with real people much. Hacking his nanny Servitors to shut them up was always an option, but he wanted to impress Paxton.

"You should take the vid again," Han told her. "I think I looked stupid."

"Do not be silly," she giggled. "Even if you did, we can fix it." Brea pointed vaguely to the ceiling. "Upon arrival you were digitally scanned and uploaded into our archival system. We can tweak your expressions until they are just right. You will have final approval, naturally."

Han blinked. "Oh."

"You will recall it was in your NDA," Brea chirped.

"Oh, sure. Right."

"You're freaking him out, Brea. Down, girl," Paxton chuckled, then made a growling sound at her. She smiled, but it never touched her eyes. Her face looked frozen for a moment, like she was waiting for something. "We're heading to the labs. Is Colbie there?"

"Yes, I believe she was just shutting things down for the day," Brea replied, frowning.

"Well, shoot. Let me just ping her, then. I need things open a bit longer, want to show Han what we're working on. He's getting a private tour. I thought a tech head like him would appreciate it." Paxton nudged him. "Am I right?"

"The LENG tech," Han murmured. "You're going to show it to me now?"

"Why not? It's mine. I can do whatever I want with it," said Paxton, shrugging. "Anyway, I know you're a busy kid. We can just get your first session out of the way quick, gives you more time to hack my shit."

Han felt all the air rush out of him. "I . . . I wouldn't."

"Of course you would. You'll try. You know why? Because I would, and from everything I know about you, we're a lot alike."

"Y-You really think that?" Han sucked down a nervous breath, his hands wet with nervous sweat.

"I do. Come on, Han. I've got your dossier, you're not just here for the program, are you? What happened with your mother was tragic, naturally you want to resolve that so you can move on with your life. But your life . . . big plans, right? Big plans that start with me?" Paxton grinned down at him, and Han could hardly believe what he was hearing, or believe his luck.

Haltingly, he nodded. "Is that bad?"

"I don't think so," Paxton replied, then did his best, guttural Michael Douglas voice. "I'm pulling back the curtain. I want to meet the wizard." It was a so-so impression.

"*The Game*," said Han. "That's one of my favorite vids."

"Mine too, Han."

"If you two are done chitchatting, let me send Dr. Colbie an alert," Brea said as Paxton pulled Han along and passed her. "I would not want to push dinner late, surely our guests are famished."

"Thanks, Brea. You're the best. Oh! And get some chicken on the menu for tonight, there's been a change of heart." He didn't give further instructions, striding into the gallery off the main courtyard. Along each side, rectangular white pedestals displayed pieces of art. Some appeared ancient, others new; some, Han noticed as he drew nearer, were holographic. Down the center of the wide corridor, an ivory banquet table was . . . building itself. Halfway done, it appeared to grow from the ground up, tiny slice by tiny slice, only the faintest machine whir indicating that hidden mechanisms below the floor were hard at work.

"This is 3D printing?" Han asked, gasping. "I've never seen it done so quickly."

"It's silicate we mine from the surface, and we can recycle it, reuse it to build whatever we need," Paxton said, sounding almost bored. "Fun little prototype, not sure it would work anywhere but on Ganymede, we can take advantage of the liquid core and magnetic field. But side projects aren't what you're here for, Han. Let's go see the good stuff. This corridor is Zone Seven, but we'll be hustling over to Zones Three and Four."

Raising his left hand, Paxton tapped his VIT screen. "You can follow along on the map if you want. I bet you've already changed all your settings and icons and tried to dig around in our system, yeah?"

Han felt his cheeks glow. He was there to impress the guy, not just suck up. "No, not yet."

"Ha." Paxton threw back his head and laughed, gleeful. "Nice. Here, we're taking that black door on your right."

They skirted along the outside edge of the pedestals and where the table was being printed. High above, a dozen or so cables held an avant-garde chandelier over their heads, shards of pink and blue and purple glass arranged like a sprawling amethyst cave crystal. Paxton only had to walk near the black door he had pointed out before and it hissed open for them. Judging by the scan Han had undergone upon landing on Ganymede, he assumed every door and zone in the facility automatically detected privileges, gatekeeping access for staff and keeping the patients out of sensitive areas. Those were tricky systems to fool or work around, but Han made a mental note to try later anyway.

He was beginning to think of his time there like a test. If he could pull off something truly remarkable, a feat of hacking or programming that impressed even Paxton Dunn, maybe the mogul would consider keeping him on.

This is an audition, he thought. *Don't blow it, don't be lame, be the kind of guy Paxton Dunn would want as a friend.*

The jitters in his hands hadn't calmed down yet. Paxton Dunn guided him through the much tighter hallways of what looked to be administrative offices. They were open plan, but still far less airy and grand than the Dome courtyard and the corridor linked to it. Cool blue tones set the feeling of being deep underwater, as if they weren't on Ganymede at all but wandering through a dark ocean submersible.

A farther black door waited beyond those desks and chairs and blue glass cubicles, and yet another tall, pretty woman was emerging from it. That door was different, huge and circular, carbon black, with a big spinning lock like the kind in Old West vids.

"Dr. Colbie!" Paxton crowed, spinning briefly to look at Han with what the boy could only describe as a "can you believe my life?" smirk. "I assume you got Brea's alert?"

"I did, however this is all a bit irregular . . ." She closed the massive door behind her and stood poised there as if to guard the way. Dr. Colbie looked like she would fit right in with the NC-17 arcade AR experiences back on the station. Han had only tried and failed twice to hack a VIT ID to enter. White-blond, long hair had been pulled into a severe bun on the top of her head, her lips painted coral red. Two razor-sharp black wings swooped out from her denim-blue eyes.

"This is Han." Paxton stepped behind him, putting both hands on his shoulders. Han couldn't remember the last time he had experienced this much physical contact with other humans.

"It's . . . it's a pleasure to meet you, Han." Dr. Colbie sighed and managed a quick, impatient smile. "I didn't think LENG would be used today, Paxton. Even for demonstration purposes I like to be warned about these things ahead of time."

"That's really great," Paxton replied dismissively. "Super. I'm your boss, though, and my authority is absolute, as you well know, so I'm going to take Han in there and LENG will be juiced up and ready to go, won't it?"

Dr. Colbie leaned back against the door, her affect suddenly flat and cold, though she seemed to subtly glare at her boss. "It's primed."

"Good." Paxton brightened instantly and walked Han forward until Dr. Colbie was forced to move out of the way. "Very good. You can monitor from your station, just to make sure us boys don't get up to too much mischief."

He almost missed Dr. Colbie's roll of the eyes and the huff she made as she strode by them. His attention had been drawn to the circular vault door she abandoned. Something pulsed behind it. An energy. A presence. Paxton pushed on his shoulders but he couldn't move. His feet had become lead, and a force drew on him, pulling as if it could suck him through the floor and into Ganymede's molten iron core.

The pressure on his shoulders eased but he still felt glued to the ground. He trembled. Paxton walked around him, and as he drew near, the black door opened. There was only more darkness beyond. Han looked into it, and it was dense, murky, thick with . . . something. The word occurred to him again. Presence.

"It's just a chair and an IV," Paxton laughed, gesturing him forward. "I promise."

Han had seen a vid once about a pair of circus brothers on Earth. They had built striped tents and packed elephants and tigers and tightrope walkers inside. From the outside, nobody could guess the wonders that one tent contained. He remembered a specific moment—one of the brothers stood outside, peeling the tent flap open, leering with excitement and knowledge as he plucked off his big weird hat and bowed, and beckoned the viewer inside.

Just a chair and an IV.

This was the smartest man, unanimously voted, in the universe. Han wasn't about to hesitate in front of him. Something in the darkness behind Paxton moved, but Han put one foot in front of the other and went beyond the door.

As soon as it closed behind him, he wished he hadn't.

11

"Smartest man in the universe my asshole."

Zurri stared with half-dead eyes at the twisty, sculpted bust on the pedestal before her. She had an eye for good art. This was not good, but it only took her thirty seconds to realize what it was meant to be. A bust of their illustrious host, Paxton Dunn, created in stone. Without bothering to glance around, she reached up and flicked it on the forehead. The way it felt against her nail was odd . . . She rubbed her thumb over the grotesque nose and realized it wasn't even marble, but some cheap printed knockoff.

"I don't think we're supposed to touch the art."

Cult girl. Of course she would be a Goody Two-shoes. Zurri swiveled, finding the woman lingering near the admittedly grand open doorway between the corridor with the statues and the courtyard. The corridor reminded her of the private jet hangars in London back on Earth.

"This isn't art," Zurri told her flatly. "It's cheap."

"Art can't be cheap?" she asked.

Zurri chuckled, then realized the woman was earnestly asking. What a walking sob story. "Entertainment can be cheap, but art always has a cost, the one you pay for it or to make it. I'm Zurri."

"I know," the woman said softly, and to her credit. "I'm Senna."

"Oh, I know." Zurri saw a familiar flicker of fear pass across the woman's face. She knew it well, the realization that a fan—or in Senna's case a critic—was connecting an image to a name. Fame was a bitch, didn't matter how it came. "It's all right. I'm not here to judge you."

Not much anyway.

"How much are you here to forget exactly?" Zurri asked, seeing the woman's dairy cow–brown eyes widen in shock. "Me? I'm not so sure. I thought I was coming just to get a little off the top, maybe I'm thinking I need a whole new style."

"I thought you were leaving," Senna replied. She wandered deeper into the cavernous space, a white trellis table sketching itself into being behind them. The whole place was weird and slightly hard to believe, so a table creating itself out of thin air didn't surprise Zurri much. She had seen stranger stuff at vid after-parties.

"I will be," Zurri said with a shrug, flicking the bust on the forehead again and smiling. It was petty, but it amused her. "I'll make sure I get my time's worth while I wait for the next shuttle. But this Dunn guy is full of shit."

"Oh?"

"He's not the smartest man in the universe." Turning to face her fully, Zurri folded her arms across her chest and sighed. "The smartest man in the universe would have found a way to build me my private wing, storm or no storm."

"Wow," the woman breathed, her eyes still huge and liquid. "This feels shabby to you?"

"Sweetie, everything feels shabby to me."

"I think it's pretty incredible," Senna admitted with a shrug. "I've never seen plants like that before. Even in Hydroponica the growth never gets that big . . ."

Damn it all, she felt some pity for the girl. "Wasn't that crash of yours a year ago? Have they kept you locked up in therapy this whole time?"

She shook her head, rippling her close-cut helmet of dirty blond hair. "I locked myself up."

"But you know me."

"You're hard to miss." Senna glanced down at her shapeless, sad shoes and then slowly raised her eyes to Zurri's. She felt suddenly chilled, like the girl was peering into her soul. "I saw what happened to you on the broadcast. I'm so sorry, I know what that feels like. The shock. The horror. The violence."

"Thanks." It was the only thing she could think to say. She dropped her arms. "I guess you can imagine it, huh? I'll bet you're one of the few who could."

"Not for much longer," Senna reminded her with a half smile. "If the smartest man in the universe lives up to his reputation. I'm . . . sorry he lied to you. I'm sorry you didn't get your private wing."

Zurri squeezed her eyes shut and waved her comment away. "I bet you never expected to string that sentence together."

"Not really, no. I didn't even have one of these growing up," Senna said, wiggling the wrist with a VIT monitor strapped to it. "I can't get any of it set up. Does it stop itching after a while?"

"No, it will always be annoying, but then you'll wake up one morning and realize you can't find your own ass without it."

Maybe it was the three vodkas talking, but Zurri was beginning to soften up a little. At least if she had to be stuck in the middle of nowhere with subpar accommodations, she could go home with the story of how she spent time with the infamous cult girl. Getting access to her was apparently even harder than getting access to Zurri. She could respect that. "I'm sure Paxton Dunn can get that thing running however you want."

"I'd rather just not use it," Senna replied, going to one of the white, squarish chairs that had just been printed from the ground up and sitting. She flinched a little. "Whoa. Weird. It's warm."

"This whole damn place is weird," Zurri countered. She stared up at the glitzy chandelier above them, watching the artificial light bounce off its pink-and-purple panes. Then her eyes slid back down to the table and the chairs being printed there. She took a quick headcount. "Eight of us."

"Three patients," Senna murmured, nodding. "Five staff."

"How do five people keep this place running? It's gigantic."

"It does seem a little . . . lonely."

A pair of stilettos piloted by a perfect hourglass woman clicked across the polish-bright tiles toward them. Zurri had just enough time to register her irritation before turning to her right, facing the larger hangar-like hall and an alcove at the very end of it.

"Smile!" A woman Zurri had not yet met crowed.

Zurri put up her hand to block her face just as that woman flashed a little camera object at them from her palm. "I absolutely will not."

"Just making sure we record this first day with you all," the woman said. She looked like she might be from South America. Maybe Spain. Or whoever grew her in a lab had been inspired by those places.

"Do I look like I want my picture taken right now?" Zurri asked, glowering.

"It is part of the NDA you signed."

She heard Senna's chair legs scratch across the floor as she shifted around uncomfortably. Long ago, Zurri had become immune to onlookers responding to her outbursts. She would never get a single thing done in her life if she constantly stopped to consider whether they felt awkward or not. "We'll see about that. Bev is incompetent but she's not that incompetent."

"I did not mean to offend you," the woman said, though her tone did not really indicate contrition. If anything, she sounded strangely flat and lifeless. "Archiving this historic program launch is my job. I handle the public relations for Paxton's brands." Then she tapped the little name tag over her left breast. "Brea."

"Senna," she heard the cult girl say. "I think we're all just tired, not really in the mood for pictures just now. I must look a state . . ."

Judging by her overall style, Senna always looked a state. Back to Brea. Zurri studied her for a moment. *God*, she thought. *Does he only hire Los Angeles tens?*

"When do we eat?" Zurri asked. She could at least get a decent meal before disappearing into her room for the rest of her time on Ganymede.

"Soon, of course," Brea replied, offering them both a mollifying smile. "There was . . . a small misunderstanding concerning dietary restrictions and—"

"Okay, that's great," Zurri interrupted. More squeaking and squirming from Senna in her brand-new chair. "From now on? Just have the kitchen send my food to my room."

"Please, you have come all this way, can you not be a good sport?" PR asked.

"*This* is me being a good sport." She crossed to the table and behind Senna, then took the chair to the woman's left. "And so help me, if you point that thing at me while I'm eating . . ."

That seemed to frighten the woman off, and she bounced out of the gallery with her dark curls flying, her heels *clickity-clacking* like chattering teeth across the tiles. A heavy, dreadful silence fell, and she and Senna sat there while the table scooted up and up and up until at last the noise of its creation ceased and they were left in even moodier stillness. Time seemed to be moving more quickly, as if Paxton had the daylight simulators cranked just a touch too high. The pleasant golden light streaming in behind Senna from the deciduous courtyard trended toward sunset orange. Above, the crystalline chandelier turned a morose shade of plum.

"Can I ask you something?" Senna asked suddenly.

Strangely enough, Zurri welcomed the break in the silence. "I suppose."

"When you leave on the next shuttle, could I go with you?"

Paxton had already screwed up her demands and let her down, and it was hard not to take pity on the cult girl. With her hunched posture and strange hair and stranger clothes, she could have been a Sector 7 bag lady shuffling against the current of foot traffic at rush hour. She wasn't quite broken, though. Close, but something in the center was holding. That made Zurri pity her, too, because Zurri knew exactly what that felt like.

"Yeah," Zurri said, shrugging her slender shoulders. "Yeah, I don't see why not." A door across the table from her opened, black and small, and two males emerged, Paxton and a teenage boy she hadn't seen yet. Paxton had his hand on the boy's shoulder like they were old, old pals. The boy wore a loosely fixed expression, as if all the muscles in his face had forgotten how to work at once. "When that shuttle comes? We'll both be on it."

"Unfortunately, you'll both be waiting for a while, then," Paxton said, overhearing. He didn't even pretend at disappointment. From the alcove to Zurri's left, double doors opened, and the rest of the staff appeared, filing in with flight attendant precision. "Predictive weather algorithms are projecting a bad week. Next shuttle won't be cleared for the LZ for at least four days. Half of a Ganymede day. Ha! Wild, right?"

"Something like that," Zurri fumed. Four. Days. The vid selection in her apartment better be incredible, or she would lose her mind waiting out the storm. She glanced at Senna, who might at least be interesting company to pass the time with; she wouldn't mind hearing stories of her life in the cult. Everyone on the station was dying to know about it, and everyone had predicted she would show up on the *Daily Bliss* to have her fifteen minutes of sad-girl fame, or that a book would get announced, but nothing. Cult Girl went into hiding, and it only extended the mystery. Then again, if Senna was there to forget all that, maybe she wouldn't be so willing to chat about it with her.

Either way, Senna's lips twisted open in what seemed like agony. She leapt to her feet, backing away from the table as Paxton's four employees streamed toward the table and Paxton steered the new kid to the chair just to Senna's right.

"Sit down," Paxton told her, stern. Then he winked at her, but Zurri caught it, too. "Everything has been handled."

12

Senna begged silently to disappear.

The chair was there to catch her when she lost her balance and tumbled downward. She tore her eyes away from the familiar boy, her chest hot and stuffy, sweat dampening the collar of her shirt. Preece, her mentor, her jailor, her father figure, her nemesis, had hijacked the craft that careened into the surface of Mars and killed this boy's mother.

She wanted to vanish. No, vanishing wasn't enough . . .

"Handled?" she breathed, eyes flying to Paxton for an explanation.

He took the chair next to the teenager's, leaning back in it with casual, boyish ease. Anju and Brea joined them, as well as a third woman with blond hair and blue eyes that Senna didn't recognize. A sleek, silver Servitor AI bot appeared, its innards encased in a shining chassis, its three-toed "feet" clacking softly on the floor as it carried in a tray of miniature stone bowls, pickled vegetables and wafers and nuts heaped inside. It set down the tray near Paxton, who immediately grabbed a handful of almonds and popped one in his mouth. The Servitor retreated the way it had come, returned almost immediately with another tray, carrying half a roasted chicken and a steaming pile of leeks and asparagus and depositing it right in front of Senna, then honked out a stilted, robotic, "You enjoy."

Even if the food looked and smelled delicious, it made her stomach turn.

"It's going to be a long experiment if you can't learn to relax and enjoy the process," Paxton teased. He caught her eye over the boy's shoulder. "Han and I had a talk, you know? Man to man. You don't need to worry about things being tense."

"Still," Senna murmured, wishing the hot chicken steam would rise somewhere else. Her guts were in knots. She could feel Zurri staring at her, gawking. She *hated* that feeling. "I just feel so awful. So, so awful. Han, I'm sorry . . ."

The Servitor made another trip back through the double doors, this time bringing Han a mountain of fluffy buns and bowls of broth, noodles steeped in lava-red oil, and french fries. She wondered if the bot had done the cooking as well.

"For what?" he asked. His face, which had been slack and less than blank, snapped back. It was like someone had jammed a new battery into his brain or something. He snatched up a french fry and crammed it into his mouth. Even before Senna could think of what to say in response, he pointed across the table and gasped. "Whoa. You're *Zurri*."

"You noticed that, huh?" The model rolled her eyes, then leaned primly away from the table while the woman delivering food brought her a plate of tossed greens, a single piece of whitefish, and a tiny serving of slivered sweet potatoes.

"You'll be a celebrity, too," Paxton told the boy, munching another almond. "This technology is going to change the world. Every world."

"I got to see it," Han boasted, grinning around at them all, french fry gunk stuck between his teeth. The Servitor had finished delivering meals, and returned to pass out glasses, then fill them. Han received what looked like fizzy battery acid, and he gulped it down the moment it finished pouring.

"Precise as ever, Sixteen," Paxton told the bot, and when it had finished tending to everyone, it simply vanished back behind the doors recessed into the alcove.

"We're all very happy for you, kid," Zurri sighed, forking the greens listlessly around in their bowl.

Senna couldn't concentrate on what he was saying. It was rude to stare, but she couldn't help herself. How could he not recognize her? Where was the rage she had seen in his eyes at the office on the station? How could he be so . . . so calm? So unbothered? She expected him to lunge across the table and pour his hideous green drink all over her head, but instead he kept on eating and talking, launching into a speech about the technology, the design, the implementation, the experience!

"I expected it to be kinda scary, you know?" he said in closing, polishing off his fries and moving on to the buns. "Thought I would feel weird after, but I feel fine. Great. Hungry, maybe, but I feel great."

Down the table, the blond woman dropped her spoon. It clattered noisily to the table, and Paxton shot her a glare. Slowly, she picked up the utensil, and let it hover over her bowl while she stared with concentrated intensity into space.

"It is a relief to hear that," Brea told the boy, smoothing the napkin across her lap. "User experience is so crucial! We will have to take a vid of your first impressions. Merchantia PR will be delighted."

But her words sounded a million miles away. Senna tore her eyes away from Han, fixing them instead on Paxton. He went on eating, ignoring her, but she could tell it was deliberate. Avoidant. They hadn't discussed the crash and come to some resolution, Paxton had used the LENG technology to change Han's memories and avoid a tense interaction. Even if it was what the boy had come for, even if he wanted to forget those things, it didn't seem right. Or it didn't seem right *just yet*.

This was only supposed to be the welcoming dinner.

The room was spinning. The crystal chandelier above them seemed to sway, threatening to detach from the ceiling and drop, crushing them, making them blood and glass and powder. She never ate meat, and now the smell of it, cooked and sweating its juicy, pungent heat, sickened her. When she breathed, the smell came with, filling her mouth, gagging her. She climbed unsteadily to her feet. Everyone was staring at her, again. *Always.*

"I don't f-feel well," she stammered. "I think the trip . . . unsettled my stomach. E-Excuse me."

She knew Paxton would try to keep her there, so she ran. Through the big open doors and back into the humid embrace of the leafy courtyard, then left following a slowly curving white ramp up to a balconied second level. Zone 2. She had seen it while studying the materials during her trip. It was rude to bolt, but Senna's frequent panic attacks had taught her the warning signs. Leaving ruined it mostly for her, staying would have ruined it for everybody.

Senna approached a coral-red door off the balconied area overlooking the courtyard. When she came close, it swished open. She clutched her nylon bag close to her chest and wandered down the L-shaped hall. The doors were unlabeled, blank and dark, and she huffed, confused. Then she noticed a door to her right glowing faintly as she passed, and when she took a step toward it, the light grew brighter and a name appeared across it.

ZURRI

She backed away and tried the next door and the next, turning the corner to the right to find that the next door glowed, and her name was there.

"Hi," a pleasant male voice greeted her.

Senna gasped, stumbling backward, then searched above and behind her for the source of the voice.

"My name is Genie, if you need anything during your stay, you can just ask me. Would you like to enter your rooms, Ms. Slate?"

"Y-Yes."

"Perfect. Should I call you Ms. Slate or would you prefer Senna?"

Pushing inside, Senna gasped again—the cozy, clean apartment had been decorated in muted ocean tones. A heavy shag rug covered the hall directly ahead, and moving farther inside she found a kitchen to her right with a counter, table and some chairs, modern but not stark, a glazed vase centered on the table with a spray of white tulips.

"Senna is fine," she told the invisible man. Marin and Jonathan had something similar in their condo, an in-home assistant, and they shouted orders at it night and day, telling it to change the temperature or turn off the lights. At first, when all that was new and she was still fresh from the compound, she had imagined a hundred fairies hidden behind the walls, rushing to do as they asked.

"Paxton tells me your pronouns are 'she' and 'her,' is that correct?"

"Yes," Senna said, walking slowly down the hallway and into the living area. The creamy ivory sofa there smelled incredible and strange. She touched it. "Is this real leather?"

"It is. Paxton's family owns and operates one of the last seven cattle ranches in Colorado."

"And this mural . . ." Senna turned to admire the impressionist painting on the wall facing the front door—just gazing at it lowered her blood pressure. She sighed at the foamy sea, the sliver of beach, and gulls like lazy checkmarks slashed across the sky. A spindly dock in the distance clung to an outcropping of rock, threatened by the crashing tides. "It's beautiful."

"You were a difficult one."

It wasn't Genie who spoke, but a different male voice. Senna dropped her nylon bag on the couch and spun to find Paxton Dunn, hands in pockets, observing her from the doorway.

His smirk bordered on a grimace. "Zurri and Han were easy. They've got online shopping carts and search histories going back years and years. But you? You've only been with the land of the living for a year."

"I was alive before that," insisted Senna, crossing her arms. "You didn't need to follow me."

"You're upset."

"You could've just . . . sent a messagey thing." She jostled the wrist with her VIT monitor.

"Right," he chuckled, taking a few bold steps into her apartment. He didn't go any farther than the table in her kitchen. "And knowing how much you love that thing, would you have seen it and responded to my *messagey thing*?"

"Probably not," Senna admitted. "About Han . . ."

"It's handled," Paxton replied bluntly, slashing his hand horizontally through the air.

"You keep saying that," she said. "And I keep not believing you. Isn't it all too fast? We just got here, we hadn't even eaten yet and already . . ." Senna chose her next words carefully, watching the way he flinched as she rambled on. "And you already changed him."

Paxton pulled one hand out of his pocket and pressed it to his chest. "Isn't that what you're here for? And *I* didn't change anything, LENG did. No offense, but Jesus, it's awfully presumptuous, implying Han doesn't know what he wants. He knows what he wants to forget, he tells me, and then LENG helps him with that. He went through the neural mapping just like you, he signed the contracts, this is all consensual."

It sounded so simple. Clinical. Senna glanced at her feet, the small feeling cresting over her again. Living in isolation with the brood, behind the walls of the compound, had robbed her of so much knowledge, so much of the easy way people barked at in-home assistants, and ordered food through their VITs with their minds, and didn't vomit when they raced up and down in the station elevators at what felt like light speed. The ignorance kept on astonishing and shaming her, and she wondered if it would ever stop.

"I explained everything about your shared connection before he made his decision," Paxton continued. His tone, she realized, was slightly apologetic, and she looked up from her feet. "He was surprised, obviously, and mad, but we had a talk. A good talk. He came around. He's a tech head like me, he wanted to be the first of you to try it. Teenagers, right?"

"Right," Senna agreed, not really knowing what he meant.

"Hey." He waited until their eyes met, and she could *feel* his curiosity, his interest, like gentle hooks behind his pupils tugging on her. "Your first session is scheduled for tomorrow morning. Is that okay? Having second thoughts?"

Senna pursed her lips and wondered. *Was* it okay? She thought of Han, of the way he looked at her across the dinner table. No rage. No pain. Whatever they were doing here, it worked. She considered, selfishly, what it would be like to be that way—emptied out of all the hurt.

"I just need to rest," she finally replied. "I'm sure it will all seem clearer in the morning."

Paxton grinned and nodded. "It usually does. I'll have Servitor Sixteen bring up something for you. Maybe just some porridge?"

"The meat was ambitious," Senna murmured, embarrassed.

"Ha! Yes, very ambitious, but that's good. You took a big swing, we like big swings here. Porridge it is. You rest up, okay? And then I'll see you bright and early . . ."

He turned to go, and as he passed through the door, she noticed a dark halo flicker across his body. An image she'd like to capture. *We like big swings here.*

"Paxton?" Using his first name felt strange. She didn't know him at all.

"Yeah?" he paused, his back to her.

"I'd like to paint again. Is there any way . . ."

He put up a hand. "Say no more. We'll find you something to use."

Before she could thank him, he was gone.

Someone was there with her in the dark. She didn't know who, couldn't see them, but she knew she wasn't alone. Senna opened her eyes with the bleary reluctance of a child peeking above the covers, dreading what they might see. Being a picky sleeper wasn't an option in the compound. You slept practically on top of one another. If someone snored, you dealt with it. If you hated the thin, poky mattress, you got over yourself and learned to ignore it. Most nights she was so exhausted from service and chores that her body didn't give her a choice; every sinew simply gave up and her brain followed suit, lights out and lights out.

But nights were bad now. Hard. Daylight hours could be filled with vids and music, eating and drinking. In Marin's apartment she had fancied herself a space-age Rip van Winkle, waking up after so many years to a universe she couldn't possibly digest all at once. They were allowed history vids and documentaries on the compound, and the more creative of the brood would make up little stories to amuse everyone before bed. Kiri and Alex had lovely voices, so they would sing while everyone scrubbed floors or set out the washing to dry in front of the massive exhaust vents belching heat from the Hydroponica levels.

Senna had missed out on not just the pop culture of her day, but of all the days before. It drove Jonathan nuts, because she never got his references, and each exasperated reaction of his would send her down a new rabbit hole of investigation. That was how she found out about Rip van Winkle, but only after educating herself on what a *Jumanji* was and why Jonathan thundering, "What year is it!?" sent Marin into a paroxysm of giggles.

But nights were hard. There was no more labor during the day to grind her down to weary dust, and no familiar, squirming bodies packed in around her to provide comfort and security. There was no hum of the steam vents, no rhythmic snoring from Somchai, no pointed cough from Preece when he caught younger brood members gossiping in the dark.

If she did sleep, the nightmares came. Nights were hard.

And nights in Marin and Jonathan's condo, and now the apartment on Ganymede, were spent alone. After a year, Senna knew alone. But she was not alone anymore. Before bed, she had tentatively asked Genie to lock her door, and she had heard a helpful chime indicating it had been done. In her fitful sleep, she felt sure she would have heard someone entering, or noticed the swishing sound of the door. But there was none of that. Just the thin specter of sleep and then a chill that swept across her torso, her left foot giving an involuntary spasm.

Senna carefully peeled the covers back and bunched them by her waist. With the portal window blacked out for sleep, the impenetrable darkness robbed her of everything. When she moved her hand across the mound of sheets, she couldn't see it. Shivering, she waited for her eyes to adjust.

It was by the door.

"Oh," she heard herself say.

It wasn't moving, just waiting. Watching. It stood in a ready position, arms flexed as if it was surprised at being caught. Just a shape. Just a silhouette. Darkness stamped against darkness, but the fuzziness around its edges gave it away. A presence. A poised and watchful thing.

Her voice was jittery as she spoke. "Hello?"

A flood of soft, pink light filled the room, and Genie's voice broke the close silence. "Hello, Senna. How can I help you?"

She blinked rapidly, blinded for a moment by the sudden clarity. There was nothing by the door. The suggestion of it remained, but only when she blinked her eyes. It had left its impression there.

"Am I alone?" she asked Genie.

"Yes," he told her, with confidence and speed that should have soothed her, but didn't. She was ignorant of many things, but she trusted her eyes. She knew what she had seen.

"Is the door locked?"

"Yes."

A beat. "Are you sure?"

"Yes, I'm sure," said Genie. "Is everything all right, Senna?"

"No."

"I see. Is there anything I can do to assist you or make you more comfortable?"

She sighed. "No."

Senna twisted toward the bedside table, and picked up the tablet there that Paxton had provided. It was just a white outline with a sheer substance in the middle, but when she touched the center, a holographic display shimmered to life.

"Can you lower the lights just a bit?" she asked Genie, her eyes traveling back to the door. When she blinked, the dark silhouette lingered. "I think I'll be up for a while."

13

In the end, it was just a very plain chair and a rolling cart with a few tubes, a canister and an IV prepped and laid out on a small tray.

Senna laughed, her throat rocky from lack of sleep. The grit in her eyes when she rolled out of bed a few hours earlier had come out in greasy chunks. "How does it work?"

It didn't seem as scary, now that she was there. She had expected wires and cuffs and a big metal helmet coming down over her head, but the room with the LENG technology was small and cave-like, cool air pumped in, circulating in pleasant, scentless puffs. Both the dense carpet and insulated walls were painted flat black. An ambient projection of a star field played on the wall across from the single white chair.

Now she knew why Han had agreed to try it so quickly, it didn't look intimidating at all. She had hoped to question him about the experience at breakfast but he wasn't there, and she had eaten alone at a new white table under the crystal chandelier, this one sized just for her. Microgreens and avocado with fresh lemon and dill had been spread across a whole-wheat bagel. The cost of such food must have been astronomical.

Paxton hovered behind her near the door. He had found her at the breakfast table and taken her on a brief tour of the labs outside where they housed the LENG technology. It had gone fast; he was eager to begin. He wore baggy pants that would have been at home on the beach and a tight black polo shirt. That day his glasses had clear rims, and she thought he looked better with the black ones.

"A memory is just a series of connections," Paxton told her. He smiled, at ease, and she wondered if he had practiced this speech for just such an occasion. Tapping his VIT, the star-field projection disappeared, replaced by a web of three-dimensional, filmy crimson lines, almost like a central nervous system but all clustered into one glob. It rotated slowly, sections of the web lighting up as he spoke.

"We can't look at your neural map and zap just one thing," he continued, then thought about it and paused. "Although that would be nice."

Senna smiled.

"Instead, we have to weaken the connections between memories and events. Once those connections become more vulnerable, we can rewrite the way you associate those memories." As he explained, some of the ropy lines on the projection turned blue, then pale blue, and then the connective tissue between them dissolved. "We reconnect A and B to D, instead of C. If C, for our purposes, is pain, and D is happiness, or just neutrality."

Different blue ropes attached themselves to the floating bit, and once the bond was strong again, the whole blob turned red again.

"So you're not erasing anything," Senna murmured, genuinely fascinated. "Just changing our associations?"

"In some cases," Paxton replied. "The more complex the memory, the more difficult that rewriting becomes. The more reconnections we have to find and reforge. Time complicates things, too. Older memories are easier to tamper with, because those bonds are already fragile. Newer memories are harder to change."

He lowered his wrist and the image vanished, the star field returning. "It will take a degree of trial and error for each of you. With Han, LENG simply had to change his association with *you* specifically. Helping him overcome the night of his mother's death will require more finesse."

"But you think you can do it?" Senna asked, half turning to gaze at him.

"I'm reasonably confident *LENG* can do it." His smile was *supremely* confident. He nodded his messy mop of dark curls toward the IV tray. "After we've isolated the correct memory junctures, we flood your system with HDAC inhibitors. It promotes new connectivity in the brain, turns on your genes, so to speak. Just gives them a kick up the ass and tells them, hey, we want to do something else with these connections, you old bastard brain, let's try something less terrible, eh?"

Senna laughed softly. "Okay, I think I follow."

"Then you're exposed to pleasant imagery and nice music, all that junk, and if LENG does it to the right memory junctures in the right order enough times, we'll have a success story on our hands."

Nodding, she wandered back toward the chair, passing her hand over the flat, expected back of it. No surprises. Nothing strange. "I thought there would be wires and electrodes and . . . I don't know, *more*."

"You'll see," Paxton replied, grinning. "There's more."

After she sat in the chair, Dr. Colbie, the blond woman with the soft blue eyes, joined them and put in her IV. She told Senna to close her eyes, take a deep breath and count back from ten, and with a light touch, she slid the needle into Senna's right arm near her elbow and then taped down the apparatus.

"A little saline to test," Dr. Colbie said with a wince. "I know it tastes bad."

Senna smacked her lip. "Ugh."

"You won't feel much until the process is complete and we're ready to administer the HDAC. It won't feel too scary, but you might get a sensation like you're really warm, like you're suddenly flushed, okay? Just relax, it only lasts a second."

"How long will the session last?" Senna asked, the funny taste in her mouth diminishing. The star field in front of her began to dim as Dr. Colbie stood up, turning her head toward Paxton in inquiry. He had been waiting and observing by the projection wall, pinpricks of light rolling over him in a dazzling spray.

"Simple stuff today, just testing some connections to see if LENG has success. Lots of connections to shake and see what happens. Erasing the trauma of the crash might mean going way, way back." Paxton rubbed his chin thoughtfully, sucking on his lower lip. "We maaay end up giving you a generally quaint memory of the compound. Not good but hazy, you know? Like a dream half-remembered."

Senna shrugged. In many ways, it already felt like that. She couldn't think badly of Mina, or Alex, or Somchai, or any of the innocent foster kids that had been pulled into that place and made to think it was safe and perfect and good. "Just . . . just don't give me any fond feelings for Preece Ives, okay? I don't want that, and he doesn't deserve that. Erase him if you have to, but never make me like him."

Pushing off from the wall, Paxton gave a curt nod. Dr. Colbie checked the IV line one last time and then left the room.

"Heard," Paxton said with a salute. "Now I think it's time you met LENG."

"Genie!"

"Yes, Zurri, how can I assist you?"

She was on her third cup of green tea, feet propped on the cubist coffee table while a muted vid of last year's fall runway in Paris played. A stunner with glowing LED leg prosthetics stomped toward the camera with a navy mesh hood pulled low over her face. The clothes were dreadful but Zurri could hand out a tap on the wrist of applause for the girl.

"What the hell is going on with my texts?" she asked. As requested, her apartment was furbished in the latest style—ultra-minimalist pastels, with the rare absurdist touch. An oversized teddy bear with shellacked yellow beetles for eyes was propped up in the corner under the vid screen. "I sent Bev my updated schedule three hours ago and it keeps bouncing back."

"Storm activity—"

"Shut up."

"Yes, Zurri."

"I want to speak to Paxton," she hissed. "Now."

She could all but hear the AI thinking through the strained silence. The next model down the runway couldn't walk to save her life, teetering on the treacherous heels with an obviously pained expression on her face.

"Paxton is currently with a patient, and is not available until—"

"Get. Him. Now."

"One moment, please."

Sighing, Zurri tapped her nails along the edge of the teacup. She loved the way that ordinarily made people shit their pants. Her nails, if long enough, could be an entire drum corps along the rim of any obliging cup.

"Jeeeeeesus," she moaned, plucking a cashew from the plate next to her feet and chucking it at the vid screen. "Learn to walk, you fucking moose. They should run you out of Paris, they should try you in the Hague—"

"Zurri?" Paxton's voice interrupted mid-rant, as crystal clear as the robot's. "What's going on?"

"Do you know Camden Zed?"

"*Who?* I don't have time for—"

"Camden Zed. Model. Dreadful shit. Anyway, why are my messages bouncing? I can't raise Bev and, God help me, I need her." She ate the next cashew and washed it down with cooling tea.

Zurri heard him try to suppress a sigh, but his annoyance was clear in his tone. "Well, we're a bit isolated here, as you may have noticed. Even communications are a pain in the ass. Have to send them out in batches when the weather cooperates. But that's how I like it. You think a shareholder is gonna come bother me all the way out here? Forget it. You just have to deal for a few days, Zurri, Bev will still be there, I promise."

"I don't *deal.*"

"Jesus. You just have to, I'll batch out all communications

when there's less noise, if I unshield our magnetic field disruptors right now, they'll be torn to shreds by the storm. Listen, I'm with a patient right now, we can discuss this later."

He went quiet, and she wasn't sure if he was still around to hear her mutter, "Oh, we will most definitely discuss this later. Prick."

"Is there anything else I can help you with today, Zurri?" Genie asked, obliviously and almost adorably cheerful in the face of their bickering. The cozy morning light permeating her room cut out, making her jump on the sofa as she was suddenly left in darkness. The vid played on, silent models walking in silent streams down a glossy silver ribbon of a stage. Through the door, out in the corridor, she heard the sirens begin.

"Another storm?" she asked.

"Rather, a flare-up of one continuous weather disruption," Genie informed her. "Paxton lowered the Dome shutters this morning, but it appears they will need to be raised again."

The lights flickered. She glanced toward the hallway that led past the kitchen and toward the front door. Flash-flicker-flash. A shape? A person? She blinked, squinted. No, it was gone. A cascade of frigid electricity danced across her arms. If there had been hairs there, they would have stood on end. The lights came back on full, and she shook her head, reaching for another cashew.

"Scheduled alert: Your LENG session begins in approximately two hours," Genie said.

"And what am I supposed to do until then?" Zurri sighed, her focus wandering to the cashew on the floor under the vid screen.

"In addition to Paxton's extensive art collection and library—"

"That was a rhetorical question, Genie." Two hours was a lifetime when you wanted to be anywhere but your mind. She couldn't stomach another runway vid. Sometimes she caught herself combing the videos for her competition. Her replacement. It was inevitable, really. One day it would be her in the background of another woman's photo, and when that day came she didn't know if she would have the strength to pose through it. Maybe it was wiser to quit before anyone saw the cracks in her smile.

She rubbed her eyes, exhausted. The same bad dreams had come, the same burst of light around her eyelids as she heard Tony explode into flames. Each morning, she woke tasting human ash. Waking hours required distraction, or chemical soothing.

Anju. Anju, Anju, Anju . . . She shouldn't have let slip the morsel about medical sedatives. Those would certainly do the trick. What vodka couldn't solve, a medical-grade sedative certainly could. She didn't want to taste ash, she wanted to bliss out and sleep, and wake to her appointment, ready for the ultimate reset, the ultimate high. What would it feel like to have her memories of Tony taken away? Good, she concluded, warm, like sliding into a perfectly heated bath, blindfold blotting out the world, the water just shy of scalding, superbly cleansing.

How to get the bliss before the bliss became the question. Not one for Genie, she thought with a sly smirk. Could that AI thing see her? Watch her? Did it wonder what her coy little expression meant? They probably kept the heavy stuff locked down somewhere, the labs most logically. Zurri consulted her chrome VIT and brought up the map, locating the labs in Zone 3, just south of the LENG facility. Clinical Offices, they were labeled.

The Han kid had droned on and on about being the first civilian to test the LENG tech, that it was bragging rights for the rest of his life. *Whatever buffers your feed, kid*, she had thought, rolling her eyes behind her glass of wine. After the drama of Cult

Girl storming off, the dinner had turned terminally dull. Han and Paxton started talking tech and her eyes glazed over, and she yearned for them to refill her glass and leave the bottle.

She forced herself to recall the mind-numbing contents of their conversation. The words *hacking project* stood out. Han was super proud of reprogramming the in-home assistant in their station apartment, apparently. That—her smile deepened—could be useful.

Standing, she dropped her silk robe and strode toward the restroom. "Genie? Start the shower. I'm going out earlier than planned."

14

Han sat extremely still in the bright daylight of his living room, groping in the gray mists of his mind.

"This might happen." He replayed Paxton's words. "Little breaks here and there, disconnections from reality. Go easy on yourself. Your mind is making new connections, repairing itself. There would be headaches, spasms . . ."

There had been both, headaches and spasms. Han hadn't woken up with the same usual impulses to check his messages, get on the forums and lose hours, sometimes days, to online spats or fall down a rabbit hole of someone else's programming, dissecting the elegance of their work, marveling at their process. He didn't want to load up his favorite VIT game and defend his high score. He wanted to sit in the artificial sunlight beamed out of the portal window, and pull on what felt like a hundred loose threads dangling from the domed ceiling of his skull.

He tugged on one thread, and an annoying question tumbled into his lap: *What did I ask Paxton to take away from me?*

Of course he couldn't remember, it would be stupid if he could. But like a loose, wiggly tooth, he couldn't help but prod at it repeatedly. *Am I hungry? Am I just tired?*

This might happen . . .

Han walked barefoot into the kitchen and went to the refrigerated drawer as if he had already done it a thousand times, as if this were all a studied routine. After finding a snack cake, he shucked the packaging, tossed the wrapper into the bin and ate the sweet, spongy disc as he navigated to the front door. Dusting crumbs off his shirt, he realized at the door that he had changed into simple black pants and a blue tee. He couldn't remember getting dressed that morning. Or had he slept in his clothes?

The door swished open, prompted by his proximity. He hadn't asked Genie for directions because he didn't want to be told Paxton was busy. Instead, Han consulted his VIT map and decided to check Paxton's office in Zone 5, nested just above and behind the big corridor with the chandelier where they had eaten dinner the night before. Han knew the way, even if it felt like his feet and legs were operating for him, without his directing them to. The hall leading through the dormitories was cold and bitterly silent.

Sometimes after an online game with his internet friends scattered across the station, he would wait in the lobby afterward, just watching his avatar idle out, swinging its arms side to side and shuffling impatiently. He would wait until he was the only one there and revel in the eventual quiet and solitude. It was the reverent kind of silence, like a gladiator standing all alone in the aftermath of the arena, or a runner taking a lonely walking lap of the track after the race. The corridor didn't feel like that. This was the emptiness that herded one away from it, so thickly hushed even a single footstep seemed like a trespass.

Han walked briskly because it felt good. The exercise pulled focus from the other thickly hushed silence, the one lingering in his head. He took a left out of the dormitory hall, around the short corner that dumped him out onto the balcony that overlooked the Dome courtyard from the east side. It must have been early still, though he hadn't checked the "time" lately. The thin, pale quality of the light filtering down from the shuttered ceiling said morning, and so did the tentative calls of the holographic birds. Down below, he spotted Brea's dark curls among the broad leaves and curved paths and statue pedestals. She was sitting on a bench between two statues, as frozen as they were, her hands flat on the bench beside her thighs, her back ramrod straight.

Avoiding her, Han slowed and quietly tiptoed down the ramp that curved into the courtyard, following its trajectory and traveling north toward what he was now thinking of as a dining hall. All the chairs and tables had been put away, leaving just the solid white rectangle plinths with various artifacts and busts. The less he thought and the more he walked, the more he felt like himself. These were just side effects, he told himself, nothing to worry about. Paxton had warned him he would feel a bit off, and he should know, it was technology *he* developed.

Still. Han knew he wouldn't feel better until he talked to Paxton about it. The reassurances would come easily, and soon they would be laughing about it and chatting about more interesting subjects, like hard storage resurgence or the Bitcoin retrospective playing at the university vid theater. He drifted toward the right of the gallery. Two shallow ramps on either side of broad white doors led the way to a walkway above that wrapped around the entire gallery. Immediately up those ramps lay the entrance to Paxton's personal office. The night before, the doors had been opaque black, but now they were clear, the situational frosting giving him privacy or a bird's-eye view of the dining hall and even out to the Dome courtyard.

He was passing by the last statue pedestal in the right row, nearly to one of the ramps, when a voice called out to him across the echoing vastness of the hall.

"Hey! Hey, kid!"

The most famous model in the universe was actually trying to get his attention. Zurri. He stopped up short, realizing he was still barefoot. His stubbed his right toe on the statue base, crumpling against it. Gasping, he flailed, trying to catch whatever priceless art he had just bumped, but the vase displayed there never tipped over, only flickered. It was a seamless holograph projected from the top of the pedestal.

"Whoa," he murmured, taking a step back. His toe throbbed but at least he hadn't smashed something irreplaceable. "Cool."

"Of course he's that cheap." Zurri joined him near the vase. She stood nearly a head taller than him even in flat sandals. Her boxy dress fell to just above her knees, a swirling orange pattern across it reminding him of orange dreamsicle ice cream. "All rich guys are. How are you feeling this morning after your, you know . . ."

Han blinked. Oh, right. The threads dangling in his mind tangled up for a moment. *I must look dumb as hell, licking my lips and trying to put a smart thought together.*

He didn't want to look stupid or weak in front of a . . . a . . .

Crap. It took a moment for him to remember just what and who she was. Mind wasn't quite right, he thought, fuzzy, everything coming to him through a thick gauze. Supermodel. That was her. Zurri the supermodel. He expected her to look worse in person, but unless she was somehow using an AR filter over her face, the reality looked as perfect as the advertisement. "I feel great, yeah. Maybe one headache but it's already going away. D–Do you have a session today?"

"I do," she replied, towering over him as she approached the vase and slashed her hand right through it. "Trying to kill time until then. *Really* kill time. Which is why I was hoping to find you."

Han's brows shot up. He swallowed and swore they could both hear the nervous gurgle. *Hoping to find you.* If for no other reason, the trip to Ganymede had now been worth it. She had seemed like, well, sort of a bitch at dinner, but maybe he had misjudged her. Zurri, *the* Zurri, needed him for something. Had Paxton Dunn erased reality itself and replaced it with something else?

"Sure." Han tried to play it casual. He cocked his hip to the side but ended up bumping the statue pedestal again. "What's up?"

Tall, imposing, now smirking, Zurri looked like a cat craning over an aquarium, ten seconds away from swiping a claw and skewering an unsuspecting shrimp. *I am the shrimp.* "You're smart with computers and stuff, right?"

Computers and stuff. Computers! And stuff! If this were one of his online friends' girlfriends, he would have been laughing his ass off, then devising a way to tell him no amount of friend circle clout was worth dating such an embarrassing noob. It began to occur to him that Zurri, someone with endless money and fame, didn't exactly need extensive knowledge of modern programming or computing to get through her day, when she cleared her throat impatiently at him.

"Yeah," he said with a shrug, again casual. "It's kind of my thing."

Very briefly, she studied his bare feet and bedheaded hair. "Of course it is." Then she smiled, hard, and nodded to her right, somewhat over her shoulder. "Those are the labs back there. I need something inside."

Han frowned. "Like what exactly? I'm not trying to get in trouble here."

"Do you want to know or do you want to help?" Zurri tilted her head to the side, and he could feel the claw extending, preparing to spear the shrimp. "I can get autographs for you and all your friends."

"Why can't you just ask Paxton for whatever you need?" he asked. Her smile wavered, the claw retracting ever so slowly.

"I want something to take the edge off while I wait for my appointment," Zurri sighed, glancing back toward the black lab offices door. "Drugs, okay? I want drugs. They have to be stored somewhere in there, and I want you to find out where, and get me inside."

"What makes you think I can do it?" Han asked, reasonably sure he could.

"You can't?"

"No." He said it too fast, and she smirked. "I can. I definitely can, but it won't be easy." Han was already planning on impressing Paxton. Finding a way around his automatic bioscan locks for the staff doors would certainly be impressive. And difficult. He hadn't even attempted to poke around in Dome security settings yet, so promising her results was premature. But Han wasn't about to say that, not to *Zurri*. He leaned to the side again, this time without knocking the statue pedestal. "I want the autographs," he said, watching her smile return. "*And* I want a VitMe."

"Fine." She rolled her eyes. "When?"

"Now, I guess," Han muttered, watching her stride to his side and crouch down so the picture wouldn't just be of his head and her neck.

"Fix your hair first," she told him.

"Like this?" He tried himself, flattening his hopelessly stuck-up hair down, only for it to spring back up.

"Jesus Christ." Zurri licked the flat of her right palm and smashed down his hair, then parted it on one side and smoothed it down. Now the trip was doubly worth it. "Get your VIT, come on, I'm over being extorted."

Han raised his left wrist, adjusted the VIT screen and made sure they were both in frame before snapping the image. With practiced ease, Zurri slapped on one of her aloof and somewhat surprised expressions, while Han pursed his lips and hoped for the best.

"There." She stood up tall again, crossing her arms and glaring down at him. "Now get me in that door."

Han hesitated, eyes scanning along the ground, up the ramp and to the doors of Paxton's office. "Genie," he said, and the assistant's voice emerged from the recessed alcove near the ramp.

"Yes, Han?"

"Is Paxton in his office?"

"No, I'm afraid Paxton is currently assisting a patient and will not be available for some time. Should I schedule a meeting with him for you?"

Han turned away, back toward the Dome courtyard and motioned for Zurri to follow him. "No, not yet. Thanks, Genie."

"That thing is listening to us all the time," Zurri pointed out, following a step behind him. "Won't that be a problem?"

"Yep." Han squared his shoulders, realizing he felt more himself again. More in the zone. "One of many. That thing heard all about your drugs, so I'll have to figure something out for that. Come on, it looks like I have time to kill, too."

15

Senna studied the ground through her fingers, both hands out in front of her, palms open, fingers tilted down.

My fingers look like rays . . . like rays of light bending toward the floor.

What was she trying to remember? Paxton put a hand on her shoulder. They were standing in the clinical offices, in the aquarium-blue serenity of the cubicles and terminals, a water feature in the corner rushing soothingly against a basin of pebbles. Something was on the tip of her tongue, something she was trying her hardest to remember. Every time she came close, pain shot across her eyes, white, hot and startling.

"How are you feeling?" Paxton asked. "We ran long; I didn't mean for your first session to be so intense."

"Just a headache," Senna murmured, looking at the spaces between her fingers again.

"That will pass. Dr. Colbie?"

She heard the doctor's heels clicking toward them. Over her white skirt and fitted shirt, she wore a loose lab coat with deep pockets that she now reached into. She pulled out two blue pill bottles and showed them to Paxton.

"How severe?" Dr. Colbie asked.

Senna didn't realize she was being asked until Paxton touched her shoulder again and squeezed. "Senna? How bad is the pain?"

"I don't know," she replied honestly. It wasn't pain exactly, not all the time, but a disorientation that made her sway back and forth on her feet. "When I try to remember, it hurts."

"Well, first of all? Don't do that," Paxton said laughingly. "That's why you're here, to forget. You have to relax, let the process settle, let those new connections we talked about form. Han was a little unsteady on his feet, too, but it shouldn't last longer than a few hours, and you need to tell us if it does."

"Can't help it," Senna murmured. Everything felt as bleary and soft as the time Marin had made her a few cocktails. *If it was something I wanted to forget, why am I trying so hard to remember?* The pain seared across her eyes again and she winced. "Bad. The pain is bad."

"Here," said Paxton. "These."

Dr. Colbie handed him the bottle in her left hand, but tugged back when he tried to take it. "Paxton . . ."

"She'll be fine. That was a long session, this will makes things easier while she recuperates."

Even blurry-eyed and weaving, Senna could tell Dr. Colbie wasn't happy. When she looked up into the doctor's face, she saw a ridge furrow over her fawn-colored eyebrows. She still wouldn't let go of the bottle, and Paxton didn't seem capable of snatching it from her.

"What we're doing here is medicine," Paxton told her through his teeth. "It's new, it's a little funny, but it's medicine. Give me the bottle, *Dr. Colbie*."

Senna noticed him reach over and fiddle with his VIT, then he went for the pill bottle again. It was just a few quick taps, but he had definitely touched his wrist. Right away, the doctor flinched from him, then spun and left them alone, walking straight out the black door, the sound of her heels vanishing, leaving only the quiet rush of water and Paxton's labored breathing. He pushed the pill bottle into Senna's hands and made sure she could grasp it before saying, "Go light on these. Just half to start, lots of water. Can you remember that?"

She nodded, and her head felt like a melon balanced on a pin. Paxton guided her toward the door Colbie had just left through. Swearing, he glanced at his VIT. "Where is Anju? She was supposed to walk you back to your rooms . . ."

"I can do it," Senna replied softly.

"Are you sure?" He glanced to his left, back toward the LENG room. "You really shouldn't be alone right now, but I need to get things set up and cleaned before Zurri's session."

"Back to my room," Senna replied, managing to lift her unimaginably heavy head and look Paxton in the face. There was that dark halo around him again. She wanted to paint it. "Half of one of these with lots of water."

A slow smile crept across his blurry face. "That's my girl. All right, you go, but raise me on your VIT if you start to feel worse, got it?"

"Got it." She frowned. It felt a bit overfamiliar. She wasn't his girl, but maybe he was just friendly like that.

Paxton approached the black door, opening it for her. When she stepped through and into the bright, bright gallery, she hissed and clamped her eyes shut. It was too much. All that light all at once, pouring into her, scouring the inside of her already tender head. Paxton must not have heard her. The door shut and he was gone, and Senna was all alone with the light and her drifting, rotating thoughts.

She put the pill bottle in her left pocket and shuffled into the blinding sear.

Back to my room. Half of one of these with lots of water.

She did not return to her rooms. Instead, she fell to her knees, suddenly weak. It didn't feel too bad to be there, eyes shut tight, hands molded over her face while she waited for the right thought to come and stir her to action. She kept circling back to it only for the idea, the will, to skitter away. *Get up, walk. It's not too bad, your eyes will adjust. Get up, walk.*

But walk where? A flicker of warmth ran across her hand, startling her. Senna squinted, holding out her fingers, watching a concentrated mote of light dance there before it bounced to the ground. It spread, bright even against the clean white tile of the floor. Either she was still hurting and disoriented and imagining things or it began to take on a shape, like the reverse of a shadow. When she looked for a source of the light, she couldn't find one, but it began to move, striding like a shadow would, only it was welcoming, warm, and winking like a flash across clean water. For a long moment, Senna stared at the "pale shadow," just breathing. She felt her pulse even out, her eyes adjusting now to the brutal light and to the shock of being pushed out of the LENG room like an infant fresh from its mother.

Birth, she thought. *I'm being reborn without my bad memories. Of course there's pain, birth is pain, too.*

She wanted to scream but stopped herself, then gradually climbed to her feet, deciding she wanted to see where the pale shadow was going. Maybe she hadn't actually *decided*—the pull was so strong it felt like the shadow had decided for her, and, helpless, she followed. The light shadow seemed to sense her newness, her fragility, and walked at an easy pace, guiding her, taking her to the right and up a shallow ramp to a walkway overlooking the gallery. They reached two transparent doors and it turned them left, around a sharp corner to an open hall that ran above and parallel to the gallery below. The nearness of the crystal chandelier dimmed the direct surroundings, and made the brightness of the gallery easier to withstand. Here, even more art was on display, white rectangles of varying sizes showing off smaller, more delicate sculptures and tablets.

The pale shadow kept up its steady, slow pace, bringing Senna to a pedestal about halfway down the corridor, pushed tight up against the right wall, which, at about waist height, became windows. Senna reached out to touch one to see if it was hot or cold, but it wasn't a window at all, just a screen showing a feed of the swirling misty ice fields outside the Dome.

At last, the light shadow stopped, still flickering and shimmering, and waited patiently next to that specific pedestal. Senna spoke to it, feeling foolish, but there was no denying that it seemed aware of her presence, modulating its pace to accommodate her. "Did you want to show me this?"

Of course there was no answer, and Senna studied the object instead. It was round and broken in two, about the size of a large man's fist. The two halves seemed magnetically locked in place, the scooped-out dish on the bottom flat to the pedestal, the other half floating above it, a gap of a few inches between them. Senna leaned over it, trying to get a closer look. Then she checked in every direction, finding that she was completely alone. A memory came to her of a tall, confident woman with dark skin flicking the nose of a stone face. A woman. A woman named . . . named . . .

Zurri. She had touched the art, why couldn't Senna?

So she did. She took the forefinger on her right hand and tried, gently, to touch the etched metallic surface of the upper half of the orb. A current passed through it and into her, hard and fast, with a force that felt like something had been shot directly into her skin. She stumbled back and made sure the tip of her finger was still there.

"I don't think you're supposed to touch the art."

Senna whirled, embarrassed and hot-faced. "I . . . I'm sorry." She expected to find Paxton there wagging a finger at her, but it was a man she had never seen before. Senna's eyes dragged across the floor toward him, the pale shadow suddenly gone. Not only that, this man was a complete stranger and Paxton had never mentioned any other staff or participants. Odd. But then, she was having trouble remembering much of anything. Maybe they had been introduced the day before, or maybe Paxton just hadn't gotten around to telling her about this employee yet.

"I'm teasing, it isn't art anyway," the man said, grinning. He wore a simple black suit, but on him it looked expensive and sophisticated.

"It's not?" Senna swiveled back to look at the broken orb again. "Whatever it is, I think it's strange. And beautiful. It zapped me when I touched it."

"Really? It's a paperweight." The man observed her from a few pedestals down from where she stood. He was of average height and lean, with a relaxed and open posture, shoulders back, hands nested in each other in front of his waist. "At least, that's what he calls it."

"He?" Senna wrinkled her nose. "Oh. Paxton." She wasn't thinking of him but of this new he. Where had he come from, and where had that bizarre, compelling light gone?

"Yes, Paxton," he said, seeming to struggle with the name.

"It's pretty elaborate for a paperweight," said Senna, gesturing to the orb. She had never seen anything hover like the top half of it did, or at least she didn't think so. When she tried to remember, the pain burst behind her eyes again. She winced and pinched the bridge of her nose. "Sorry if I seem off. I just had a treatment done in the labs."

"There's no need to apologize," he replied. "Or explain. I know what goes on here."

Eventually the pain dwindled and Senna dropped her hand, squinting down the floor toward the man. "Have you had it done? The LENG process? Procedure . . ." She shrugged. "I don't know what to call it."

"Me?" He laughed. "Oh, no, no, I would never. Do you mind if I ask what it was like?"

"Remembering anything hurts right now," she admitted.

His expression softened and he took a single step toward her as if to come to her aid. "Then don't try to remember anything. Or maybe just one thing . . ."

"Hm?"

"Your name?' He smiled again, left hand scratching idly at the right.

"Oh! Senna." She snort-laughed and shook her head. People usually recognized her. She remembered that much. "You've never seen me before?"

"Just around the facility," he said. "And right now. My name is Efren."

"Efren," she repeated, and when she did, tiny wrinkles appeared at the edges of his eyes. They were both quiet then and he ruffled his hair, perhaps nervous. Perhaps awkward. He had lovely hair, she thought, immaculate yet careless, so black it was almost blue. Golden-hazel eyes. Brown skin. Lips made for smiling, and a brow too quizzical to be serious all the time. He looked like he laughed often and with his whole body. *Beautiful.* She kept using that word. Did babies feel this way, too? Heart-soft and welcome-eyed, seeing everything with a glow across it, uncomplicated, untainted by judgment or comparison. Did everything new start out beautiful?

"There I go again," she murmured, somewhat dazed. "Off."

"One can hardly blame you for that," said Efren. "Given your reasons for being here." He had an accent like Paxton's, British but more pronounced, and with the touch of vague interference that came with bouncing around countries or prolonged time on the mishmash of the station.

"I'm supposed to be going somewhere, I think. I keep forgetting . . ." Senna gazed around at first the orb, then the "window" and then Efren. He seemed forlorn, or maybe in pain, a line tight between his eyebrows. Must have felt sorry for her. But it would come to her eventually, the destination . . .

Back to my room. Half of one of these with lots of water.

"My room!" she cried out, then covered her mouth. "Sorry, it just came to me. I'm supposed to be going back to my room to rest but I got distracted and took a little detour."

"I'm glad you did," Efren said. "If you don't mind my saying so, Senna, you really don't look well. Perhaps I could walk you to your rooms, with fewer detours this time."

Senna nodded, patting the pill bottle shoved into her pocket. Half of one. It would all come back, Paxton had assured her. It would just take time.

"All right," she replied. "Someone was supposed to walk with me anyway."

"Ah, yes," Efren said as he approached, waiting for Senna to tentatively dislodge herself from the wall and fall into stride with him. She glanced around for the shadow of light, but it had vanished. "One of Paxton's dollies, I imagine. Which one? The doctor or the assistant?"

"Anju." It felt like scraping dry bone to dredge up her name. "What do you mean 'dollies'?"

They ambled down the walkway, toward an archway she hadn't noticed at the end, it traveled under a gap that would take them back out into the Dome courtyard, but on a second, higher level. "Don't tell me you haven't noticed . . . All of his employees are tall, slim, perfect, same make and model just with a few settings tweaked."

"Everyone I've met has been nice to me," Senna protested, frowning. "You don't need to be rude about them just because they're pretty."

"Oh, they're nice! Lovely, yes. Perfectly nice." He laughed and put his hands in his pockets and their elbows bumped. "Nothing wrong with their personalities, but Paxton likes things to look *just so*."

"And what about you?" Senna asked, looking up at him as they walked. The humid, lush scent of the Dome plant life rose to meet them. "You're the outlier."

"Well spotted, eh? Nothing gets past you." His hazel eyes twinkled, and she huffed. He was teasing. "I'm not like Anju and the rest because I'm not Paxton's employee."

"Then what are you? What do you do here?"

At that, he hesitated, half shrugging before changing his mind and bobbing his head side to side as if weighing possible answers. "It's complicated."

"Meaning you think I'm stupid."

"No! Meaning I don't want to get you in any hot water, let's just say I keep the technology running smoothly," Efren hurried to say. They started down another ramp, this one curving toward the ground level of the Dome. A huge, hulking tree arced over them, mist clinging to its trunk, an augmented-reality toucan watching them from its hefty branches. "Everything here is proprietary. You, me, the tech, even that fucking toucan is probably proprietary. You're going to hear that word so much here you'll grow absolutely sick to death of it. What matters is that I'm not Paxton's employee, but he does need me, and so I don't have to fit into one of his adolescent male fantasies."

"Surely he couldn't run this place without his staff, however they look," Senna pointed out. It was becoming easier to follow a thread, to stay on one topic without her thoughts turning into a jumble mid-word. Paxton was right. It did get better and easier. "Maybe he needs you, but he needs the others, too."

"True, true. He would try to run this place entirely on his own if he could," Efren assured her. "I'm sure he's tried."

"You know him well," she said. "From what all the programs and vids say, nobody really knows him well."

"*Knew* him well," Efren corrected. That same pained, distant expression crossed his face. "We're no longer close, and that's for the best. What do you think of this place? Astounding, isn't it? Hard to think otherwise."

"Beautiful," she replied, picking her word of the moment. "It doesn't seem possible, or real."

"Paxton is a visionary," Efren agreed, guiding her through the maze of mosaic trails, sculptures and leafy impediments.

"You admire him."

Efren drew his head back, his mouth twisting to the side. "No, Senna, I wouldn't say that I admire him. *Pah*. Listen to me prattling on while you're half-blind with pain. You were better off alone and dazed, maybe. I'm sure I've said enough, and I'm also sure you're far more interesting."

Senna grew quiet, and imagined she always did when people said things like that. It was still hard to remember what she had been like a few hours ago. Had a man ever said something like that, and had she demurred? Had it always felt as if explaining her story, her past, was like choking up a stomach full of bloody bile?

"It's complicated," she finally said.

Efren belted out a laugh, and just like she thought, he laughed with his entire body. "I deserved that," he sighed. "I won't pry, not when your head is all strange jelly."

They had navigated the path back to the other side of the courtyard and the twin ramp that led up to the second floor, but on this side to the balcony outside the dormitories. "I think I can find my way from here."

"I'll stay a while, if you get lost again, come find me," Efren told her, and it made her want to get lost on purpose. There was something about his warm, sure smile that comforted her. If she were a more suspicious person, she would allow herself to think they had met before.

Senna found her rooms, and when she made it inside, she exhaled a shuddering breath. Her entire diaphragm felt pinched, like she wasn't holding in her whole breath, only a little. Something in reserve. Something new sat on the kitchen table. It had a big silver bow on it, which was the only way she knew it was a gift. If it had been there that morning, she would have already opened it.

Under the gleaming bow was a new and pricey set of paints. Real paints. She reached for a brush, and then for the vial of turpentine. When she popped open the lid, the scent nearly made her knees buckle. Memories. The compound. A hard sensation in her cheeks, like something had gotten wedged there, tears that she couldn't quite cry . . . The way the brush slid into her grasp, it was obvious she hadn't forgotten how to hold the tool, and she hoped she hadn't forgotten how to use it.

An alert blared from her VIT. The screen lit up, and she watched a message scroll across the lock screen. It was from Paxton.

> Enjoy the new paints. I can't wait to see what you create. Maybe you can show me something tomorrow over our dinner date. xo

Senna glared at her VIT, mouth dry, stunned. Dinner date? She couldn't remember agreeing to meet up with Paxton for dinner. Had she? Would she? Pulling out a kitchen chair, she dropped down into it and felt the pills rattle around in her pocket. She rolled the bottle onto the table next to the paints and scraped again at the dry bone of her memory, but nothing came to her but the pain.

Our dinner date.

She must have said yes, or maybe it was a misunderstanding, but then she *was* having trouble remembering so very many things.

16

Han pounded his fist on the bench, stumped.

"I thought I had it," he muttered, glancing away from the flat black projection and white text hovering over his VIT. A portable keyboard sat on his lap, some of the key labels worn away from use. Across from him on her own bench, Zurri tore her gaze away from the canopy of trees arcing over them.

"Forget it, kid," she sighed. "Maybe I can ask the blond one for the good stuff. She seemed like more of a pushover."

"This sucks. I thought I had it." Han chewed the edge of his left thumb. They were nearing the end of Zurri's free time before her appointment. Full day had arrived in the Dome, and rather than gather in one of their rooms, which seemed suspicious, Han and Zurri sat right out in the open. They picked a secluded bend in the mosaic tile trail through the courtyard, one shielded on four sides by dense foliage. Zurri alternately stared up at the artificial light filtering through the leaves and scrolled idly on her

VIT. "This OS uses the same skeletal structure as the generic Merchantia in-home assistants, like the kind we have at home. I thought I could use the same way in . . ."

Zurri stood and checked the time on her VIT, and Han held up one of his unchewed fingers. "One more try?"

"I'm just about out of time," she told him. "How does . . . how does this stuff work anyway?"

Han smirked. "You really wanna know?"

"I've seen people hack all kinds of shit in the vids, is it anything like that?" She mimed bashing away on a keyboard, hunched over, eyes bunched up in concentration.

"No, not at all," Han said, straightening his back and hearing a soft pop. Okay, maybe the hunching part was a tiny bit accurate. "I have a bunch of scripts already downloaded to my VIT, just text files run through a scrambling program, nothing contraband scanners would pick up. Script kiddies upload them to black VIT dens, and then you can take whatever you want."

"Sounds illegal," Zurri chuckled.

"The scripts aren't," Han protested. "What you do with them can be, I guess. The one I use at home works like this—if you contact the Merchantia help desk, they walk you through problems, and sometimes they need to remote into your VIT or your home console. They use global admin IDs that can access most Merchantia products, so this script picks one of those as a log-in, then tries all known passwords for that ID that have been used. MSC has an algorithm for generating passwords, so there isn't an infinite combination. Make sense?"

Zurri flopped her open hand back and forth, so Han beckoned her closer. It was still wild that she was Who She Was and she was there, listening to him drone on about hacking. Surreal. He couldn't really think about it too hard or he would start to sweat even harder. While she was bird-watching on the other bench, he had already surreptitiously looked at the VitMe of them four times. None of his gaming friends were going to believe him, or any of this. He couldn't wait for the storm to pass and for Paxton to batch out their communications. He already had dozens of messages queued up on the server.

"Here." He pointed to the display projected above his VIT. Text scrolled and scrolled, dozens of password inputs and failures every second. "See? I ran the script again just now. It's trying to log in with ID MSC192_RICO!J20 and those are all the password attempts."

"If I mess up my password twice trying to get back into my messages, I get locked out for a while," Zurri pointed out.

"Admin IDs don't flag those systems," Han replied. "Besides, it doesn't matter. The Dome won't even accept these admin IDs, Paxton must have set up his own in-house security IDs, or maybe he's the only admin. I can try to trick him into giving me his admin name, but that seems like a long shot."

"And not exactly subtle," replied Zurri.

"Wouldn't matter." Han killed the script and pointed above their heads, then to the bench he was seated upon. "I'm sure Paxton already knows what I'm up to. We're not trying to get access to a big MSC server, any fishy log-in attempts would be obvious when there's, you know, like eight of us total."

Her dark eyes went wide and she swatted him on the shoulder. "You could've told me that before!"

"I don't mind if he knows," Han said. He hoped he sounded cool, unbothered. Hell, he had just shown Zurri basic hacking methods, so he was *feeling* very cool and unbothered. Another thing his friends would never believe. "I hope he does know I tried. I'm gonna crack this before my time here is up. Just imagine his reaction! A teenager breaking into his automated security system and messing with all the locks. Legendary status, for sure."

Zurri didn't seem impressed. In fact, she crossed her lean arms over her chest and rolled her eyes. A pair of brightly colored birds swooped low behind her, then disappeared back into the trees. "You are way too obsessed with him. He's a creep."

"He is not!" Han heard the whining note in his voice and glared off to his left. "He's brilliant. You couldn't make all of this." He gestured to the Dome surrounding them. "I couldn't. Nobody could. Of course I want to impress him, I want to *be* him."

"No, kid, you really don't. He's isolated himself out here for a reason. Only a genuinely weird person would do that. Where's his family? His friends? He doesn't even meet his adoring fans." She chuckled and waited until he reluctantly glanced toward her. "Other than you, mm? You don't want to be like that."

"Where are your family and friends?" he asked.

Zurri narrowed her eyes. "Fame is isolating."

Going quiet, he closed the projection on his VIT and shifted on the bench. His butt was beginning to get sore. This was stupid anyway. He didn't need her permission to do what he knew was right for himself. She was a stranger, and judgy, and what did she know about Paxton? Nothing. "Anyway, I'm already like that, I just see my brother, and have my games and my online buddies. It wouldn't be so different, and at least I would be doing something great. Something important."

"Birds of a feather," she sighed. Her VIT chimed softly, warning of her impending appointment. "Just think about what I said. You can do great and important things without turning into a mini Paxton."

"Can I still have my autographed stuff?" he asked softly.

"Yeah, sure, kid. And if you really do figure it out, then you can have another VitMe, if at first you don't succeed and all that, right?"

She took the path to the right, leading back through the maze of trees and flowers and shrubs to reach the labs on time. A few of the heavy, riotous blooms off the trail matched her orange dress, and bobbed as she walked by, stirred by the speed of her gait and the confident swish of her arms. She almost ran headlong into someone coming around the corner, but didn't seem to notice, head high as she left him with the stranger in their quiet little glade.

"Hello," Han greeted the man, frowning in confusion. "Have we met?"

"Is that it?"

Zurri stalked in a circle around the chair, observing it from every angle just in case she was missing something. "Like . . . is this a joke?"

Near the comically intense vault door leading into the black LENG room, Paxton and Dr. Colbie watched her. They wore twin expressions of benign amusement. In her mind, Zurri had taken to calling the women working for Paxton the Jane Does because she was never going to remember any of their names and they all had the same dead fish hollowness behind the eyes. Probably a side effect of prolonged exposure to Paxton's bullshit. Of all of them, the blond one in the room, Dr. Colbie, irritated her the least so far.

"I assure you, this is not a joke. What were you expecting?" Paxton asked.

"I've been to nail techs with more interesting chairs," she

replied. "This is supposed to revolutionize therapy? It's not even an Eames."

"It doesn't have to be. The chair isn't the important part," Paxton explained, using the slightly exasperated singsong tone of a failingly patient parent. It was a tone she did not appreciate. If she were paying for this experience, this would be the moment when she threatened to ask for her money back. She couldn't wait to excoriate him to the press when she returned to the station; the social media feeds would light up for days.

"So where's the important part?" asked Zurri, pausing near the extremely nondescript and apparently unimportant chair.

"There," he said, pointing to her head. "And all around you. It's in the walls. Under the floor. Hidden in the ceiling."

Her eyes slid from his to Dr. Colbie's. "Is he for real?"

"Oh, one hundred percent." She smiled, and the twinkle behind it almost charmed Zurri. "The LENG technology is incorporated into the room itself, and since the scanning apparatus is a bit on the secret side, we didn't exactly want to have it out where anyone could snap images. Proprietary, as you might expect."

Zurri tapped the face of her VIT. "Clever. So how does it work?"

"You sit down, we put in your IV, and then we use the neural map Kris took back on the station to begin modifying your memories," explained Paxton. "Or do you want the technical version?"

"No, thanks." Zurri spun on one heel and lowered herself into the chair. "I've had enough of that for one day."

"Do you need me to review the potential side effects again?" Dr. Colbie asked, approaching from Zurri's right while pulling on medical gloves. Her all-white outfit from the day before hadn't changed.

"Just like a hangover?"

"Similar." Colbie smiled. "Have you taken anything today? Consumed any alcohol?"

"Unfortunately, no."

"Then we're clear to begin."

Even after the needle was nestled in her vein and secured there, it didn't seem like enough. If everything important and useful was hidden in the walls, then how was it close enough to be effective? She didn't purport to be a doctor or even vaguely science-minded, but it didn't add up. Briefly, she considered it might all be placebo. Maybe this song and dance just tricked one into thinking they had undergone some kind of treatment. Well. She was too smart for that. The minute this was over she would start retracing her steps through the memories she had relived in detail during the neural-mapping session.

"See you on the other side," Paxton called, waving as he and Colbie disappeared behind the heavy, circular door. It shut with an authoritative thud, final and chilling.

She hadn't expected the darkness of the room to feel so close or so claustrophobic. At least she had the star field projected against the wall in front of her. It soothed her to concentrate on that, following one comet tail after another, watching them zing into infinity, pixels, blurs, and then nothing. Gradually, she became aware of a deep, bassy thrum emanating from the floor. It sounded and felt like a generator starting up, whirring and whining but also churning, a relentless *ka-thum, ka-thum* that plucked at sinews inside of her she hadn't considered in a long time, or maybe she never noticed them before. Primal. Alarming. The projection of the stars narrowed, the edges shrinking inward, eating away at the image until it was like looking down a small, circular hallway.

Electricity along her arms. An alertness in her body. This was new to her but old to the species.

Then came the fear.

Was it starting? Had they started? Zurri swiveled her head from side to side, realizing they hadn't given her an out. What was the safe word? Where was the OH SHIT button? She clutched the arms of the chair and looked toward the door. A presence. She stared back at the figure waiting there. Another projection like on the station? It didn't resemble the glossy, white, sexless augmented-reality robot that had been there for the neural mapping.

I am LENG, it said.

It wasn't the cheerful, rueful voice of the station LENG. Her eardrums contracted, her head suddenly filled with thunder. It was a voice that had come from below the ground, below all grounds. A voice from the core of a world. It came closer, a blurred, black halo leaping from its edges. Just a silhouette, but her instinct assigned it features, hollow eyes, gaping mouth, fingers just too long . . .

Jesus God holy Christ get me out of here!

I am LENG, it repeated, moving in stutters to the star-field wall, where it should have occupied space and the stars should have appeared all over it. Instead, it repelled the light, and nothing touched it, and even the projected stars bent strangely around its parameters.

You will give me what has been promised, it told her. *I have come to consume.*

The pressure built in her head. The tight instant before a sneeze. Coming up out of deep water too soon. She closed her eyes, but it was there behind her lids, too. *It, it, it.* LENG. The name didn't encompass it, insulted it, even. She hated it, but she wanted to look more, not to see it, really, not to understand it, but to peer into the cold, constricted vastness it inhabited.

You will give it to me, or I will take it, LENG said. *And taking is pain.*

It was already pain. It was *all* pain. Her molecules vibrated. Something was wet on her face, and it dribbled down into her mouth, salty, warm and warning.

Remember, it demanded. *Remember, and I will take it.*

"I? You?" Zurri cried, desperate, her teeth throbbing, as if her gums were receding at its presence, fearful of it. Every cell of her fearful of it. "You're not you. Or I. What *are* you?"

I am not I *or you*, it agreed. *No word encapsulates. Yesterday I was a harvester, today I am a traveler. I have been given a map—your map. Walking the landscape of your map begins now.*

The thing came nearer, swallowing the vanishing tunnel of stars. Every juddering footstep of it toward her gave an answering pulse behind her eyes, burrowed into her brain. The noise was incredible. *Unsustainable.*

Another warm gush into her mouth. *I'm going to die here.*

And then she saw him: the man on fire, the body bursting into flames, gouts of red flowers growing at warp speed from his chest. Ash in her mouth, heat rising, bathing her face . . .

"Tony!" She screamed his name as if she could stop him, like she *wanted* to stop him. Maybe the fire made sense. Maybe it was cleansing. No . . . he had hurt her and broken her trust, given her far too much to carry around; she didn't know what he deserved. She only knew what she deserved: to be free from the pain he had caused her.

He came to you, LENG said. Its too-long fingers stretched out toward her, and Zurri became rooted to the chair. *Give, give unto*

*me, and I will take it. I am hunger. I am always hunger. I am hungry
for the inadequate feast of your sorrow.*

Memories forced their way to the surface like steam hissing
through the cracks of widening fissures. Weeks before he broke
into her condo, Tony had arranged a birthday dinner for Zurri.
All her friends would be there. Her favorite Italian place on the
top level of the station. The reservation, even with the power of
her name behind it, had to be made six months in advance. She
actually dressed up, actually tried. Her favorite space peridot necklace, a spritz of discontinued perfume from a long-gone French
atelier, heels that lengthened her already sky-high legs . . . Then
she glided into the private room reserved for the party and discovered it would just be her and Tony. The first appetizer arrived, sweetly divine watermelon salad, her glass of Nebbiolo
untouched as her stomach tied itself into strangling knots. She
had to fire Tony, she thought, listening to him guzzle wine, listening to the loud, wet breath of an overexcited, oblivious man.

Zurri pretended to take a call. "This is really sweet," she had
told him through pinched lips. "But I have to take this."

I have to take this, LENG repeated. Its presence, the sense of its
weight and size, the threat it posed, pinned her to the chair. Its
fingers reached her eyes and entered, and Zurri felt it searching
through her thoughts. Seeking, seeking . . . Then the scooping,
the taking, skittering pinpricks of untold needles tickling raw
nerves.

The pain was incredible. *Is this cleansing? No, no, no, God, it's
agony.*

This wasn't what she wanted. This wasn't what Paxton told
her to expect.

She gasped and gasped, and couldn't find enough air in the

room. Then its fingers retracted, Zurri blinked her watering eyes, and when she opened them again, LENG was gone. She slumped forward, emptied, a brittle shell. Her hands shook on the armrests as the star field overtook the wall again, white blobs placidly and predictably traveling on their paths, going nowhere.

For a moment, Zurri fell into a meditative state, her mind completely blank. She had attempted to achieve such a thing at a Buddhist retreat once, but sitting in a hot, crowded room in an itchy, cheap wrap dress was boring and she hated it. But if this was where it led . . . if this was nothingness . . . She raised a trembling hand and placed it over her chest, and waited to feel her wildly beating heart. Instead she felt a steady rhythm, a thumping that told her the emptiness was just fine.

The door to her right wheezed, the heavy bolts released, the seal breaking. She climbed to her feet, still in a trance. Vaguely, she knew there had been fear, that something strange had come to visit her and taken bad things away. Now she tested those vacant spaces, exploring them like the shiny skin revealed below a scab. Had she been frightened before? What had she seen?

If she couldn't recall, did it really matter at all?

17

A prettily sparkling chime woke Senna from her sleep, a sound like someone had learned to play a waterfall as a musical instrument. She had gotten to the leather sofa somehow, and now peeled her cheek away from the supple ivory surface, her head lead-heavy and throbbing. The blue pill bottle sat on the coffee table in front of her, the cap jauntily poised on top but not screwed, half of a pill and a few telling crumbles just beside the bottle.

Gingerly, she prodded her temples, and found that the pain had gone. The chime sounded again through the lifting fog of grogginess.

"I am sorry to disturb you, Senna, but Anju is at the door. Should I allow her to enter?"

"One second," she murmured, stretching stiff arms over her head. "How long was I asleep?"

"Approximately four hours."

"Whoa." She frowned and carefully gained her footing, then

shuffled across the carpet to the hallway leading to the door. "What time is it?"

"Dome time three forty-seven p.m.," Genie replied. "Would you like me to arrange lunch, or would you prefer to choose from your refrigerated options?"

"I'm not hungry, thanks." Senna pushed the hair from her eyes and hoped she didn't look like too much of a mess as she approached the door, and it slid open to reveal Anju, all radiant smiles in a black, fitted frock and jangling gold earrings.

"Oh!" She cocked her head to the side. "You poor thing, did I wake you up?"

"I took a nap," Senna admitted. No use denying it when the proof was right there smooshed across her face. "I was tired and a little headachy after my session. Did you need something?"

"I brought these for you," said Anju brightly, holding her arms out flat in front of her, several clothing items folded neatly over them. "They should be your size!"

"O . . . kay." Puzzled, Senna took one of the garments and held it up, finding a baby-pink dress not much bigger or different than Anju's. "What is this for exactly?"

"For tonight," she said simply, as if Senna were a wayward child being reminded of schoolwork. When Senna's only response was a blank expression, she added, "For your dinner with Paxton?"

"Right." Senna had completely forgotten. "About that—"

"He can be fussy about these things, he likes to dress up," Anju raced on, ignoring Senna as she placed the pink dress back across Anju's arms. "His one embarrassing concession to station life, I guess."

"It's just dinner?" Senna asked. "It's not . . . it's not like a date or anything, right?"

Anju stared at her in wide-eyed terror. Meanwhile, Senna stared back, wondering who exactly this woman was, how she had come to be on Ganymede. The impending dinner and the dresses Anju had brought as some kind of sisterly offering didn't seem so important anymore. The man she had met, Efren, seemed disparaging of Anju and the other staff members, skeptical. She couldn't yet tell if that was earned. And here Anju was being very thoughtful, or thoughtful in the way that she knew how.

"Where did you grow up?" Senna asked.

Anju wasn't prepared for that one, clearly, her eyes going unfocused as she continued holding out the clothes. Weren't her arms getting tired?

"On the station," Anju replied through a tentative smile. "Like you." Then she scrunched up her face and sighed. "Sorry, I'm sure that sounded creepy. Paxton gave us dossiers on all of you so we wouldn't bring up anything that could trigger a memory relapse. I spent most of my time in Sector 3."

"There's housing there?" Senna felt more at ease. She absolutely did not want to talk about dinner, but she was genuinely curious about where Paxton's staff had come from, and how they wound up so far from home. "I thought that was the tech and manufacturing sector."

"There's housing if you work insane enough hours." Anju chuckled. "And my parents did. So did—do—I. But I'm not here to talk about—"

"And your parents? What were they like?" Senna pushed. "I didn't really know mine, but I suppose you must have read that in your dossier, too."

At last she lowered her arms, holding the dresses to her stomach with a defeated hunch to her shoulders. "I didn't see mine much, they were hooked into the MSC promotion pipeline hard.

Mom was from Kerala, Dad is American. He was off station a lot, running science missions out of the satellite HQ."

"They must miss you," Senna pointed out, trying to be nice. "With the distance and the storms here, I can't imagine you get back home much."

"No," Anju agreed. "I never get home. Here." She thrust a different dress, a darker mauve one, into Senna's hands without asking. "You should wear this one. It's a nice shade with your hair."

"Anju, I'm sorry, but I don't remember agreeing to dinner tonight. I can't remember him asking, and I don't remember saying yes."

She nodded and took a step back into the hallway and away from Senna's door. "That will happen with the memory stuff. I should go."

"I'm sorry for all the personal questions—"

"We're just not supposed to get close with patients, is all," Anju assured her, giving what felt like her first genuine smile of the interaction.

"But it's okay for me to dine alone with Paxton?"

The smile vanished. Anju left quickly, one notch below a full-out gallop. "Dinner's at seven in his office, try not to be late. He hates when girls make him wait."

Three hours later, Senna put on the mauve dress and her same shapeless shoes and shuffled out the door. Things remained fuzzy in her mind, but three things stood out as true: Anju had gone to the effort; she wanted answers or at least clarification from Paxton; she didn't know what else to do.

The dress, stretchy and clingy and not at all her usual style, was the nicest thing she had ever worn on her body after the fancy VIT from Agent Tiwari. Senna had stood inspecting herself in the bathroom mirror, hair curling around one finger while she twisted back and forth, realizing she had the wrong underwear for the outfit, but none better to change into. Over the dress she wore a loose, cottony beige jacket that hid the obvious outline stamped around the butt of her dress. She felt more like herself once she pulled on the jacket, swaddled and undefined.

On the way out the door, she passed the paints still on the kitchen table and stared at them longingly. She would have preferred to stay in and just paint. Images burned to flow from her heart to her hand, but they would have to simmer awhile longer.

Just to make sure she had things right, Senna checked the facility map on her VIT and then navigated to the balcony outside the dormitories. A walkway wrapped around to the right that would get her to Paxton's officer faster, but she chose to go down the ramp and through the courtyard instead. The "sun" was setting, and the rosy-orange glow smoldering through the Dome seemed like it deserved to be experienced. If she was going to paint again, she would need to fill herself up with color, get drunk on it, remember what it was like to speak only in that bright and imperfect language.

The courtyard was full of inspiration, empty of people. Empty, that is, until Senna reached the bottom of the ramp and let her eyes wander up toward the walkway. She saw the hint of a shadow there, and hands wrapped around the railing. Following the pale-blue-and-white-mosaic trail to the right, she turned and shielded her eyes, and caught sight of Zurri standing in the center of the suspended walkway, frozen and staring. She didn't look well.

Twenty minutes to seven. That was enough time. Senna took the stairs up to the catwalk as quickly as she could, and even then it felt like she was moving through oxygenated pudding. Everything was in slow motion since her nap. It would get easier, both Paxton and Dr. Colbie had assured her; healing the brain took time.

"Hey," Senna called as she reached the top, out of breath. She saw a tendon jump in Zurri's jaw at her greeting, but nothing else. "Are you all right?"

She approached with her hands out in surrender, loath to startle her, sensing the fragility of a wounded animal, and one perched on a precarious ledge. The fall was long and while probably not fatal, certainly painful. None of the architecture was exactly up to standard Tokyo Bliss Station code—this was Paxton's house, and his rules, and nobody had come to inspect and scold and levy fines.

"Zurri?" The whites of Zurri's dark eyes were dyed crimson. She wasn't blinking. "Should I get Dr. Colbie? Zurri?"

For a moment, Senna stood with her in silence, watching the deep pull of her lungs, her chest rising and falling like she had just sprinted. Leaning toward her slightly, Senna craned to see what Zurri was staring at, and found herself looking directly toward Paxton's office. The once-transparent doors there were now darkened, frosted a deep maroon.

"This sky," Zurri finally said, and Senna breathed a sigh of relief. "Doesn't it remind you of fire?"

Senna chewed the inside of her cheek, choosing her response carefully. They were all there for different reasons, but Senna had seen part of Zurri's reason on the live *Daily Bliss* broadcast. That man had jumped right in front of her and set himself on fire. If Zurri had entered the program to forget that, then it wouldn't be right to remind her of the trauma and damage the process.

"I think it's quite pretty," Senna said, with exploratory gentility, as if she were talking her, quite literally, down from that open ledge. "Are you feeling okay tonight?"

"I don't know," replied Zurri, and her right cheek flinched. "I keep trying to remember. It's like gathering string, I chase after it, bundle it all up, then when I finally have it in my hands, it just falls to the floor again and unravels. Then I'm chasing it again, trying to remember."

"We're not supposed to do that," Senna reminded her. "When I tried to remember, it just made my head hurt, it got so bad Dr. Colbie had to give me medicine."

Knuckles tightening on the railing, Zurri swiveled to face her. Her eyes had become so dry that tears welled in the irritated corners, glossy and ready to spill. "What kind of medicine?"

"Um, I think it was called Talpraxem or something. I only took half of one and it knocked me out for hours. The side effects didn't sound great either, or the warnings. Do not take while pregnant, take at mealtime, store in a dry place . . . ," she rattled off.

"Talpraxem is serious stuff." Zurri blinked, and Senna felt like she had won a small victory. "Can I have it?"

"Have it? A-All of it?"

"Sure, or whatever you're willing to spare."

Senna scratched the back of her neck, glancing toward Paxton's office. It had to be almost seven. *He hates when girls make him wait.* "I suppose I could share, but maybe I should clear it with Dr. Colbie first."

"No, don't do that," Zurri laughed. "Don't snitch. I've taken it before, Senna. I've taken everything before. I'll come by your apartment later."

Senna didn't see herself winning the argument and nodded. At the very least, someone would be checking in on her. That made her feel better about going to dinner with Paxton, in fact . . .

"How about in two hours?" Senna said, giving herself a clear-cut time limit for the meal.

"Sure." Zurri smirked, then looked her up and down. "Why are you dressed up?"

"I'm not," Senna insisted, tucking a piece of hair behind her ear.

"That's a twenty-thousand-yuan Bethany Li bandage dress. The spring 2268 collection. I know because I wore it in the campaign." One of her dark, well-sculpted eyebrows lifted. "You are one weird mystery, Cult Girl."

"Don't call me that." Senna grimaced, pushing away from the railing and storming off.

She could practically hear the gears churning in Zurri's head while the model landed on something suitably mean to say. Instead, she just called, "I'm sorry, okay? I won't call you that. We'll pick this up later, Senna. I want to know where you got that dress."

And I want to know where Anju got it.

"And, Senna?"

"Yes?"

"Girl code stuff, just be careful with Paxton. I've known a lot of men like him. They're takers, and they don't take rejection well. If he gives you any trouble, you come to me and I'll sort him out, all right?"

Senna looked down at the dress she was wearing. So Zurri thought this was a date, too. She simply nodded, and frowned, and decided it was good to have someone as worldly and intimidating as Zurri on her side. *Girl code stuff.* That was a new one for her. Senna ran her hands down the fine fabric of the dress. What was Paxton paying these people? Maybe that was a totally normal item for someone with Anju's job to have. After all, Paxton was astronomically famous and wealthy, maybe he expected all of his staff to wear high-fashion clothes to work.

Or maybe your brain isn't so soft after all, and you know exactly why she has it. Because it was a gift from him.

That wasn't fair. Anju was a competent woman in a high-powered job; if she wanted to save up her money to splurge on clothes, then that was her right and her business. Judging her for it was the exact bullshit Senna had spent a year drumming out of her head. That kind of indulgence, that kind of consuming, was everything Preece hated and railed against. On the compound, members of the brood wore their plain, scratchy pants until thin knees broke through thinner fabric. Then those holes were meticulously mended, and the process began again. Without a VIT, without a life outside the compound, Senna onced marked time that way, by the give on the knees of her trousers, by the proximity of fresh air to knee skin.

She toppled to the left, holding herself up by the stairway railing. A hot, white knife of pain shot through her eyeball, stabbing back into her brain. *I'm remembering,* she thought. *I'm not supposed to remember.*

Life on the compound and Preece remained, but when she tried to picture the faces hovering above the thin patched pants, her mind throbbed, furiously bereft. Nothing. They were gone. Gone because . . . because . . . Senna slid to the stair below her and sat. Gone because she had asked Paxton to rip them away. They all wore blurry masks, voices garbled nonsense, ghoulish half-human golems wandering the vanishing corridors of her memory. Preece remained, the lone face in a sea of half-remembered personalities.

Senna waited until the pain passed, and then she forced herself up and half ran the rest of the distance, huffing and puffing, weak in ways she was constantly discovering. Through the gallery, where the Servitor was setting out identical bowls of soup for Brea, Anju, and Dr. Colbie. They smiled at her with muted curiosity, like she was a passing tram. Han didn't notice her trot by, enamored of a mountain of pasta drenched in red sauce. Senna smelled the garlic as she sailed by.

Up the ramp, to the doors. They were crimson, brighter than they were before, as if her two-minute lateness had angered the man inside. Marin and Jonathan sat her down to watch *The Wizard of Oz* once. "You're like a newborn baby," Marin had teased, dusting their popcorn with seaweed flakes in the kitchenette. "You don't know anything. You haven't seen anything!"

Jonathan liked it. "We get to be your tastemakers. We'll only show you the best stuff."

Here was the Great and Terrible Oz, only the curtain was red and Senna had seen his face, while the outside world on Earth and the colonies and the station wondered and speculated, in awe. From their limited interactions, Senna got the impression that he *wanted* to be seen. Why did he hide from the public? Why choose a moon of Jupiter and not some expansive and lavish lab on the station? He could afford to buy out half a sector if he wanted to. Now was the time to ask, she realized, during this dinner she couldn't remember wanting.

The doors swished open, the man behind the curtain would see her now.

Paxton had changed into a smart blue suit without a tie, the cut of the pants slim and high, showing a sliver of silvery gray socks. When she stood in the open doorway he looked up from where he had been fiddling with his console. His resembled Marin's, recessed into the surface of his desk, routed through his VIT for convenience, a three-dimensional, projected display hovering inches above where the technology was nested into the wood. Of course, Marin's desk wasn't real wood, but Senna assumed his would be something outrageous and imported from Earth. It certainly looked expensive, the desk curved and dominating the back half of the space, darker whorls and knots in the surface giving the flat, glossy plane the look of wind-blown sand.

"There you are," he said, making the display vanish and striding toward her with open arms. "Right on time."

Senna smiled. She was at least two minutes late.

"And looking *gorgeous*. I like the coat, too. Adds, you know, your own spin." To get to her, he had to walk around a small, obviously temporary black table and chairs, where their meal had been laid out. "May I?" he asked, gesturing toward her jacket.

Senna trapped her fingers in the too-long sleeves of it and bit down on her lip. "I'd rather keep it on. Chilly."

"I can have Genie adjust the temperature in here."

Senna shook her head no.

"Sure! Sure, okay, no problem." Judging by his expression, it was at least somewhat a problem, but he spun back toward the table with a flourish, and Senna decided to take the seat on the right. The office itself was less grandiose than she expected, with decidedly fewer vanity sculptures. Immense digital frames hung on the walls, cycling through various photos, most of them aerial images of the Dome as it was being constructed. His desk held a variety of smaller frames faced toward the chair, and a statue bust. The only light in the office originated along the back wall, which was a false window like the one on the upper walkway overlooking the gallery. It showed a meadow at sunset, pale grasses stretched to infinity, an obligingly scenic wind rustling the field so that it resembled one massive, pastoral wave breaking against a pre-storm sky.

"I thought you might want to try your luck with the chicken again," Paxton said, pulling out her chair. Unnecessarily, in her opinion, but Senna let him do it. It was the first time any man had tried. Her face felt tightly nervous, as if any expression too extreme, good or bad, would crack it. "There's butter noodles, too. Didn't know about wine. Are you . . . Do you . . ."

"You tell me," said Senna, half joking. Without asking, he spooned a helping of noodles onto her plate. The authentic non-soy dairy smelled intoxicating. "Do I drink? Seems like you know everything about me."

Paxton hid a laugh behind a cough into his fist. "True enough. We like our research. Can you blame us? We're fiddling around in your head, seems like we should have the lay of things. Hard to navigate a forest blind, and the mind is the densest, strangest forest imaginable."

He held up a chilled bottle of white wine and tipped it questioningly toward her.

"No, thank you," she replied, and he poured his own tall, cylindrical glass, visibly disappointed. "It still doesn't sit well with me. I just never developed a tolerance, Preece wouldn't allow us to try. Even just aspirin was a big deal. He had to source it himself."

"I confess, even with all my vast resources, finding information on your group was a challenge," Paxton told her, adjusting his glasses. He sipped his wine and watched her listlessly twirl the noodles around her fork. "You're the only source of knowledge now. The last of your kind."

"Nobody needs to know what went on in there," Senna insisted. If he wanted to get her to eat and drink with him, this wasn't the way. Any mention of the compound and the brood soured her stomach and hitched a knot in her throat. "I'm already starting to forget some of it. I thought it wouldn't bother me, but . . . aren't you worried that if anyone can do this, it will make life less meaningful? If you can just erase anything you want from your past. you're making it harder for people to grow, aren't you?"

"What a shocking thing to say," Paxton whispered, adjusting in his chair. "No. Absurd. Human beings are not their pain. One unforeseeable misfortune shouldn't derail a person's life forever, or even a few years, that time—all time—is precious. LENG is offering choice and control. We curate our lives in every other way—our social circle, our news feeds, our wardrobes, our diets, our skin, our hair, why shouldn't we curate that which affects us most?" He paused and furrowed his brow, glancing up at her with his chin tilted down, his eyes barely visible behind his spectacles. "Are you having regrets about coming here?"

"I don't know," Senna answered honestly. "I'm beginning to worry I made the easy choice, not the right one."

Paxton shook his head. "This is just something new, of course it's frightening. People are always resistant to change until you prove that it's inevitable."

Senna smirked. "You want to create utopia."

"And that's . . . good?" Paxton sounded hopeful. Clearing his throat, he recited, "Thomas More said something like, 'Things will never be perfect, until human beings are perfect.'" He waited, and Senna only smiled slightly. "Of course from his seminal work *Utopia*?"

"I haven't read it," she confessed. Although it sounded like something right up Preece's ally. She assumed his definition of "perfect" differed wildly from Paxton's, who now gazed at her askew, as if she were very simple or very pitiable, neither option she liked. "It is good, of course it is. Only . . ." Well. She had come for answers; she might as well do her best to get them.

More than just the philosophical implications of LENG were on her mind. There were more immediate, practical concerns, too. Senna put down her fork and sighed, rubbing her eye. "Can I ask you something?"

"Anything."

"Did I . . . did I agree to this? I don't remember you asking, or me agreeing."

Paxton snorted into his wine. "Jesus, who do you think I am? Of course I asked."

"How did it go?" she asked. "Show me."

His thick, dark brows rose almost to his hairline, but after a moment he relented. "You were about to start your session. Dr. Colbie made a joke about you not being able to stomach our chicken last night." He paused, eyes searching along her face. "She said, 'Sixteen is going to be inconsolable. It worked under a two-Michelin-star chef on the station.' And I suggested you try its chicken again, but not with Han there to make you nervous. Then I invited you to do it here, now, and you said you would."

"But how did I say it?" she pressed, watching a line crease itself above his nose.

"Is this an interrogation?" Paxton chuckled, pouring himself more wine. "Senna, if you don't believe me, I can show you the security tapes."

She hadn't thought of that. Shaking her head, she exhaled deeply and pointed to her glass. "Okay, maybe a little wine."

"Atta girl."

It did taste nice, the wine, bubbly and not too sweet, with a strange zing that Paxton told her was its dryness. That made sense, it did zing her tongue in a way that made her thirsty for more of it. After she had tried the noodles, which were superb, and the sous vide chicken, which was odd at first but eventually delicious, Paxton offered her more wine and she declined. The fizzy, blurring effect was beginning to distract her.

"This is . . . strictly professional, right?" Senna asked. "This dinner? It's not a date, is it?"

Paxton shifted in his chair and dumped the last of the bottle into his cup. "I don't know, is it?"

"It's just . . . I think I should focus on my recovery," Senna told him, the wine making it feel like there were obstacles to navigate in between words. Even her thoughts were weaving. "And I don't know how to do any of this stuff. Preece didn't allow it, and it hasn't come up since I've been free."

Paxton regarded her over the smudged lip of his glass. "He didn't allow it?"

"On the compound there were men I liked and other women, too, but there were strict rules about it. Preece had some passionate ideas about overpopulation."

"Really?" Paxton drained the cup, smacked his lips and put his cup down a little harshly on the table. "A guy like that? I figured it was all a sex thing. It always is, in cults. A paternalistic figure, total control, and everyone there to dote on him and make him their idol. Sex always enters into it, why wouldn't it? For someone like that, it's the tool of ultimate control."

Senna's toes curled in her shoes, the comment delivering a sobering shock to her solar plexus. Smartest man in the universe he might be, but he certainly didn't know everything. *Not even everything about little old me.* "Thank you for dinner," she murmured.

"Senna, don't do that. It wasn't serious. You know how cults are . . ."

"Yes, I do."

Her first impression freshly onto the grounds was correct, she realized. She didn't like him. There was something unpleasant about his voice, she was beginning to feel, a subtle yet pervasive whine, like every word was a plea. A plea to like him, a plea to like the so obviously unlikable.

Look at me, don't look at me. Love me, wonder about me. Look at me.

The lights flickered, and Senna pushed back from the table. Maybe one day she would get to finish a meal without cutting it short and storming off, but she refused to feel guilty for this—Paxton had crossed a line. She might not know anything about dating or men or women, but she knew when something made her feel like that, it wasn't to be ignored. Too many times on the compound she hadn't listened to that feeling, and let Preece bowl right over her, overrule her, reduce her instincts to childish fears. Some fears were childish, it was true, but not the ones that curled your toes in your shoes.

Paxton dodged away from her, toward the doors, grumbling to himself. It seemed he wasn't going to fight her on it, and that at least was a relief. She watched the pictures change in the frames on the wall behind him while he went to open the doors. The ice fields, desolate and untouched; a single rover brave against the threatening expanse; the robotics construction crew breaking ground; the skeletal suggestion of the Dome in its earliest phases; a group shot after facility completion and a half-dozen smiling faces; a silhouette against a cold, white void.

A shadow.

"Senna, can we discuss this? It wasn't meant to be a jab, don't let this ruin our dinner."

In a memory or a nightmare, a voice redolent with malice whispered to her. She stared at the shadow in the frame, but in the next instant, it was gone.

18

Han flaked crusted sauce away from his chin and groaned, jamming the heel of his hand into a knot that had formed between his shoulder blades. Beside him on a white plinth, an abstract bust of Paxton Dunn sat at about shoulder height.

"Just relax your arms, please," Brea was saying. She had her recording device resting on the palm of her hand, her brown curls pushed back behind her ears with a patterned gray headband. "Try not to fidget."

As soon as she said that, his urge to fidget worsened. Han sighed and glanced at his VIT, wondering how long this was going to take. Then his eyes wandered to his right, up the ramp, to the closed, red doors of Paxton's office. He didn't like that Senna had gotten invited to dinner with Paxton. That was supposed to be *his* time with the mogul. What did they even have in common? Han decided it wouldn't happen again. Tomorrow night, he would be the one picking Paxton's brain over dan dan noodles. What would Paxton's private office look like? Cool as hell, he guessed. He had to get inside.

First, he just had to get Paxton's attention.

The artificial sunset dousing the gallery with lavender and ochre light flickered, and Han groaned. Paxton had never lowered the immense shutters encasing the Dome, the storm raging on outside. Cocking her head to the side, Brea waited for the sirens and the darkness, but it was just a flicker.

"Oh, good." She brightened. "We can proceed." As she filmed him, she began to circle, capturing more of the facility and a more dynamic shot as she started up with the questions. This was part of the experience, he told himself. He balled up his hands into fists, hating being on camera. Even when he gamed with his closest buddies, he used a rendered avatar instead of his actual face.

"Can you say your name for me, please?" Brea asked, firm but friendly. Her voice was low and had a rasp to it, and an accent that might have been Spanish. Mostly he just knew the flat, boring station accent, although one of his gaming squaddies had grown up in Australia for a while before transferring to Tokyo Bliss. Han was always jealous of his cool voice and the way he said *reckon* instead of *think*.

"Han Jun," he said, flinching when he had to look into the camera apparatus. "But everyone just calls me Han."

"How old are you, Han?" Brea prompted, pointing to her mouth with her free hand and giving an exaggerated grin. *Smile.*

His voice sounded dumb when he talked and smiled but he did it anyway, just to make it all end quicker. "I'm fourteen."

"What are your impressions of the facility so far?"

"I haven't done much yet, but so far it's the best thing ever. I was the first person to test the new LENG tech here, so that was pretty stellar."

"That sounds *very* stellar," Brea corrected, slightly scolding. "What was it like meeting your hero, Paxton Dunn?"

Now *that* was a question he didn't mind answering. "He's nicer than I expected, way nicer, and—"

The light flickered again. This time the storm won, and harsh red light speared through the gallery. Emergency indicators flared on the ground alongside the walls, and Brea muttered something unintelligible. Diligently, she kept the camera fixed on Han while he cowered against the statue pedestal.

He still didn't feel one hundred percent after his first session, and the sudden sirens and flashing lights made him want to curl up into a ball. Finally, Brea gave up, storming off as Genie's voice flooded the echoing hall. "Please remain calm," he instructed. "The facility is detecting abnormal wind activity. Please remain calm and follow instructions."

"*Abnormal?* Stay here," Brea snapped at him, clicking away swiftly in her heels, vanishing through the lab door behind Han. After their meal, Dr. Colbie had gone that way, too, while Anju disappeared up the ramp toward Paxton's office, then took a left toward Zone 6, which the map labeled staff-only areas, housing for them and R & D labs. Brea would probably just go consult Dr. Colbie and only be gone a minute or two. Nobody emerged from Paxton's office.

Han covered his ears, wincing as another burst of Technicolor pain came with the piercing red lights. Something warm flashed across his hand, then again, an insistent pulse. When he lowered his right hand to observe it, he watched what looked like the reflection off a VIT or spectacles bounce to the floor. It danced back toward him, hovering over his foot, then zipped a few inches across the floor, just in front of him. He took a small step toward the uneven, pale circle, and it moved on, but waited for him. Looking around for the source of it, he couldn't imagine any of the ferociously bright sirens making that kind of reflection, a glimmer he would expect to see in the middle of the day, not a darkened crisis-alert mode.

"Updated alert: Abnormal debris detected outside facility. All-staff call, severity level nine. Please remain calm and follow instructions," Genie boomed again.

"Nine?" Han repeated. That didn't sound good. "Genie? What am I supposed to do?"

The assistant's voice shimmered up from Han's VIT monitor. "Remain in place, a staff member will direct you shortly."

The insistent little light hovered over his shoe, then away from him again, as if egging him on. Han squinted, trying to pass his hand over whatever would project the light, but he couldn't find the source.

"Weird," he muttered. "Where is that coming from?"

A memory tugged at him, of a long-ago day, bright, a pleasant, grassy scent on the air, his fingertips dipping into cool water. A pool. He had seen little reflections like the one dancing around his shoe at the koi pond. It was by the university and the botanical garden. Distorted laughter; orange-and-silver shapes moving beneath the glassy water surface; reeds pushed by artificial wind; a university student fluttering a throaty shakuhachi, ancient music echoing in a cavernous space station sector. For just an instant Han almost forgot about the alert, because he knew it was strange that he would have gone to the koi ponds alone, but he couldn't remember who had gone with him. There had to be someone . . . He preferred staying in his room as much as possible, so someone must have convinced him to leave the condo. There were things he had memorized, core truths that weren't facts but something deeper. There were facts you learned and facts that lived in the body, aspects of life that weren't true so much as innate. You needed those innate things to stand up, to keep standing, but something had come loose.

Who did I go to the koi pond with?

It didn't help that the sirens and lights kept on, and Han wanted to turtle his head down into his shoulders to escape the noise. And the light kept . . . mocking him. He didn't know how it could mock him, but it did.

"Genie said to stay here," Han groaned, tossing up his hands and letting his head fall back loose on his neck. That sent his gaze spinning across the ceiling and then to the walkway above the gallery. He noticed a shape up there, a person, and wondered if maybe it was Zurri.

"Hey!" he called. "Zurri?"

It wouldn't be Senna; she and Paxton were still in his office. The silhouette was far away, but tall and thin, so maybe it was Zurri after all. It waved back to him, then beckoned. When he glanced down again, the light was gone. Han took the ramp up to the second level, slowing his gait a bit while he crossed in front of Paxton's office. Just in case. But the doors didn't open. He kept going, wondering who had been up on the balcony waving to him. The small light was already mostly forgotten.

"Hello?" he called. "Who's up here?"

The flash of lights and the emergency glow along the floor were enough to see by, but it wasn't much. Han reached the spot where the silhouette had been, but they had left and moved on. From up there, Han had a clear view down to the black door of the lab offices. Brea hadn't reemerged. His eyes swept the gallery on his level again, and the bridge in the Dome that faced it, then to the right, and the corridor that wound around into an area he hadn't explored. He noticed the figure moving along the far end of that corridor, back again, moving swiftly away from the tall window to his right that offered a scrolling a view of the Ganymede ice wastes. The figure hugged the wall to the right, moving west, avoiding the ramp that curved down into the leafy maze and toward that unexplored area of the compound. On his VIT map, this area was reserved for staff. He saw the shadowy silhouette begin to disappear again up ahead and plunged after it, feeling as if he were chasing a ghost.

Similar to the opposite side of the courtyard, the overlook he ran through led to a hall. On their side of things it split into the dormitories, but here it burrowed deeper to the western side of the second floor. They passed a single door on the left side, Han's proximity making a sign across it glow faint white and read STAFF ONLY.

Han noticed something shiny on the floor, illuminated by the pulse of lights outlining the walkway. Genie warned everyone to stay in place again as Han bent down and picked up a single gold earring—a wide, hammered hoop.

Footsteps approached from behind, fast, and carrying the signature sharp click of the heels the staff wore. He spun and collapsed back against the door as Dr. Colbie and Brea raced by, the doctor's blond hair uncharacteristically disheveled. Neither of them paused to acknowledge Han as they hurried down the corridor. Carefully, he followed, the cold earring cradled in his palm. The two women stopped at the end of the hall, standing in front of a waist-high transparent railing. Here was the edge of the facility, where the outer shell of the Dome itself was visible, the thick, curved wall encased in the safety shutters protecting them all from the storm.

Shuffling up behind the two women, Han found himself stumbling into an ongoing argument. Something was wrong.

Dr. Colbie tapped furiously on the face of her VIT, glancing up toward the Dome wall, another snarl of blond hair falling loose around her neck.

"—this protocol is level eight, I have the authority," Dr. Colbie was saying heatedly.

"It is day two, the patients are still in a disoriented state, how will this look?"

"Search your fucking database, abnormal debris is exactly what you think it is, if she's out there . . . if she's out there . . ."

She?

That was when they noticed him creeping ever closer and both shut up abruptly, Brea offering him a tired "what can you do?" smile. "Han," she cooed. "These are unusual circumstances, can I escort you back to your rooms? You will be more comfortable there while we handle this situation."

"What situation?" he asked, frowning. "What's going on? Is it the storm?"

The facility rocked. Lightning cracked above them, startling Han, and he closed his fist, hard, the earring jabbing into his hand. When he opened his palm and looked down at it, a bead of blood welled there, smeared across the gold. The earring had a clamp instead of a sharp hook, jewelry made for someone with unpierced ears.

"Han?" Brea prompted, taking him by the shoulder.

"What was that sound?" he asked, a little dazed, the sirens making mush of his brains. He let his head fall loose again and stared up at the curved ceiling of the Dome, high above, and watched as the security shutters gradually began to lower, massive industrial petals that gently stacked as they retracted, revealing the stark white mists of Ganymede.

"What's going on?" Zurri had arrived, appearing down the

corridor in stilted, slow-motion frames, the flashing lights revealing and deleting her with each step. "Can you shut that thing off? It's giving me a migraine."

She had changed into a thick robe, fluffy and so white it glowed in the uneven darkness of the sirens and alert.

"They're lowering the shutters," Han told her, pointing. "Severity level nine."

"What the hell does that mean?" Zurri demanded, coming to stand beside him and folding her arms across her chest.

Brea's smile looked brittle enough to snap in half. "If the two of you could return to your rooms—"

"The fuck I will, what is severity level nine?"

More footsteps, these decidedly without high heels. Paxton rolled in like a storm, thundering down the hallway with leaden steps, glasses crooked and mouth ferociously tight as he elbowed Brea, Zurri, and Han out of the way and went straight after Dr. Colbie. The doctor remained at the end of the hall, eyes glued to the ceiling as the shutters revealed more and more of the transparent Dome outer structure.

"Could've overridden this from my office but I wanted to see the circus in person," he grunted, clamping a hand down on the doctor's left shoulder. "What do you think you're doing?"

"Is everything okay?" a mouse-quiet voice asked. Senna. Han's vision blurred a bit as he whirled to look at her. He felt a pressure build behind his eyes the closer she came and the more of her face he could see. But it passed, and then she was huddled close to Zurri, shooting furtive glances at him and then farther down the hall toward Paxton.

"Nobody will tell me anything," Zurri muttered. "It's absolutely ridiculous. Mayhem."

"Brea, get them out of here!" Paxton thundered, blindly gesturing over his shoulder at them.

"All right, all right, you heard the man." Brea pretended at a laugh, attempting to herd them with both hands. Han allowed himself to be pushed a few steps, but as soon as she got within spitting distance of Zurri, the model clucked her tongue.

"Touch me and I will sue you into the next galaxy, bitch."

"The scanner has to be wrong," Dr. Colbie was saying while Paxton grabbed her by the left wrist. She cried out, her arm wrenched at a nasty angle while Paxton himself slapped her right hand away and fiddled with her VIT screen. "It has to be wrong. Did you see? Tell me you saw it."

"It's day two, you absolute moron," Paxton hissed. "You will not ruin this for me."

The shutters paused, hesitating, and a creak like the complaining of ancient trees rippled through the corridor. Then the petals began to unfold again, and the shutters inched back up to protect the Dome barrier again. An insistent, piercing beeping began, rising from Paxton's VIT, accelerating, fluttering like a heart beating wildly out of control.

Brea had gone still, and Han felt Zurri and Senna holding their breaths, as if they all knew and didn't know what was coming, and dreaded it.

"Can't this fucking thing go any faster?" Paxton screamed, raking a hand so viciously through his hair Han was shocked a fistful of tufts didn't tear loose.

The beeps were one sound now, on top of one another. Han squeezed the earring in his hand again and held his breath, too.

About sixteen feet of unshuttered barrier was still exposed when the mass hit the Dome barrier, hard. It smacked into the transparent, curved edge near the very top, impacting with the muted thump of a bird diving into a window. Quiet for them, dulled by the thickness of the barrier, but Han felt the crunch of it in his bones. Cold that cruel did unfeeling things to the body. He couldn't make out much, not with the speed of it all and the spike of fear and adrenaline, but he knew he saw a suit meant for exterior exploration, white and padded, and he saw dome strike Dome, the helmet just a hundred spider-webbed cracks glittering with frost, and behind those fractures, a still-living face, screaming silently before the storm picked up Anju again and carried her away.

19

"Just another thing to forget," Zurri sighed, snapping open the Talpraxem bottle and shaking out two into her palm. The tiny pink ovals glistened under the kitchen light, but Zurri waited to toss them back, angling into her chair while her fellow inmates stared holes into the table. The storm warning sirens had ended, though the facility remained shrouded in gloomy half light.

"It's horrible," Senna murmured, emerging from the darkened hall and returning to the kitchen. She had changed into a sack of a T-shirt dress with her same long coat over it. Zurri couldn't blame her for wanting to immediately change out of a dead woman's dress. "Just horrible."

"You knew her for twenty-four hours," Zurri told her. "You'll manage."

"I can still be upset!" she replied, voice muffled as she pulled her knees up to her chest and nestled her chin into them. "It can still be sad."

"Something weird is going on," the boy said, dropping a blood-smeared earring onto the table.

"You think?" Zurri was tempted to swallow the Talpraxem, but it didn't seem like the prudent thing to do until official word came down on why one of the Dome employees had just pancaked against the facility exterior. She shivered, then checked to see if either of the other two had noticed her discomfort. Nope. Senna was still buried in her legs, a human egg balled up in her chair, and Han was too busy fixating on the earring. The other woman's apartment was about as cutesy as she expected, themed in a soothing ocean theme with a big mural in the living room and sea glass set into the table.

"I hate this place," Zurri sighed, letting the pills clatter onto the table.

"Go on," urged Senna, staring across the table at Han. "What's weird?"

"Besides people flying into the windows like confused birds?" Zurri stood up and crossed to the refrigerated box, helping herself to an aluminum cylinder of white wine. The Talpraxem was for later, but she didn't have to spend this time with them completely sober.

"Let him talk," Senna murmured. "Go on, Han."

The kid hesitated, dark eyes hovering on Senna's face as if he maybe didn't want to tell her specifically, then took a steadying breath and shrugged his bony shoulders. "I saw something tonight. A . . . shadow thing. I thought it was Zurri, but it couldn't be, because she showed up later and it was definitely ahead of me. Leading me somewhere."

"I've seen it, too," Senna assured him. She had gone pale, and flinched when Zurri opened the wine with a crisp *crrrack*. "The shadow was in my room; it was watching me sleep."

"I don't know about you two, but I can't take three more days of this," Zurri muttered, taking a long sip. The wine wasn't going to put a dent in her anxiety. She didn't want to say that she, too, had seen the shadow, or thought she had, glimpsing it briefly, when the storm made the power flicker. "Locked down until further notice, can you even believe that shit?" She rolled her eyes. "Dunn is going to wish he never built this place when I'm done annihilating his ass to the press. He'll have to call it off now. He can't keep this experiment going when someone just died."

"He can't do that." Han tore his eyes away from the earring. "He can't."

"Kid, I know you're his fan club president or whatever but this is serious," Zurri told him. "I want an explanation from him and then I want out."

"You can't," Han pointed out. "The storms." Then he tapped his VIT with two fingers. "None of my messages are going out. Even if Paxton wanted to send us home early, he can't. You saw what happened to Anju, do you want to climb in the rover right now?"

She made a face and dumped the rest of the wine down her throat. "I just know I don't want to be here anymore. I'm not going back in that LENG room, I'm staying right here. I mean, Christ, can either of you remember what goes on in there?"

"No, I can't picture it," Senna replied, pouting out her lower lip. "Does this feel like what you expected?" Senna asked.

Both Zurri and Han shook their heads no.

"There are . . . blanks. I can feel the voids. It's like my head is going to burst whenever my thoughts wander in the wrong direction, or if I try to remember my time in the LENG room." Senna played nervously with the ends of her oversized coat, and she could sense there was more coming as the woman chewed and chewed it over. "There's another man in the facility, I've only seen him once, but I didn't see him tonight with everyone else. Do you think . . . do you think maybe he had something to do with Anju?"

"I met him, too," said Han, spinning the earring slowly with his right forefinger. "He seemed nice enough."

"Hold up, there's another person here? Why haven't I met him?" The door chimed softly as Zurri's voice rose and Paxton stepped into Senna's apartment, rubbing at the weary line etched between his brows. "Perfect," she said, standing. "Maybe you can explain what the hell is going on here."

"Thank you for being patient." Paxton stood in the hall, a few feet from where they had gathered at the table. He seemed particularly intent on Senna as he pursed his lips and then announced, "We've reviewed the security footage. It looks like what happened this evening was a terrible accident. Anju logged a concern with one of the north-end shutter depots, a thermal regulator failed, and ice jammed up the track. Our maintenance suits have clip-in systems to prevent something like this from happening, but it looks like her clip failed or the wind was too powerful for it. I'm just . . . I apologize that you all had to see that. As you can imagine, we're reeling. Anju has been part of the team here since the early days, and we're all going to miss her."

"How awful," Senna murmured. "I'm so sorry, Paxton."

Zurri frowned. She knew vague corporate speak when she heard it; it had been spouted at her thousands of times whenever some intern fucked up and made a shoot run hours too long, or a hungover director slept through call time. "What was your assistant doing out there? Don't you have maintenance Servitors for that?"

Switching to rubbing his eye under his glasses, he said quietly,

"We all wear a lot of hats around here, Zurri. Maybe you can save the accusations until after we find a way to recover her body. If . . . if we can at all."

Silence. Han and Senna wilted, convinced. Zurri wasn't so sure. She watched Paxton carefully, vigilant for any signs of deception. Annoyingly, he just looked tired, impatient to be away from them. That scanned, at least.

"Are you calling off the program?" Senna finally asked in a tiny voice. To Zurri, she almost sounded hopeful.

"No," Paxton replied firmly. "We can resume in the morning. I know we've all had a bad shock, but Anju believed in what we're doing here as much as I do. She understood the dangers of working at a facility like this, the dangers of pushing the boundaries the way we are." His voice shook with real emotion, but Zurri forced her eyes not to roll. "I just ask that you all stay in your apartments for now, while the staff shifts gears. Sixteen will deliver any food you might need, and your updated schedules will be sent to your VITs."

At that, he gave Senna one more furtive glance, which she was too distraught to notice. What was up with them? Zurri stowed it for later.

"Zurri? Han?" he prompted, dismissing them.

She stood in her own time, subtly collecting the two Talpraxem and hiding them in her palm, then taking her mostly empty can of wine with her to cover the movement. While she rounded the table, Han swiped the earring off the table and brought it to Paxton, presenting it to him with what felt like a tacky flourish.

"Senna says this was Anju's. I found it on the floor."

"Thanks, Han," Paxton murmured, taking the earring from him and slipping it into his pocket. "And I understand that this could affect your healing and progress here, so if anyone would like to update their neural maps to include tonight's tragedy, that can be arranged."

Called it.

"Classy," Zurri muttered, passing him in the hall.

"I'm simply offering," Paxton replied, cold.

It didn't seem like he was following them out. Zurri let Han leave first, lingering a little in the doorway. The protective hairs on the back of her neck were standing up, the ones that recognized a fellow woman in need.

"Good night," he told Zurri firmly, refusing to budge.

"Senna, are you going to be okay if I go?" she asked, ignoring him.

"Sure," Senna said around a yawn.

Zurri narrowed her eyes and shook her head, backing out the door with her eyes locked on Paxton's. The smallest, strangest smile appeared on his face. *I'm watching you*, she thought. *One of us has to.*

20

Paxton couldn't shut down the experiment and make them leave, he just couldn't. Not that he wanted to stay on a secluded moon base where people were dying and creepy shadows roamed the halls, but what Paxton said was true—this was new tech, new tech developed in secrecy in a dangerous location. It was insulting to assume Anju hadn't known and accepted the risks of coming onto such a project. Han wasn't superstitious, or religious, or stupid; there would be an explanation for the shadows he and Senna had noticed. Probably just a side effect of the therapy. He should probably tell Paxton about it—they were the guinea pigs, and their feedback had to be invaluable.

And he wasn't going to let some ridiculous, benign hallucination chase him away from his dream.

He knew Paxton was impressed with him finding the earring and returning it. Sure, it was a sentimental gesture, but it still had meaning, right? And anyway, Han was pretty sure Paxton had given him a quick, approving glance. Fatherly. Han struggled to remember what that even felt like, the pride of a father. Come to think of it, he couldn't produce his father's name. Weird. His memory just needed time to heal. He knew he had a dad, or at least a donor dad, but it was like the assumption of oxygen—of course it was there, it had to be, or Han wouldn't be breathing and alive.

Another side effect. All of this was data, crucial data, and accordingly he consulted his VIT and opened a fresh notes file and began logging all the observations he wanted to share with Paxton. He would get another one of those knowing little looks, and just like a bar filling up in a video game, Paxton's approval would rise.

"You're on Ganymede with Paxton Dunn." Han rounded the corner away from Senna's apartment, backtracking down the hall to where his rooms were, head down as he typed furiously on his VIT. "Don't lose sight of that, man . . ."

"And what an action-packed prospect that has turned out to be, mm?"

Han stopped short, nearly barging headfirst into Efren. Stumbling back, he dropped his VIT midsentence and stammered out an apology. They had only met briefly in the courtyard, and Han wasn't sure how he felt about the stranger, who seemed largely to avoid everyone else. Han couldn't imagine what he was doing at that time of night in the guest wing. Was he the one gesturing to Han on the balcony? Was he the one leading him up to the gallery just before Anju died? Senna had suggested he might have something to do with the accident, but Paxton's explanation dismissed that, and it sounded like nobody in particular was to blame.

"Oh, hey," Han followed up after his muttered *sorry*. "What are you doing here?"

"I'm here looking for you," Efren replied simply, as if that were the most obvious thing in the world. Given that he was waiting almost directly outside Han's door, it perhaps was. "Because Paxton is about to put this wing into lockdown, and I don't agree with that decision."

Han frowned, exhausted, emotionally a little brittle and wrecked, and squinted at the man. He dressed like a futurist preacher, or something out of a grimdark comic vid, but his face and hair made him look like he could be one of Han's web language tutors. "Someone died, it's probably just a temporary security measure."

"Maybe," Efren countered. "But Paxton is a grown man, you can stop doing his work for him."

"For him? What do you mean?"

"He's a powerful man, he doesn't need you to stick up for him when he's about to deprive you of your liberty," Efren said, sighing. "Your liberty, and potentially so much more. I realize there has been a loss, but none of you is responsible, correct?"

"Correct," Han said slowly. Lockdown. That did sound bad, but surely Paxton had his reasons. Han didn't know why he should listen to this guy over the man who owned and operated the entire facility, and who so far had been pretty cool and generous.

"So why would you need to stay locked in your rooms?" Efren pressed. He was leaning toward Han ever so slightly, as if this answer did greatly interest him.

"Maybe it just . . . I don't know. Maybe it isn't safe to have us wandering around right now."

Efren snapped his fingers and pointed. "*Maybe it isn't safe.* Now we're getting somewhere. If it wasn't safe for Anju, why would it be safe for any of you?"

"It was an accident," Han said flatly. "What happened to her was an accident, Paxton looked over the security footage."

"Interesting." Efren dragged out the word, tapping his thumb thoughtfully on his lip. "Then that footage still exists on server storage somewhere, just waiting to be found. Listen to me, young man, and listen closely, Paxton is going to notice that you're not in your rooms very soon, and if he's going to put you all into captivity, then I think you deserve to see that footage for yourself, don't you agree?"

"I . . . guess." Han shrugged. "Well, yeah. Yeah, it isn't fair to keep us locked up when we didn't have anything to do with it. It's not like I'm going to go outside and try to repair anything. And Zurri sure as hell isn't, either."

Efren nodded, smiling crookedly. He reached over, but stopped himself from patting Han on the shoulder. Instead, he turned and began to walk back the way Han had come. "Do you know what undoes all so-called great men?"

"Old age? Tax evasion?"

"Ha!" Efren snorted. "You really are clever. No, Han, it's hubris. Now then, good luck finding that footage. If anyone can, it's you."

Han shuffled closer to his door, watching his own name light up across it. "I could tell him that you're doing this. That one of his employees is trying to undermine him . . ."

"I sincerely hope you do," Efren called back, strolling away. "What was that inane chestnut of Paxton's that always got quoted? Ah yes, 'If something gets you out of bed in the morning, then it should keep you *from* bed until it's done to the best of your ability.' Just keep that in mind. Your hero said it, so it must be true."

Zurri waited with her door half-open, listening for the moment Paxton left. She heard his footsteps vanishing down the corridor and out of the guest wing about twenty minutes after they had been shooed from Senna's apartment. Those girl code hairs had gone up on her neck, and she wasn't going to ignore it. She had a strict policy against fixing wounded birds masquerading as people, but they were all vulnerable, they were all having their minds tampered with; Senna wasn't necessarily a friend, but Zurri didn't see the harm in checking on her before bed.

It was a miracle the girl had lasted this long outside her cult compound. They hadn't prepared her for anything in there, Zurri was realizing. Pairing a thrifted, oversized jacket with a Bethany Li couture piece demonstrated that pretty clearly. In a distant, wistful way, Zurri envied her naivete. It had to be re-freshing to know so little about the outside world, to hear the name Bethany Li and think: *Who?* Maybe that was why Paxton had fixed his eyes on Senna and not her—Senna was practically raised in total isolation. She had a strange, interesting purity, ut-terly sheltered from the reality of Earth life and real station life, all but grown and reared in a lab.

Paxton would never want someone worldly like Zurri, some-one who would absolutely call him on his shit.

Zurri whispered, "Genie? Can you let Senna know I'm here?"

"You have been instructed to return to your rooms," Genie replied, at obnoxiously full volume. Zurri glanced up and down the hall. Still clear. "Please follow outline procedures, normal scheduling and access will resume at Dome time eight a.m. Lockdown precautions are now in effect."

"Lockdown? Uh-uh. No thanks. Get her for me, okay? It will only take a minute," Zurri insisted, glaring up at the invisible guardian, assistant, doorman and butler. At least real bouncers could be bribed. "I just want to see . . . We're all shaken tonight. I wanted to make sure she's all right."

"She's fine."

Zurri closed her eyes and groaned. To her left, Paxton swaggered back down the corridor, Anju's earring in his hand, his thumb running across it worriedly, as if he could mark his print into it.

"Clearly we got off on the wrong foot, Zurri," he said, glibly apologetic. "Let me take you to your rooms, we'll open an egregiously expensive bottle of whatever you want, and if it amuses you, go ahead and pour it down the drain. Otherwise, we can share it and I'll answer all your questions. By the end of the night? Well, by the end of the night, I think we could even be friends."

"I'm not your friend," Zurri said, swiveling and cocking her hip to the side. Even in flats, she was taller than him, and she could tell by the way he almost pulled something straightening his neck that it bothered him. "I'm nothing like you, Dunn."

"I wouldn't say that. You're rich, I'm fuck-you rich. You're famous, I'm an icon. Our great purpose is to be the inspirers, to make the masses think: 'One day I'll be just like them.' But they'll never be us, will they? You were born with beauty, I was born with vision. We serve the same function." His hand pivoted back and forth between them as he talked. Zurri felt those hairs on the back of her neck go up again. Danger. Paxton held up

Anju's gold earring with both hands and gradually bent it until it was halved. "You just need to learn to be more . . . flexible."

She didn't care about Anju one way or another, but that seemed crass. "Man, you've got mental problems. That woman *died* tonight. Your employee. Your responsibility. She died."

Paxton tossed the bent earring up in the air and caught it, repeating the motion a few times as he considered her words. "Did she?"

Danger.

Zurri's room was the opposite direction, and she decided it was time to go, and if lockdown kept him the hell out of her rooms, all the better. Something in her right peripheral vision moved swiftly, blurry fast. She saw a mass of brown curls and the hint of a smile, and then a hand lashed out to take her by the shoulder.

Brea. She had come up behind her silently while Paxton distracted her. For once, she wasn't wearing heels. Zurri jabbed with her elbow but Brea seemed to anticipate the move, sidestepping easily before jabbing something at her. The zap from a black tool in her hand hit Zurri in the sternum, and she felt the world spin as she collapsed, held and dragged before everything went dark, before she even hit the ground.

21

Senna set up her easel facing the mural of the sea. As soon as she smelled the hard hit of the turpentine, her head swam with nostalgia, the sweet and the bitter.

"These are my personal paints from London," Preece had told her, pushing a metal basket toward her across the mess hall table. On the compound, they used one huge room for eating and sleeping, shoving the long cafeteria-style tables and benches to the side at night and rolling out their sleeping pads. "When these are gone, they're gone," he had warned.

She was sixteen then and had never painted a single thing in her life, couldn't name a single painter, had never been to the university district to see a single gallery exhibit.

"You can paint whatever you want," Preece had added, showing her the brushes, the tubes of paint, the little vial of turpentine needed to clean the paint-soaked bristles or thin out the pigment.

"Whatever you see, whatever you feel, whatever you dream, paint it, as long as it's true."

Every year on her birthday she received a few more canvases. Nobody else was allowed such an extravagance. The others, now washed-out faces on copycat bodies in her mind, received extra food or sometimes replacements for their worn-out clothes. Never cake or ice cream or any sweets at all.

"I could waste money on unhealthy frivolities," Preece would tell them whenever someone whined about the restrictions. "Or we could all eat next month, the choice is yours."

What he said was true. Senna laid out the paints on the coffee table behind her, and unscrewed the cap on the tube of black paint, drawn to it. Marin had tried to get her to use a tablet to draw and sketch, but Senna needed the tactile feel of the brushes, the sound of them swishing across the canvas, the scent of the paints and all the slight variations in their texture and application. It was also true that some of the other brood members began to resent her for the gift of the paints. It was often whispered that Senna was his favorite, a petty exaggeration that Senna never allowed herself to believe.

Until, a few years later and losing control of the children he had raised, Preece hijacked a passenger transport headed to Mars and . . . and . . .

Senna fell forward against the canvas, brush in hand, paint sweeping across the blank square as she felt the void LENG had hollowed out push back. It had its own form, the gap in her memory, not empty but solid as a shield. Impenetrable. She had almost managed to stumble up to a memory, but now the pain was incredible, and she closed her eyes, mentally backing away.

Coward.

It was gone. Whatever it was, she had to let it be gone. It was terrible enough to bring her to this place, isolated and dangerous, and ask a stranger to rip apart her memories and patch them back together. Anything that bad deserved to be respected and left alone, like a bristling beast growling out its warning song from the back of a deep, dark cavern.

She couldn't remember falling asleep on the floor, or dreaming, or waking. Sometime later, the ambient lights set for night, Senna crawled to her feet, dried black paint smeared across her hands. Stumbling back a few steps, she took in the image on the canvas. Her painting. It was the silhouette of a tall, lanky creature, no eyes or features, just oozing tendrils for fingers.

The shadow.

So Han had seen it, too. Zurri had, too, she suspected, but she also assumed the model was too proud or embarrassed to admit as much. Senna wanted to assign it to the treatment, but she couldn't do that.

I saw it the minute I arrived. It's always been here. Senna considered its presence in her bedroom, the yawning pit of fear that had opened up under her as she watched it watching her from the doorway, darkness living outside of darkness, formless and yet with its own intrinsic density.

She amended her thought. *No, it hasn't just always been here. It's always been.*

Han mouthed along to the lecture as it played through his vid console, a gamer's delight of candy, cheese-coated crisps, a rainbow of mochi and a sixty-four-ounce Mega Slurp of sugar-free soda waiting to be devoured on the coffee table beside him. How Paxton had managed to get actual Mega Slurp cups from Earth, he didn't know, but the mad lad had done it. Even if it was just for nostalgia points, Han could respect it.

Which is why he wanted to find nothing. Uncomfortably, he hoped his third attempt to gain access to Paxton's Dome security systems failed.

Why are you doing it, then, if you're sure Efren is full of shit?

Good question. Han hovered between two extremes that were both extremely his brand—total devotion to his mortal god, Paxton, and a strong desire for the truth. It was why he enjoyed hacking in the first place. Exposing truth, exposing scandals, letting all the muck and grit and dirt come to the light . . . that was a noble pursuit. The want of truth was, in itself, a good thing. It was part of what made him like Paxton in the first place, when he first discovered his inventions and his philosophies years ago—he didn't parade around on red carpets on the station or on Earth, models dripping from his arms. There were rumors that he had been married twice, and those relationships dissolved quietly, the women amply paid, locked into NDAs and never heard from again. No juicy tell-all vids appeared, and Paxton remained quietly on Ganymede, minding his business, pursuing his solitude and his science.

That was what Han wanted to be—a man left alone with enough time, money and peace to listen to the wisdom of his dreams, and then turn that wisdom into invention. Even if it was something small, he wanted to be a contributor, not just a consumer. In his short lifetime, disease-dissolving coatings had been developed for implanted chips in the body, Paxton had built his reality-defying facility on Ganymede, there were even whispers of first contact, just a fungal spore, but even that was something astonishing.

He could do astonishing things, too, staying in an astonishing place, mentored by an astonishing man . . . But those things had to be proven true. Han didn't like the uncertainty Efren had planted in his mind. He needed to know that he could trust Paxton's word, that this lockdown was just a silly precaution, that what had happened to Anju really was just a sad accident. The lecture played on. A classic. This was Han's psych-up music, the quick, precise voice of another of his idols, acclaimed chef turned travel vid host turned astrophysicist Cecilia Fan, giving a lecture two years ago at Yang Hall on the station, filling to capacity the university's largest venue.

". . . and once we had eyes on that troublemaker, that naughty little gremlin"—that part always made him chuckle, and her audience joined in on the recording—"a once-putative theory became amazing, undeniable fact. Now we had proof of trans-Neptunian objects whipped into a frenzy by a black hole. A black hole no bigger than a kumquat." She paused there to approximate the size for the audience, and there was more laughter and then applause as Cecilia pulled a funny face. Han wasn't looking at the vid screen, but he had it committed to memory. "How much could that really do? you ask. Oh, just a lot. It can do *so much*, my friends."

Han trailed off, no longer mouthing the words of the lecture as he stewed over the text screen hovering above his VIT. Third time had to be the charm. He reached for his Mega Slurp and sucked down a few fizzy gulps, waiting for inspiration. What did he know? Facts. Truth. Efren worked for Paxton in some capacity. There was obviously bad blood there. Efren had to know some of the ins and outs of the facility, and he believed the security systems could be cracked, and cracked specifically by Han. Han didn't know if there was anything interesting to be found in that security footage, but he knew a lure when he heard one—

Efren wasn't just encouraging him, he was daring him. Efren even had the balls to refer to Paxton as a "so-called great man," which were basically fighting words, and Han looked forward to proving him wrong.

And he had mentioned hubris. Hubris. That had to be the real clue.

What would be a stupidly arrogant choice of admin log-in? he wondered. What would a man, blinded by hubris, do? He brought up one of his scripts and ran it, then tried a few different variations on *admin* or *administrator* for the log-in nickname. Log-in? *Admin*. Password? *Password*.

No luck. Good to know his tech idol wasn't a total fail of a human being.

Log-in? *Administrator*. Password? *Qwerty*.

Nothing. Han cracked his knuckles and shoved a coconut-covered black licorice mochi into his mouth, chewing with chipmunk-big cheeks. "Okay, okay, let Cecilia's wisdom flow through you, Han. You're just warming up."

Log-in? Paxton. Password? Ganymede.

Han blinked. It wasn't right, but he was receiving a different rejection error. He had gotten the log-in nickname correct, because now it was prompting him to retrieve his password, not his password *and* his log-in information.

"Holy whoa," he murmured, coconut dust falling into his lap. "Okay, okay, okay, Han. *Think.*"

While one success tasted sweet, it also smacked of bitterness. Efren was right. That was a dogshittedly idiotic admin name. Anyone, including someone on their tenth total try, could guess it. Was Paxton lazy or just confident? Maybe his password had layers upon layers of encryption. Maybe it was a personal refer-ence nobody could possibly guess. The details of his life remained largely a mystery, so how would anyone guess his favorite dog's name or his second wife's birthday?

He tried a few more variations on simple, expected, universal passwords, but they were all duds.

"We've observed what a supermassive black hole can do, but what about a black hole the size of your fingertip? Or the size of a pinhead? Everyone always wants the big kahuna, right? Much sexier, those monster black holes! Those poor miniature black holes, always the bridesmaid, never the bride!" Cecilia's speech continued in the background, slicing in and out of Han's concentration as he puzzled over the hack.

What if I'm going about this all wrong? What if I don't need to know about him, what if I need to know about me? He knows everything about us, everything about me . . .

Zurri and Senna weren't trying to test Paxton's systems (well, Zurri was, but that was beside the point, and she wasn't attempting the hack personally)—no, it would be Han. Paxton would know that. Grabbing another mochi, he bit it in half and chewed, glancing up at Cecilia and saying a silent, tongue-in-cheek prayer to her. What if Efren wasn't actually working against Paxton, but with him? What if it was an elaborate test? Han gasped, remembering his first chat with Paxton when he arrived at the Dome.

I'm pulling back the curtain. I want to meet the wizard.

The Game. A Fincher classic, in which a man gets involved in a complicated web of quests, each intended to question his reality and push him to unravel a whole mess of secrets. If Paxton was a fan of that vid, then maybe he was taking inspiration for it, *testing* Han. It was wild, pointless, a lark, but Han tried his hunch anyway. Paxton had taken a neural map of his brain, he had the technology to carefully alter his memories, to zero in on individual connections between thoughts and associations. Anything was possible.

Log-in? *Paxton*. Password? *HanIsKing*.

The text began to scroll. The password went through. Han clenched his entire body, the half-eaten ball of mochi plopping into his lap.

22

Zurri stared at the vid of her own face, not believing the words coming out of her mouth.

"What Paxton is doing here is simply mind-blowing!" Her face crumpled into shy giggles. "Oh! Can I say that? I said it. It's incredible. Paxton is incredible. More than just healing and hope, I've found so much more here. I've found connection, back to myself, back to others."

This was a nightmare. There was no other explanation for it. She struggled against Brea's hands, clamped like two fleshy vices around her upper biceps. Brea's fingers dug in, hard, squeezing a pained gasp out of Zurri's throat. It was no use. The girl didn't look strong but she had a *grip*.

"First of all," Zurri breathed, dazed still from the shock Brea had given her to her chest. It had knocked her unconscious for just an instant, but that was long enough for Paxton and Brea to get the other hand and wrap a tight gag around her mouth. That gag was off now as they held her hostage in the LENG room, and they would regret removing that scrap of cloth. "I would never say any of that, not a single word, you demonic little fucker. Let *go* of me."

"Let her go, Brea, but watch her," Paxton said.

"You're going to regret that," Zurri slurred, stumbling away from them both. Regret it like she regretted pounding that can of wine. "What the hell is going on here? How can you make me say those things? Is that a deepfake?"

"No," Paxton chuckled, stepping out of the way as Zurri swung, trying to knock the tablet showing her vid out of his hands. Brea lunged forward, landing a blow with the flat of her hand to Zurri's neck. She went down.

"Not the face," Paxton warned. "The others will notice."

Zurri tried to push herself up from the ground, the star-field projection bleeding across her face and shoulders as she did. Jittery, weak, she could only muster a tiny glob of spit, but she hacked at Paxton's shoe.

"Rude. That doesn't seem like the Zurri I know." He tapped the shiny edge of the tablet, dangling it mockingly over her head. *Crazy.* He was crazy. She should've known. She should've listened to those prickles of danger warning her that this guy was a psychotic mess. "It's not a deepfake, Zurri. It's you. You said it today after your session. Don't you remember?"

Of course she didn't remember. She spent the morning hatewatching old runway vids, having a leisurely brunch and then trying to convince Han to outsmart the security systems for her. Then she had her appointment, and then . . . a blank. A strange, murky blank that rested heavily on the tip of her tongue, anxious to be spoken but impossible to define. Just a blank, and then she remembered a sky like fire. Standing on the walkway. Senna in her conspicuously expensive dress. Anju smashing into the window.

A growl welled up from the base of her belly. She wanted to kill him. She was *going* to kill him, or sue him inside out, whichever was more expedient. The vid played on. It was an impromptu, candid interview. She was standing at the base of the stairs leading to the suspended walkway in the courtyard, her orange dress matching some of the flowers in the background.

"This place is unbelievable." She was laughing, reaching to caress one of the blooms.

Paxton's voice, friendly, conversational, answered from behind the recording device. "Nice, right? "I have a fondness for the prehistorics. Cycad, staghorn ferns, gingko . . . it's wonderland," he said. "It's Eden."

"So what now?" asked Zurri from the floor. "You keep me imprisoned here and send that off to the station? Why? It doesn't . . . none of this makes any sense! We came here *trusting* you."

Paxton shut off the vid and crouched down to her level, Brea hovering nearby, her mean little black Taser device aimed and ready. "I wouldn't want you to live that way. Imprisoned. No, I wouldn't want anyone to live like that. Brea? Get Dr. Colbie, please."

"Brea? Brea, wait! Help me." Zurri's eyes flew to the other woman's, imploring. She wasn't going to do whatever Paxton wanted without a fight, she was not letting this crazy white psycho win. "You don't have to do what he says!"

"Yes," Paxton muttered. "She does."

Brea didn't even pause to consider Zurri's pleas. She left the LENG room and returned a moment later, heaving open the heavy vault door, Dr. Colbie's white jacket a bright flare in the dark room. Colbie had always seemed nicer than the others, or at least more compassionate.

"Dr. Colbie—"

"Don't bother, Zurri. She won't listen to you." Paxton stood with a sigh, rubbing his lower back and flicking his head toward Zurri. Dr. Colbie didn't look as certain or as willing to cooperate as Brea. She fidgeted by the door, an ominous syringe cradled in both hands.

Maybe Dr. Colbie wasn't a total lost cause.

"Get her up," he told Brea, and she came at Zurri again with the Taser device. "Put her in the chair. We'll do this again, and again, until we get the Zurri we want."

Zurri gasped and hissed through her teeth as Brea grabbed her by the arm and hauled her to her feet, shoving her toward the chair. The star field rolled across them, constant.

"Is this how he gets you to do what he says?" Zurri cried, directing this primarily to Colbie. The doctor glanced away, back toward the door. "He puts you in this chair and messes with your head? We outnumber him. Just stop complying!"

"We can sedate her," Dr. Colbie said softly, her voice almost hoarse. "But to put her through the process again so soon, Paxton—"

"Do. It." He jabbed his finger in Zurri's direction. "Try to calm down, Zurri. Try to think of how content you'll be when you aren't constantly up my ass about everything. It'll be a new, gentler you, and we'll all be happier for it."

"Why?" Zurri murmured, feeling herself tumbling toward defeat, toward giving up. *No, there can be no losing against this guy, he's going down no matter what.*

"Because I create the world." Paxton chuckled to himself. "Because I control everything on Ganymede, including you. I offered to do this the friendly way, Zurri, over whiskey. You chose this."

"No, I didn't!"

"Agree to disagree."

Brea brandished the Taser as Dr. Colbie shuffled over, heaving a labored sigh before taking the syringe and holding Zurri's right arm, sliding the needle in while Zurri stared up at her, protesting with wide, glossy eyes.

"Just stop listening to him," Zurri murmured, knowing she had seconds of lucidity left. "This isn't right, girl. You know this isn't right. What he's doing here to you? To me? It's not okay. It's monstrous. *Fight back.*"

"I can't," Colbie mouthed, silent, her back to Paxton while he remained close by, observing, his mere presence quietly threatening.

"Warm up LENG," Paxton muttered, turning and striding toward the door, the back of his head just visible through the narrowing, blurry tunnel of Zurri's vision. She had gotten her sedatives after all, she thought darkly, feeling the familiar sensation of the world shrinking in on her.

"Let's get on with it." The door opened and Paxton saw himself out. "I'm tired of interruptions."

Han had expected a clean, elegant system, something far more sophisticated than the in-home assistant OS he had hacked at home. Was it wrong to feel disappointed? Paxton had other things to worry about, Han reminded himself. He was creating never-before-seen technology. He was changing the universe. Some messy programming nobody was supposed to see didn't exactly rate as a cardinal sin.

Unless it was meant to be seen. Unless it was meant for Han. *The Game.*

This was pure rush, the dopamine flood from solving a difficult puzzle times one hundred. His hands shook; he started to sweat. *I'm in, I can't believe I'm actually in.*

Through the sudden buzz it was difficult to concentrate. He had gone snooping for a reason, but it was like breaking into a multilevel, dream-stocked tech store and only stealing one measly memory stick. There had to be so much to find, so much to discover.

Later, he promised himself. He would clear up this stupid claim of Efren's and then really sink his teeth into Paxton's data. And so he navigated to the main server, checking directories and subdirectories for any labels that might logically store the security footage. He assumed the system would create a folder for each day, then chunk the data into modest sizes to make it easier to view. Or . . . if this was Paxton's log-in, he could just review recently accessed files.

Han smiled, finishing his Mega Slurp and typing fast. Just as he thought, Paxton's activity in the last hour led him right to the correct subfolder. Everything there was labeled by Dome time, making it easier to track down the correct file. It made sense that Paxton would want to keep anything work- or facility-related synced with the day and time back on Tokyo Bliss Station. Most big companies with satellites or a colony presence kept things in relation to station time for ease of sharing and interoffice connectivity.

Wiping the condensation off on his pants, Han sat back against the sofa, his legs crossed underneath him as he let the footage play, approximating the correct time to be just a few minutes after the end of dinner, since he had seen Anju there at mealtime. He set the playback to 1.5 speed. There was no sound, but Paxton had accessed a file displaying activity in a narrow gray maintenance shaft in something labeled Quadrant 3, Zone 6. Zone 6, Han recalled from his map, sat near the staff quarter, but this appeared to be a subterranean level, almost unfinished, with exposed pipes running along the ceiling.

On the footage, an unskinned Servitor leaned over a hatch near a sealed door, welding. Anju stepped into frame behind it, already dressed in her space suit. The Servitor stopped what it was doing, and stood upright to listen to her. Han grunted, wishing there were sound. Something else joined them in the frame, gliding up from behind Anju. A man.

Han wanted to believe it was just an artifact from crappy capture, or a trick of the light, but it had too much form, a silhouette of a man standing behind Anju, crowding her. Even the Servitor seemed to notice it, its chrome, beak-like head turning to regard it, round aperture eyes growing wider at having seen it. Anju did something on her VIT and the Servitor went still, powered down, and then the man placed both hands on her shoulders, and Anju interfaced with the hatch on the wall. He let go of her and turned to leave, giving Han a brief glimpse of his face.

His stomach dropped. Efren.

Efren walked away, a placid expression on his face. When he was out of frame, the sealed door flew open, a spray of ice scattering across the interior floor, then calmly, Anju walked out into the hazy white unknown.

His mouth had gone dry. The footage played on, but there was nothing more to watch. So Paxton had viewed this footage and deemed *that* an accident. Han's heart clenched in his chest; Paxton knew that Efren had spoken to Anju just before she went willingly out the hatch. He had lied to their faces.

What the hell is going on?

"Genie?" asked Han.

"Yes, Han, how can I assist you?"

He drew in a deep, ragged breath. Was he really doing this? Was he really going to confront his hero? If the most brilliant man in the universe didn't have an answer for this, then maybe he wasn't so brilliant after all.

"Where is Paxton right now?"

The AI had to think it over, giving an unusual pause. "Paxton is currently meeting with staff in his office, but the facility is on lockdown until Dome time eight a.m. tomorrow. Would you like me to schedule a meeting with him for you?"

Right. The lockdown.

"Where is Efren, Genie?" he asked, shaking.

"That information is currently unavailable."

Han's eyes wandered back to the text hovering above his VIT, glowing faintly in the low light of the living room. The gears in his mind started spinning, faster and faster, an anxious itch bothering him at the base of his neck. Was this lockdown a coincidence or was Paxton trying to take care of Efren himself? Maybe it was for their own safety. In that case, he should've been honest. He should've been, but wasn't. They were allowing him access to their brains, and there he was, lying to them. How could Han trust him to use the LENG tech on his memories ever again?

He deserved an explanation.

"Lockdown," Han repeated under his breath, then dove back into the Dome security systems. He was, after all, using Paxton's own admin log-in. Surely that granted him the power to lift the facility-wide lockdown . . .

He heard a quiet *ka-shh* from the front door, the override lock releasing.

"If you think Paxton will not notice your *extracurricular* activities, Han, you are mistaken. Please reinstate the lockdown protocols." Genie had never taken that bossy tone with him.

"Nervous?" Han smirked and stood, deciding that on his walk to the clinical labs he would see about tweaking Genie's parameters, too. It couldn't hurt to have friendly eyes in the sky.

Han is king, baby, he thought, another rush of adrenaline coasting through his body as he approached the door and it slid open. He only hoped he wouldn't run into Efren. *Hail to the king.*

23

Senna had just finished obliterating the shadow and painting the entire canvas flat black when she heard a strange sound at the door. Sitting on the couch, barefoot, she had been letting her brushes soak in turpentine solution while she stared at Anju's pink dress, now folded neatly and placed on the center of the glass coffee table like an offering.

It didn't seem right to keep the dress, and she had forgotten to give it back to Paxton before he left. In all honesty, she had just wanted him out. When he asked for a hug before going, she obliged, feeling sorry for him. When the hug lingered too long, her hands limp at her sides, she regretted indulging the request.

Senna stood and laid out her brushes on a towel to dry, wiped her hands and scooped up the dress. Maybe it was silly, but she didn't want to see it in her apartment anymore. She hadn't found any use for the messaging system on her VIT, since none of her communiqués were clearing the storms anyway. A few times, she thought to check in with Marin, but none of it went through. That wouldn't affect intra-Dome messaging though, she had been assured.

Returning the dress would give her a chance to set some boundaries with Paxton, too. His interest wasn't subtle, and the attention made her uncomfortable. It was the way he looked at her, too probing, like he was trying to see through skin and bone, like he was trying to peel back the flesh to see what was underneath.

"The facility is on lockdown until Dome time eight a.m. tomorrow," Genie reminded her as Senna approached the door.

"I just want to return this to Paxton," she replied, pausing near the kitchen and slipping on her shoes. She always tilted her head up slightly when she spoke to Genie, as if he lived in the ceiling above her rooms, when in truth she had no idea where "he" resided. "Can you tell me where he is? I'll be quick about it and come right back."

"Paxton is currently in his office," Genie told her. "But you have been asked to observe lockdown protocols."

Senna gave a *hm* of curiosity as she approached the door and found it slid open as quickly and freely as it always did. "Seems lockdown is over."

"It is not," Genie assured her.

"Well, like I said . . ." Senna stepped out into the darkened hall. "I'll be right back."

The straight, empty halls of the guest wing squeezed in on her, strange and cold, like a place abandoned. Senna held the dress slightly out in front of her, unwilling to keep it close to her body. Now that its owner was gone, it took on a slightly haunted quality. Clothes could be so intimate. She wondered what Anju had done in that dress, where she had gone. Maybe she had been a wild child on the station, staying out all night before consigning herself to the quiet, isolated focus of life on Ganymede. Or maybe she had a husband somewhere, or a wife, and this was what she wore out to their anniversary dinners. The more she considered the possibilities, the heavier her heart became. What a senseless, stupid loss. Anju had been nothing but kind to her, and Senna didn't care what Zurri said—it was perfectly understandable to grieve someone, even if their acquaintance had been a short one.

How awful that Anju's parents wouldn't learn of her death until the storm that had killed her moved on.

Senna tiptoed swiftly out of the guest wing and onto the balcony overlooking the Dome courtyard, a view traveling east to west. No AR birds flitted through the canopies, no reedy insect calls filled the still paths below. Without its dynamic, artificial light and dynamic, artificial life, the courtyard held the sinister emptiness of an after-hours exhibit. Back on the station, Marin couldn't convince her to leave the condo and go to the museum at the university, but she did show Senna how to navigate the VR tour of their exhibits, borrowing a friend's pricey VR goggle set and letting Senna spend the afternoon perusing dinosaur skeletons, Viking canoes and real sarcophagi on loan from Earth museums. The program did not simulate other human beings wandering the corridors with her, and she found the experience unsettling, alone with the ancient dead. Even if it was just a virtual tour, Senna couldn't help but obsess over what the Vikings or the Egyptians would say, knowing their preserved bodies were now on display two hundred fifty thousand miles from home. When it was over, she was subjected to Jonathan's elaborate Egyptian aliens theories, while Marin, increasingly drunk, heatedly pointed out that they were now colonizing space, and no pharaohs in flying saucers had turned up to protest.

For the rest of the month, Senna had nightmares of the mummies waking up and slowly, inexorably, hunting her through the echoing halls of the museum.

With that in mind. Senna willed herself not to think about the shadow thing she knew lurked in the facility. It had appeared too many times—and now to other people—for it to be just her mind playing tricks. But she had stayed walled up in Marin's condo because of her fear of other people, for fear of their judgment and scorn and pity, and now she was in a place where everyone knew her, there were no more excuses, and if a memory of a mummy and a shadow could give her nightmares, then surely keeping a dead woman's dress in her possession could do it, too.

She turned the corner to the right, hoping to take the faster path to his office that ran along the walkways that overlooked the gallery and dining area. The shutters had been drawn down tight, however, blocking off that door and the faster route. From the balcony, the way through the huge double doors opening onto the gallery from the Dome appeared clear, so she would have to take the ramp down into the courtyard and follow the less-appealing path through the twisting, leafy turns.

At the bottom of the ramp, she caught sight of a shadow dodging behind a tree and froze. But *the* shadow had never hesitated to show itself or approach; in fact, it never showed any kind of fear.

"Who is it?" she whispered. "I know you're there."

"You looked like you were on such a mission, it didn't seem right to interrupt," Efren called back, stepping around the cocoa-brown trunk of the broad-leafed tree and leaning against it. "We're on lockdown, you know."

"You're the one hiding," Senna said back. Now that she wasn't where she was supposed to be, she felt bolder. "Did you know Anju well? I'm sorry about what happened to her. It must be hard on you all."

Efren wandered out farther onto the path, the light in the Dome perfunctory, warehouse-thin and unflattering. Even under that unfriendly cast he looked handsome, put together. He wore the same black suit, his hair falling soft as ravens' wings around his ears. Senna had the strangest desire to stare at him and keep staring, and she wondered if that made him feel the way she did when Paxton stared at her. Vulnerable and squirmy.

"I'm part of things here," Efren pointed out, "I'm not on lockdown. Anyway, I won't tattle, if that worries you." He came closer, but maintained a respectful distance from her. Senna continued holding out the dress in front of her, as if afraid of its contamination. "Your sympathy is appreciated, but I didn't know Anju well. None of us really did." His smile changed, deepening, welcoming. She realized he was appraising her back, but it didn't unsettle her. It was the oddest thing, the way she wanted to study him closely, as if drawn in, as if he had tossed hooks behind her eyes and begun gradually to pull. "I didn't have you pegged as a rule breaker."

"I'm really not. I was brought up to love rules, all kinds of rules." Senna gestured with the dress toward the right, toward the path she needed to take to Paxton's office. "I'm returning this dress; it belonged to Anju."

She shivered, wishing the birds would come back, and the comforting mundanity of their little calls and squeaks.

"You don't like the Dome at night," he observed, falling easily into step with her as she began to tiptoe along again.

"It's too quiet," Senna replied. "It's all too quiet. Can I ask why you didn't know Anju well? There's so few of you here, I thought it would make you all close."

They walked on, Efren no longer looking at *her*, his eyes fixed on the leaves bobbing around them as they passed. Senna couldn't tear her eyes away from him. Was this attraction? Marin had told her that when she met Jonathan, it was love at first sight, though Senna couldn't imagine how anyone could be in love with Jonathan, let alone instantaneously. Maybe that worked in his favor; the love came before Marin ever had a chance to hear him speak. She liked Efren's profile, it was even better than his face head-on, his nose bent in a way that reminded her of ancient coins.

"We couldn't get close," Efren explained in his strong, magnetic voice. "Not for a number of reasons. Her loyalty to Paxton, for one. And her . . . I wouldn't call it disinterest, that doesn't capture it." He glanced down at the floor, almost tripping. After steadying himself, he sucked in his cheek and sighed, wrestling with something. "It doesn't matter how hard she tried, she couldn't see me."

"So cryptic," Senna sighed. They had skirted the outer edge of the gardens, coming to the tall doors opening onto the gallery. Here the light changed, not brighter, but milkier, hazily pre-dawn, the purple crystal chandelier sending a kaleidoscope of pale violet shapes across the empty floor and between the statue pedestals.

Efren's gait slowed as they crossed from courtyard to gallery. "I don't have to be." Then he stopped altogether, quarter turning to look at her, though for a flash his eyes lingered to the left and up the ramp, in the direction of Paxton's office. The doors there, visible from below, glowed red.

"You're making me nervous," she murmured. "What's going on?"

"It's only . . ." The light hung differently around Efren. She had noticed it with Paxton, too, but where a curiously dark halo sometimes clung to Paxton's head and shoulders, Efren absorbed the light, pulled it in, the way her attention, too, was drawn to him. For a moment, he struggled, then he unleashed another one of his smiles on her, only this time it was sad, and knowing, and Senna braced for bad news. Nothing good ever came after a smile like that.

"You're about to see something you won't understand; I want to protect you from it, shield you, but I can't. I can tell you to turn around and go back to your rooms, I can tell you to run, but there's nowhere for you to go. Warnings won't matter, you're here now, so what's coming is coming." Efren almost reached to touch her shoulder, then stopped himself. "The storm isn't just outside, Senna, it's in here, too. You can't see it, but it's already swept you up."

Senna backed away from him. "You're not making any sense."

"Not yet," Efren told her, sliding his hands into his pockets with a sigh. She was frustrated with his spooky, oblique nonsense. Maybe she had misjudged him. This wasn't instant attraction after all, but repulsion. All the men here were insane. She coasted away from him and to the right, walking swiftly toward the right ramp leading up to the overlooking walkway and Paxton's office. "Senna?"

She paused at the base of the ramp, listening.

"I look forward to meeting you again."

"Sure, okay. I need to go. Good night, Efren."

Now she was just weary. After Paxton took the dress back and she made it clear that she didn't want anything romantic between them, she would take one of those Talpraxem Zurri loved so much and sleep and sleep, and nothing would stop her from escaping this whole miserable night. In the morning, she would order the greasiest thing available and wait for the winds to subside, then she and Zurri would get on that shuttle and leave Ganymede far behind.

Brighter red pulses bloomed behind the doors, rhythmic, slower than the beat of a heart but hypnotizing. Did she say something? Ask Genie for help? Her presence triggered the proximity sensor. What was wrong with the doors? Weren't they supposed to be on lockdown? The long glowing panel behind Paxton's desk swirled with colors, crimson and gold, muddied with what looked like gore and tissue, an amniotic slurry creating the pulses she had noticed through the semi-translucent doors. There was another rhythm, too, breathing, labored, harsh, and a fleshy percussive note, what sounded like someone slapping their own naked belly.

You're about to see something you won't understand.

It took a moment for Senna's heart to connect to her eyes to connect to her brain. The dress fell out of her grasp and slithered to the floor at her feet, the fabric pooling making more noise than her silent squeak of confusion and terror.

I can tell you to run, but there's nowhere for you to go.

Senna covered her mouth with both hands, but her fingers had gone numb. A naked woman writhed on the ground in front of Paxton's desk, on all fours. She would have been staring right into Senna's eyes from that position, but she didn't have a head. Where a face and hair and eyes should have been, there was nothing, just a bundle of loose, unconnected wires, but her body moved as if she were whole and sensate. Pants around his knees, Paxton huffed and groaned, slamming his groin into her from behind.

Senna began slowly to back away, but Paxton glanced up

from the woman's back. Their eyes met and his mouth went slack, yet it hardly put a hitch in his rhythm. An image of her own mindscape appeared to her, a perfect pink bubble of chewing gum stretching thin, and something poking at the taxed, rubbery surface from within. This—this grotesquerie under an unnatural red glow, in perpetual silence, his breathing, her helplessness—scratched at an itch Senna hadn't thought to feel yet. The void in her mind, the gap in her teeth that wanted prodding . . . Was she remembering? Was she taking something back that the LENG technology had tried to erase?

A silent tomb bathed in red light. A single man's labored breathing. Her, paralyzed, surrounded by death, powerless to stop what came next. Suddenly she could see Preece standing there, his eyes wild with all that he had done and with the one last thing he meant to do. The ship. The crash. Connections re-formed. Senna knew that if she did not find a way to escape, then she would go down with him. There was only one thought in her head: I cannot let him take me down, too.

"Fuck," he muttered, wiping at the sweat on his brow. He yanked off his glasses and threw them on the floor, rubbing his hand over his face. "This complicates things."

Someone was behind Senna, silent and quick. She felt it just before the tip of something sharp and cold pressed against her neck.

I cannot let him take me down, too.

When it was over, what would be left that was true? Would any real, unclouded parts of her remain? Even while the pain built at the base of her skull, even as LENG's endless black fingers curled into her brain, she tried to hold on to some tiny piece of her essential nature. But what did that mean? What was she—*who* was she—without her memories?

"What are you doing to me?" she asked weakly, voice no stronger than a whistle through broken teeth.

I am taking. LENG's voice shook through her every sinew. *And this time, I am taking everything.*

24

"Hey!"

Han hadn't expected to find Zurri breezing through the halls with the lockdown in place. Then again, he was the one that had sprung all the doors, so he couldn't exactly start pointing fingers. They almost collided as she came around the corner from the overlook balcony, returning to the dormitories.

"Hi," she said, gazing down at him with a serene expression. He noticed a bruise near her wrist, her knuckles were scraped, and her clothes were rumpled, like she had just rolled out of bed. Not exactly the picture-perfect Zurri he was used to seeing.

"You've, um, your hands . . ." He pointed to her scuffed knuckles. "I think you're bleeding."

"I hadn't noticed, thanks." Zurri regarded the backs of her hands and then her nails. One was badly chipped. She seemed . . . different. Calmer, somehow, or maybe it was just that she had never grinned at him like that, open and friendly, without a hint of judgment or snark. Maybe she was just tired.

"Are you all right?" he asked.

"I'm great." Zurri gave him a thumbs-up. "Never better. I was just catching up with Paxton, he was telling me the funniest story about meeting me on Tokyo Bliss Station. He's *so* hilarious."

"He . . . is?" Han glanced over her shoulder. Was someone pointing a rifle at her head and making her say this? Just a few hours ago she was railing against Paxton at Senna's kitchen table. "Is this a prank? You hate Paxton."

Zurri's thin brows met over her eyes. "What? No, come on, kid, I'm completely serious."

"Sure," Han replied, rolling his eyes and edging around her to leave the guest wing. "Sure you are. God, I'm not that gullible."

Shrugging, Zurri continued on her way, lifting her hands again to study the torn skin there as she went. It wasn't until she had vanished around a right corner that he noticed she was missing a shoe. Han filed that away, then spun one-eighty and found his way out onto the darkened walkway. Whoever had designed the lockdown atmosphere for the Dome got points for extra creep factor. Han decided to move fast, to not think about it too hard, and to find Paxton before he could get too spooked and retreat to his rooms or, worse, run into Efren. He was acutely aware that a staff member had just let Anju walk out the airlock; if Efren could come for her, he could come for Han.

Once Han had found his way through the courtyard and into the gallery, he noticed a light on above him, shining out dim but noticeable from Paxton's office. The doors were slightly ajar, and then closed as he watched, Paxton walking out and pausing until the office sealed itself shut behind him. There was a worn-down stoop to his shoulders, his dark curling hair mussed and greasy, and he wiped off his spectacles on his shirt as he slumped over to the ramp and began to descend.

There was his chance. Han inhaled through his nose, squaring up his shoulders and neck, marching right up to Paxton only to be met with a bemused roll of the eyes.

"Someone's been a busy boy," he drawled, stacking his spectacles neatly back on his nose. "Figured out the little puzzle I left for you, then, mm?"

"So it *was* a test," Han breathed. The surge of excitement was almost enough to distract him from why he'd come. "Just like *The Game*. Does that mean you wanted me to find the security footage, too?"

"No, no," Paxton chuckled weakly, draping an arm across Han's shoulders and steering him back around and toward the black clinical lab door. "Even I couldn't have seen that one coming, but that's why we do trials, right? I couldn't have known LENG would . . . well. Or that her protocols were that weak. That's my bad. It doesn't matter. Anyway, I'm glad you're here."

"Glad?" Han frowned. "You lied to us, Paxton. What was that shit with Efren on the footage? Why didn't Anju fight back against him?"

Pausing, Paxton rearranged them, standing in front of Han, both hands perched on his shoulders, staring down at him with the fatherly sternness of someone about to deliver a lecture. "Jesus, you remind me so much of myself, it's actually creepy."

"I do?" Han smirked. "Really?"

"You're observant and clever. You're fearless. You see a problem and you don't think, 'Whoa, okay, slow down, that's too big for me to tackle.' You just throw yourself at it. It makes you reckless, too. Which, sadly, is now a problem." He grimaced and tossed a scathing look toward his office doors. "Too many problems. But it's fine. It's all fine. I'm handling it. It's going to be a long, long, fucking long night, but tomorrow it'll all be handled, and we can finally do things right around here. Get some peace and fucking quiet."

Han shook his head. "What's going on around here, Paxton? I'm . . . honestly, I'm scared. First Anju, and these shadow things. I keep seeing shadows everywhere, a shadow like . . . like a creature. Senna saw it, too. What does it mean? Is it a side effect?"

"You're a Cecilia Fan fan"—he chuckled breathlessly at the stupid repetition—"right?"

"Yeah, but what does she have to do with—"

Paxton slung his arm around Han's shoulders again and continued guiding him toward the door. Han tried to drag his feet, but Paxton pushed, insistent. "Her 2268 speech at Yang Hall. Classic. Beautiful stuff. Practically poetry. I met her a few times, you know? She didn't realize it was me, but she was nice. Didn't have to be. Some of those lecturers are real assholes, but Fan is all right. Anyway, she likes to theorize about the capabilities of the smallest perceivable black holes. You must have your own theories . . ."

"I'm a teenager not an astrophysicist," Han protested, the black door growing closer. "I guess it would just bend light and warp space but on a small scale. Listen, it's cool, you know? You talking about this stuff with me, but I still don't understand what—"

"And if it was small enough," Paxton barged into his question. "Let's say really tiny, we're talking Planck length, could you contain it?"

They didn't go through the door, and Han tried not to make his relief too noticeable. Paxton swiveled to face him head-on again, waiting for his answer. When Han hesitated, eyes shifting to the empty gallery and everywhere else but Paxton, the man asked again, "If a black hole was small enough, could it be contained?"

"Theoretically? Um, sure."

Paxton nodded, slowly at first but building speed. "And if you could contain it, what could you do with it?"

"I don't know," Han replied, squinting. "What *could* you do with it?"

To Han's right, the black door slid open.

"You already know, Han," Paxton said, weaving from exhaustion, his eyes bright and irritated, shot through with crimson. "But I'll be happy to show you again."

25

Zurri tore out of sleep like someone had waved a wand over her and a curse had been lifted. She hadn't dreamed. She hadn't, she realized with a jolt, even been aware of her own body's existence until she came abruptly awake.

Where am I? she wondered, examining her surroundings. They felt brand-new, but tingles ran from her fingers up to her scalp as she ran her hands over the luxe blankets. Cozy. Tasteful. It matched her minimalist, haute aesthetic. Right at home. She placed a hand over her chest, feeling her breath rise and fall, the automatic and unthinking miracle of a living body, so intrinsic that thinking about it too hard made her feel clumsy, like she would bungle it if put in charge of actually directing her own lungs to expand and contract.

Gradually, a sense of familiarity spread across her. Right. Ganymede. She had arrived at the facility just two days ago. Day three. How long was she meant to stay? Zurri stretched and yawned, pointing her toes, raising her VIT to check the time and consult her calendar. More and more it all came back. That must have been one hell of a night of drinking, though she didn't feel a booze hangover coming on. What could make her sleep like that? She'd find the evidence soon enough, she reasoned, strewn about the kitchen or the living room sofa.

> Good morning, Zurri! It's another beautiful day on Ganymede.

The Dome scheduler on her VIT greeted her, pink text sprayed with glitzy confetti.

> It's recovery day, please practice meditation or mindfulness. If you need guidance on these methods, please contact Dr. Colbie in the clinical labs. The hard part's over! Now allow your mind to heal. Your appointment with our PR specialist, Brea, is scheduled for Dome time 1:00 p.m.

In a black peignoir trimmed in lapis-colored marabou feathers, Zurri found her way down the hall to the living area. A kaleidoscope of pale stars played on the vid monitor there, a tray of food waiting for her, a vivid green matcha latte steaming steadily beside an egg-white omelet and roasted brussels sprouts. She crossed to the coffee table, eyes sweeping the ground for bottles, booze or otherwise, but the apartment gleamed. Spotless. The kitchen, too, showed no evidence of recent debauchery.

Zurri squeezed her eyes shut for a moment, trying again to recall the events of the night before. If she was having this good a sleep and morning because she was sober, then why couldn't she remember much?

Her food was getting cold. She decided to sate the pleasant stirring hunger in her stomach, and ate until she was full. Afterward, she only felt better. Was waking up always this easy? Gradually, she became aware of an ache in her neck, and when she massaged it, the pain radiated out in startling waves. That was a deep bruise. Weird. Zurri wiped her mouth and strode briskly to the bathroom across from her bedroom. It emulated a clean Japanese *onsen* aesthetic, bamboo lamps glowing in the corners, the pebbly floor and spa tub done in slate gray speckled with blue. A wide, arcing fern soared across the doorway, shading it like an awning. Just inside the door and to the left, two floor-to-ceiling mirrors flanked the stone sink. Frowning, she inspected herself, turning to try to appraise the tender spot on the back of her neck and scalp.

Slightly shiny. Greasy. She smelled the pads of her fingers, detecting a faint medicinal twinge. Her knuckles seemed scuffed and peeling.

"Genie?" she asked slowly, the word occurring to her before its function did.

"Yes, Zurri, how may I assist you?"

"Did I get black-out drunk last night?"

"You did not," Genie replied.

She lifted a brow. "Are you sure? Did I fall down in here or something?"

"You did not fall down in your rooms, no. Would you like me to notify Dr. Colbie of any injuries?" the in-home assistant asked.

"No . . ." Zurri shrugged, the area between her shoulder blades tender but bearable. "No, I guess it's nothing."

"Your health and comfort are our highest priority," Genie continued. "If you require assistance, do not hesitate to ask."

It *was* odd. Why couldn't she remember how she got that bruise? Thinking about it too hard made her woozy, and she grabbed for the sink, steadying herself. "You know what? I think I will go see Dr. Colbie. Is she available?"

"Yes, Dr. Colbie can see you, her agenda is open until after lunch."

A moment later, dressing in the bedroom, Zurri felt another stab of pain coast down her spine as she pulled on her shift dress.

"Shit," she muttered, reaching to cup her lower back. "That's vicious."

In the medicine cabinet she found only over-the-counter pain medication. Not even fixings for a mimosa in the refrigerated box either to take the edge off. That didn't seem right. She would've asked for a full liquor cabinet. Her rider, via Bev, would have made that explicitly clear.

"Genie?" she asked, toiling over this question in the kitchen, tapping her foot in its faux suede moccasin impatiently. "What happened to my booze?"

"You asked to have it removed, Zurri," Genie replied flatly. "Would you like me to have that decision reversed? Sixteen can deliver whatever you require in a matter of moments . . ."

"No? No. Huh. I'll be damned." *Past Zurri was either smart as hell or crazy.* Maybe it wasn't such a bad idea to lay off the sauce until she sorted out what was going on with that bruise. And why she felt dazed in a vaguely euphoric way, like her toes weren't quite touching the ground. Breakfast had been good but not *that* good.

As she reached the door, a message alert chimed on her VIT. She checked it as she stepped out into the hall, distracted.

COMPLIANCE REQUIRED: INDICATE BELOW YOU HAVE READ
AND RECEIVED

This is a Dome-wide update—the following topics have
been deemed sensitive. Please avoid discussing these
items with your fellow patients, as it may hinder their recovery process.

With Senna Slate, do not discuss the following:
» The Dohring-Waugh Cult, and her association with it or
its leader, Preece Ives

With Han Jun, do not discuss the following:
» The crash of the *Dohring-Waugh* passenger craft onto
the surface of Mars
» Close family associations, such as parents or siblings
» Criminal activities related to cyberattacks and hacking

Zurri indicated that she read and understood the instructions,
receiving an immediate message of gratitude from the system.
Right, the program. Her fellow inmates. No, fellow *patients*. The
place between her shoulder blades throbbed again, a tight line running from there to the top of her skull. Senna existed in her mind
only as a general idea, a small, sad thing with a sad past and sweet,
unsteady nature, cotton candy ephemera with a tragic haircut. And
the kid, Han . . . skinny nerd with big heart eyes for Paxton. A
mini mogul and, she seemed to remember, a fan of hers.

Even before she could lower her wrist and take another step,
she was intercepted by a flurry of yellow fur and slender, flailing
limbs.

"Watch it!" She jumped back, the door to her apartment hissing back open before she could tumble against it. Fur and limbs resolved into two distinct forms—one a fluffy golden dog and the other a teenage boy with a mop of dark hair. Han. They both skidded around to regard Zurri, although only the dog looked somewhat contrite.

"Oops, sorry!" Han was holding a bright red ball. "Paxton gave me this AR dog, new tech, totally proprietary and Dome exclusive. Isn't she incredible? So lifelike, it's wild. I'm teaching her to fetch! Check this out . . ." He threw the ball down the hall, and the dog gave a single excited bark, spun around and then leapt after it, bouncing down the hall with as much elastic energy as the ball. She cornered the ball, missing it six times before at last snapping it up and returning to them with her head held high, tail swishing proudly. When she dropped the ball into Han's hands, it disappeared, just an illusion of the augmented-reality app Paxton had designed. He was right, the tech was unbelievably lifelike. Surreal.

"Best part? No allergies and no drool," Han said with a laugh. "How are you feeling?"

"Feeling?" Zurri frowned.

The kid made a fist with his hand again and when he opened it, a ball appeared, the dog coming forward to close her jaws around it. They gently wrestled for the ball while Han peered up at Zurri. "You were sick. Paxton said you needed a few days to rest so we left you alone."

"Oh." She reached instinctively for the bruise on her neck, trying to solve a puzzle with too many missing pieces. "I guess I'm better now. I mean, I feel fine except for this weird bruise. Why did he give you a dog?"

Han beamed, giving up the fight for the ball and letting the dog have it. He patted her big, broad head fondly while she gummed the ball and covered it in slobber. "It's Paxton's code, jacked right into my VIT. He always wanted a dog but couldn't because of his allergies or something. I'm the first person to have it. Technically it's his dog, but now she's mine."

Her eyes slid between him and the dog and back again. "Are you sure about this? Paxton *gave* you his dog?"

"Yeah, why not? It's just an AR dog, I can handle it. Lula even leaves AR poop behind, and you'll see it, too. Paxton is going to update the Dome VIT parameters so even you guys can see it. Wild."

Zurri snorted. Right, he had a huge ego, this kid. Not as grand as hers, but few could aspire to those heights. "You know dogs, even fake ones, are a lot of work. Tons of responsibility. They shit, like, all the time, and you have to be the one to clean it up. You cool with that? Because I am not cool with stepping in virtual poop."

"Whatever." He shrugged. "I'll get one of the Servitors to 'clean' it."

"Oh? You rule this place now, huh?" She had to laugh; he seemed completely at home. Zurri didn't know *what* she felt. Sore, for one. She eyed the hallway behind him, still anxious to grill Dr. Colbie about that mystery bruise, and now her illness and the days of convalescence it required. She knew she was there for memory treatments, but this forgetfulness struck her as extreme.

"Sort of." Han tossed the ball up and down in one hand while Lula wiggled with anticipation beside him. "Paxton said I can stay on for as long as I want, even after the program is done. Like a mentorship. She'd really be *our* dog."

That was less amusing than his strutting peacock attitude. Her teenage years had been full of misadventure, getting drunk with fellow models in their cramped Tokyo apartment, chasing boys and sometimes girls, sneaking into bars they were way too young for, flirting with attendants to get into VR parlors showing racy matinees. Eighteen-year-old Zurri would have gone completely mad trapped in a tiny moon compound with only adults for company. "How long would you stay?"

"Maybe forever, I don't know."

"Forever?" Zurri shook her head. "You're joking."

Han crossed his arms over his narrow chest. "Why? I'm not joking. I'm smart enough, Paxton says I'm a genius, that I'm wasted on the school back on the station."

"What about your friends?" Zurri replied without thinking. "And your family?"

She winced. Shit. One of the forbidden topics. She decided not to fumble more by trying to cover up what she had said or blurt out an apology; that might only make it worse. Hopefully he just wouldn't notice. But Han did notice, and he paused, gazing up at her with dark and distant eyes. Then he gave her a lopsided grin, the consternation vanishing in a blink. "Stupid. What family?"

26

"You don't need to do that." Senna scrambled out of bed, shorts and shirt and hair rumpled. She slept so deeply now that every sunrise felt like a clap of thunder, a snap of the fingers right in front of her face. Even before she could orient herself or stretch, corn-yellow light had begun to suffuse the walls, creeping up from the bottom edge and gradually making the room glow like a lantern.

She reached for the nearest sock on the floor and held it tightly to her chest, as if that one little action could ward off the embarrassed flush bleeding across her face. But the sock went unnoticed by Anju, who had just bustled into the bedroom and begun pacing and tidying.

You're his personal assistant, thought Senna. *Not his maid.*

"Really," Senna added. "I'm perfectly capable . . ."

"It's fine," Anju snapped at her, bending to scoop up Paxton's black jeans and fold them neatly over her arm. "It's totally fine."

Her brown hair was swept up into a seashell shape on her head, her bright, perfectly tan skin dusted with coral-orange rouge. Heavy golden hoops dangled from her ears, though to Senna one looked a little misshapen, not quite a perfect circle, as if someone had trampled on it.

"I . . ." Before Senna could finish her thought, Anju strode up to her and shoved a clean dress into her arms.

"Should I have the rest of your things moved here?" Anju asked, her smile tight and stretched. "I already cleared it with Paxton. You brought so few items, I doubt he'd even notice them in the closet."

"No." Senna frowned and shook her head. She still wasn't sure why she was there, or where "there" was. A bedroom . . . Paxton's. When she took the dress from Anju, the woman spun and retrieved a few more socks, then disappeared into the walk-in closet across from and to the left of the bed. It was a simple, clean room, minus the rogue socks, with walls that could be calibrated to show any scene or project any light, an orb-like black fixture hanging from the center of the ceiling. Below it, a mirror-black circle of a rug opened up like a hole in the otherwise white tiled floor.

Two dark cubed tables flanked the goliath of a bed, but his bedroom was otherwise empty.

While Anju clattered around in the closet, Senna held the dress to her abdomen with one hand and ran her palm over her shoulders with the other. She was feeling for evidence, for traces of what had happened the night before. Closing her eyes, she sank back into her thoughts, letting the room around her go quiet. Paxton. Had they kissed? She touched her own lips, but they didn't feel any different. Were they lovers? What was she doing in his bedroom?

She shivered, cold at heart. If she was there, if she was waking up in his bed, then she must feel something for him. Out of the strange cavern of her thoughts, a single refrain rose to comfort her: *The most brilliant man in the universe wants you. He's chosen you.*

"I'm so lucky," Senna heard herself say.

"Did you need something?" Anju's voice carried through the wall of the closet.

"No! No . . ." Shimmying out of her pajamas, Senna pulled on the dress and watched it swish around her knees. "Why did I say that?" she murmured. *I'm so lucky.* She could remember being a little girl, sitting on a freezing table while a hazy fog of a man thumped her knee with a triangular hammer. Her foot would swing out and it made her giggle. "How did you do that?" she would ask, amazed.

The unremembered man had given her a warm, fatherly smile. His voice came out flat, atonal, as if someone had vacuumed all the life and personality out of it. "It's a reflex. Some movements are just intrinsic to the body."

Like a hammer striking something in her head, when she pushed against the name Paxton, against her memories of him, like a foot kicking she heard, *I'm so lucky.*

I'm so lucky spoken in a voice not her own. A loud, terrible voice that took up all the space in her head until it almost hurt. The door opened and Servitor Sixteen entered, startling her. The chrome AI bot came with a tray clamped in its three-fingered hands, its three button-like eyes glowing blue, flashing when they scanned across her. Senna huddled back against the bed while Sixteen deposited the food on the cube table near her.

"Thank you," she said, out of habit.

"You enjoy," Sixteen replied, torso and legs somewhat out of sync as it turned and left.

"Pax should really replace that thing." Anju appeared, patting the side of her head, though no hair had moved out of place. Senna wasn't hungry—in fact just the smell of the orange juice on the tray made her want to be sick. Instead, she found herself drawn to Anju, with her perfect hair and perfect face. Her perfect body. Senna felt terribly misshapen and average by comparison, especially in her loose dress, while Anju's glittery gray frock could have been a quick coat of paint. *Pax. She knows him so well, and she's so otherworldly, why would he pick me over someone like this?*

A throb built at her temples, pressure, her brain pressing hard against its confines. A thought, a dream, a revelation was trapped in there, a sudden painful swell like a bubble caught in the throat. Senna's teeth chattered. *I'm so lucky.*

"What?" Anju asked, consulting her VIT, becoming aware of Senna's rude gawking.

"You don't belong here."

"Excuse me?" the other woman scoffed.

Senna shook her head, passing her palm back and forth across her mouth, the redness over her face deepening. "I'm sorry, I don't . . . I'm not feeling like myself today."

Apparently gifted with infinite patience, Anju smiled gently and came to take Senna's forearm, squeezing it. "This whole process is difficult, Senna. You're doing fine, just don't push yourself too hard. Sit, okay? Have something to eat, it will help."

"I'm sorry," Senna mumbled, refusing to sit and refusing to eat. "I shouldn't have said that to you. There's just . . . so much missing. Time. Memories."

"It will get easier," Anju assured her, taking the orange juice and pressing it into her hands. "You have to eat."

Their eyes locked over the juice, and Senna felt herself begging silently. She couldn't decide what she was pleading for, mercy maybe, or understanding. An explanation. Her stomach churned with acid, but she managed one single sip of the juice. That seemed to please Anju, who took a step away and then nodded, returning her focus to her VIT before heading for the door.

"Take however long you need," Anju called over her shoulder. "Your schedule is wide open. You're free."

Senna put the juice back on the tray and collapsed against the edge of the bed. Her head fell into her hands, and she squeezed her skull lightly, in pulses, as if feeling for open, bleeding, raw cracks. They were there, she knew, but on the inside. So many blanks. Time. Memories.

"I'm so lucky," she whispered, shocked by hot tears racing down her cheeks. If she concentrated, she could chart their path over her skin, though they fell slowly . . . so slowly . . . more like snowflakes on an icily still night, heedless of gravity or the shape of her bone structure, falling, falling . . . It seemed to take an age for them to run, salty and lukewarm, between her lips.

She raked her hands through her hair, and something gave. When she pulled her fingers lower to see, chunks of hair had come away, trapped under her fingernails. That bubble in her throat burst, panicked shivers racking her body. She stared at the dark blond hair drifting in tufts to the floor.

"What's happening to me?" she murmured. *You're so lucky,* the voice not her own reminded her. *Lucky, lucky, lucky.* "What's happening to me?"

Senna arrived at the black door to the clinical labs with her hair tucked neatly behind her ears. She couldn't stop fussing with it, which only seemed to make more strands fall out. Every time she noticed one coiling on her sleeve, she felt another clench in her stomach.

This isn't right.

That was her shield, she decided, against the hammer-to-knee reflex of her mind insisting she was lucky, just so lucky. This didn't feel like luck. It took her a moment to recognize the tall, gorgeous black woman approaching from the other end of the gallery. Before the name and personality clicked, the shape and quality of the woman's eyes were familiar. Senna didn't recognize Zurri; she recognized the same glint of fear, the same tenting of the brows that hinted at constant trepidation.

"My hair is falling out," Senna blurted.

Zurri's eyes widened and she laughed, craning her neck back. "Good morning to you, too, Senna."

A dog and a young man blew like a dust devil into the gallery, the fluffy golden dog somehow running and performing circles at the same time. Han. Again the delay, the hiccup in her brain like a fog of sleep lifting before each individual thought could become clear to her. Shapes in the mist.

"You here to see Dr. Colbie about your hair?" Zurri asked. Senna noticed her feeling along her own scalp then, but she kept her hair shaved down close to the skin, so any fallout would be far less noticeable.

"Yes, I think I must be really stressed," Senna sighed. "Or maybe it's from the treatment. Do you think it could be a side effect?"

"Senna, I can hardly figure out what day it is, you're asking the wrong person."

She frowned. "I don't like this. None of it seems . . . normal. Isn't this awfully extreme?"

"We're on a moon base getting our bad memories wiped clean," Zurri pointed out. "What part of that sentence seems normal to you? This is what we signed up for."

But her voice trailed off, and Senna heard the note of confusion in her voice. "Is it? Why are you here to see the doctor?"

"Found a bruise on my neck," Zurri replied. "Which . . . okay, it's not normal." She shot a furtive glance in every direction, then leaned down, lowering her voice. "This morning I woke up and couldn't remember where I was. I asked for all the booze to be taken out of my room, too. Does that sound like me?"

"We're here to get our memories wiped clean," Senna teased back with a sigh. "You're asking the wrong person."

"Shit, good point." Zurri lowered her voice even further. "Did you get the alert on your VIT about verboten subjects?"

"Verboten?"

"Forbidden." Zurri gestured her along impatiently.

"Oh. Yes. What about it?" Senna asked. Before she found the courage to pick herself up off the floor in Paxton's room and clean up her tearstained face, her VIT had warned her not to discuss Han's family, and to avoid any mention of fire, stalking or assistants to Zurri. Those seemed like easy enough subjects to avoid until they were well enough to leave the base.

Han and the dog sprinted together out of the gallery and back into the courtyard, vanishing into the leafy pathways. Had the dog always been there?

"I . . . I sort of want to know what it is they said about me." Zurri licked her lips. "What you're not supposed to mention. I think I want to know."

"That defeats the whole purpose of being here," Senna replied. "If we're going to experience all these awful side effects, it had better be worth it, right? Why would you want to undo the treatment?"

Zurri swore under her breath and glanced away. "I don't know. I just . . . I guess it's human nature. Can't leave well enough alone, right? I prod at things. I'm a prodder. Listen, this one model I know, she hated her lips, wanted them totally re-done. It started with fillers and injections, then getting the shape changed with tattooing, more injections, and more. She wound up with a dead girl's lips sewn on her face, a total transplant, and she hated those, too. It ruined her career, ruined her. All over lips, and she had looked just fine to start. Beautiful, even. Not perfect but indelibly her."

"What are you saying?" asked Senna, wondering what was taking Dr. Colbie so long to notice them waiting outside the door.

"I'm saying a correction can go too far, it can become an obsession, and before you know it, one minor change is you in a shady Old Manhattan clinic with a corpse's lips sewn all crooked on your face. Did I ask for too much?" Zurri inhaled through her nose, gazing up at the ceiling. "Is this my Old Manhattan? I can do that, I can go too far. Maybe I asked them to erase too much."

"Or maybe it wasn't you," Senna murmured.

"How do you mean?"

"Crap." She ducked her head, trying to swerve behind Zurri as she caught sight of Paxton up on the walkway above the gallery. If she was so lucky, then why did the sight of him make her entire body clench? *You woke up in his bed, what the hell is wrong with you?* Maybe it was just nerves. She didn't know love, she didn't know romance. And yet . . .

Some movements are just intrinsic to the body. Who had told her that? His face must have been erased for a reason.

Predictably, Paxton had spotted them, waving, changing course to walk in their direction. "I don't want to see him right now. I have to . . . Just tell him something. Tell him I had to do something. Anything."

Zurri pivoted to watch Senna scurry away. "Why don't you want to see him? He's nice enough. He might know about your side effects." She frowned, going on and on while Senna slipped away. "Do you know what? I'm having a recovered memory of him . . . which is ironic, considering what we're doing here. I think we met at a party maybe. He made some dumb crack about being the smartest man in the world and we all just stared at him. So awkward."

"Just . . . make up an excuse! I'm sorry! Thank you! I'm sorry!" Senna tried not to run, but just a glimpse of Paxton sent a flurry of nervous tingles down her spine. She couldn't look at him, and he called something she couldn't quite make out as she followed Han and Lula, escaping into the courtyard. She blinked, and lightning flashed across the backs of her eyes, white-hot forks like veins stamped into her vision as she dove behind a tree and tried to catch her breath.

This isn't right.

"This is your life, worry-free!" It was . . . her own voice, coming from somewhere deeper along the path. Senna dodged out from behind the tree and followed the sound, hugging herself. It grew louder as she took the blue-and-white-mosaic path to the right, along a tight bend and into a more private grove of sheltering fronds, with two benches placed across from each other, nestled between statues. A pair of lovebirds cooed in a tree above the left bench, where Han was engrossed in a vid playing on a loop, hovering above his VIT. At his feet, the fluffy dog rested her chin on the ball between her paws.

Senna clamped both hands over her mouth, watching herself smile into the camera, wearing a loose white crop top she didn't recognize and tan pants cinched at the waist, her hair swinging cheerfully around her face as she leaned casually against a statue pedestal.

"Hi, I'm Senna Slate. I'm sure you recognize me, most people do. But I didn't want to be known just for my pain, who would? Therapists and psychologists told me I was a lost cause, but I have a new start and a new life now, thanks to the LENG program at the Dome on Ganymede. The state-of-the-art technology here developed by Paxton Dunn and administered by a team of qualified MSC professionals can help you overcome even the most traumatic experiences." It had looped back to the part she heard through the leaves. On the vid, Senna grinned and lifted up her hands, gesturing to the Dome ceiling as the camera panned to take in a broader view of the facility. "This is your life, worry-free!"

"What the *fuck*?"

Han shrieked, freezing as she stomped up to the bench, the dog nosing curiously at her ankles. "Whoa! I'm sorry . . . You're not supposed to see this. I mean, duh. Obviously. Shit. I'm so, so sorry, it's just Paxton uploaded the new ads he finished and he asked me to watch yours and give him ideas. He values my feedback, you know?"

"*You're fourteen!*" she screamed, lashing out at the vid, her hand passing right through it.

Han's mouth fell open and he went pale, staring down at his lap while the vid fizzled out, leaving them both in stunned silence. "I didn't make it," he said quietly.

"I don't remember saying those things!" Senna balled up her hands into fists. "I wouldn't say that! I wouldn't . . . I don't . . ."

She pressed those fists into her eyes, grinding. "What is happening to me?"

"Don't cry! Hey . . . I'm really sorry, please don't cry," Han pleaded. "Listen, okay? Hey, listen. I'll tell Paxton to delete the footage. I know I'm only fourteen, but he wants me to stay on and be his apprentice. If that's the case, then he should respect what I say. I'm sure he would get rid of this if he knew it would upset you so much. He . . . he really cares about you, Senna."

She almost raked her hands through her hair but didn't want any more of it to fall out. "I don't care about him! I don't *know* him!" That vid of her was proof enough. Something didn't add up. Why would she not remember filming it? How well could the treatment be working if only fragments of her mind remained? "You shouldn't stay here with him, Han. You should go back to your family."

"I don't know why you guys keep saying that." Han grimaced, standing. Lula rearranged herself to settle beside the bench, away from all the shuffling feet. "There's nobody out there for me, I don't *have* a family."

Senna didn't care about the instructions she had been given. Would it hurt him? Would he even believe her? She brought her VIT up to eye level and dove into her recent messages, bringing up the advisory from that morning.

"Look." She pointed. "We're not supposed to discuss your family, right? Then that means you have one."

"Maybe they're dead," Han pointed out, his lower lip bending. "M-Maybe that's why I'm here and why I want to forget about it. You're not supposed to do this! You're sabotaging me!"

As she pointed at her messages, another appeared, this one from Zurri.

I told him you were PMSing and needed to lie down but he
said you weren't? Kinda weird. Anyway, he's still looking
for you.

Senna let out a frustrated groan and tore at the VIT strapped
to her wrist. "This is how he can find me, right? This thing
tracks us."

"If you have the implant—"

"I don't. Thank God." Senna didn't know why she lacked the
implant, only that she did. That knowledge still remained, but
not how she had avoided getting one. Blinking, she saw a flash of
a screen, a form she was filling out on a tablet, something about
VIT implant policies interfering with her religious beliefs. Was
she religious? *It's all gone, he's taken everything from me. And for
what? Some rosy advertisements?*

"Good riddance." Throwing the VIT down on the path, she
hoped it broke. "Don't tell him you saw me."

"But—" She saw Han kick her discarded VIT into the bushes.

"I have to write down what I know, what I remember."
Senna picked a path, and took it, and hoped it was the right one.
"I can't let him take any more."

27

Dozens of Earth vids had taught Han what getting called into the "principal's office" meant, but this was his first time really getting the flavor of that feeling. Those were all pre–space migration vids, when kids and teenagers crowded into nondescript brick buildings and shoved one another into lockers, ate in a shared cafeteria and did their homework on paper.

Fly casual, he told himself, wondering if whistling would be too much and give him away. *Like your namesake.*

"I know you saw her," Paxton was saying. Behind his spectacles, his eyes drifted off toward where Han had hidden her VIT. "The camera feeds will pick her up, but you can just tell me what happened." He turned back to face Han, a mild, half-disappointed frown tugging at his lips. "She's not in trouble, neither are you."

Han didn't know where his loyalties lay exactly. There was nothing *wrong* with Senna per se, but something weird and squidgy happened behind his eyes whenever she came near, like he couldn't quite see her correctly. Interference, he thought. By-product of the therapy? Was something about her changed or erased from his memories? That would explain the dodgy feeling he got around her. On the other hand, Paxton had given him a dog, and offered him a place to stay, giving him the opportunity of a lifetime. A dream handed to him on a silver platter.

"Maybe she should be in trouble," Han muttered.

Paxton laughed through his nose. "Oh?"

It was easier to look down at Lula, so he watched his own hand stroke across her forehead and then outline her bushy eyebrows with his thumb. "What happened with my family?" he asked. "Senna said . . . she said I have a family, but that can't be right. I don't remember them."

Paxton stared at him for a moment. "Han? Come with me. I want to show you something."

"I'm really not in trouble?"

"Trouble?! Ha. Jesus, no." Paxton veered back around toward the gallery, walking slowly, letting Han make up his mind and catch up. "It's the opposite of trouble. It's a reward."

Han's eyes lit up. "Can the dog come? I think I'm getting attached."

"She should stay here, I think. You can toggle it in the app."

A reward. What would it be? Just getting asked to stay on at the Dome was reward enough, and Han didn't know how he had earned it. The days ran together, a blur, something Paxton warned him about before and after each LENG session. That Han couldn't remember what exactly went on during the treatment hours was normal, too, Paxton assured him. They were still measuring how long a full recovery would take; Han, Zurri and Senna were, after all, the LENG therapy pioneers. He just remembered Paxton keeping him long after a therapy session, asking if Han was interested in a mentorship program.

Paxton had just finished typing something on his VIT when Han caught up to him. Servitor Sixteen clanked past them, going back toward the direction of the benches.

"Make sure you get it to my office," Paxton told the Servitor in passing. "How did you feel after Senna mentioned your family? Disoriented?"

"No, not disoriented, just confused." Han fell into step with Paxton, trying to mimic his cool, casual swagger. They walked beneath the wide-open archway leading into the gallery. The table and chairs for lunch were being printed as they entered. "Is she right? Do I have a family?"

Paxton's head bobbled back and forth, weighing the question. "You did, Han. You wanted me to erase those memories. Your mother died tragically, and you couldn't escape her memory. Her voice is used almost universally for in-home assistants. She's the voice of the elevators on the station, of the default text-to-speech program for VITs. Our company—my company—hired her for all of it. How could you leave your own house, when she was everywhere? Waiting to ambush you. It was paralyzing."

"I can't remember her at all." Han frowned. "It's like I was raised by ghosts. I remember the Servitor nannies and tutors, but nothing else."

"That's because in truth there wasn't much else," explained Paxton, leading Han around the in-progress table and toward the doors set into the alcove beneath the upper walkway and Paxton's office. "We're so alike, it's tragic. You're half–bubble boy, I was all bubble boy. My brother was born with a whole litany of problems. Back then they didn't know as much about extraterrestrial pregnancy protocols. Alec didn't live to see ten, so when I came along, they were cautious. *Extra* cautious."

"I'm sorry about your brother," Han replied.

"My parents panicked if I developed as much as a sniffle," he chuckled, the doors opening at his approach. "They kept me in isolation, and let me assure you that a bunker in the French countryside is not a thrilling place for a young man to grow up. It was my entire world until I was eighteen; there, I had nothing to do with my time but study, and work. And dream. My father liked to joke that my dreams grew so big because my world was so small."

Han felt like those words could've been his. "Wow, yeah, I know what you mean."

"Now it's easier for me to just be here, not alone but somewhat apart. The marvels of the station and the colonies appealed to me, but not everything that came with it. The people, mostly. That doesn't mean isolation isn't sometimes lonely."

Han hadn't laid eyes on that part of the facility before. A transparent enclosure housed an industrial kitchen, a labyrinth of vents, stainless steel countertops, islands and convection ovens. Maximized for space, eight partial Servitors worked on magnetic rails built into the floor and ceiling, pinging back and forth across the kitchen as they managed about a dozen different steaming pots. They flew past one another with absolute precision, pincer-like arms raising and lowering to avoid collisions.

"Where the sausage gets made," Paxton joked. "Literally. Now you'll see it figuratively." He took a sharp right, leading Han toward an unmarked silver door just to the right of where the kitchen enclosure began. "I'm going to show you how LENG really works."

"No way," Han breathed. "That's . . . But nobody . . ."

"I know," Paxton chuckled, and manually input a password and log-in into his VIT to open the silver door. Han shivered, overwhelmed with a sudden tremor of déjà vu. "About your family—"

"Yeah," Han sighed. "It's heavy. I don't know what to think. There's really nobody left?"

"You have a family here if you want it. You're a smart kid and you can handle yourself, but I don't want to see you end up like me—"

And there Han made a huffing *pah* of incredulity. Who *didn't* want to be like Paxton Dunn?

"Well, not *exactly* like me. I could've built this facility on the station, but I'm selfish, and I like my little kingdom here. It's been more interesting with all of you here." Paxton motioned for Han to follow him down a tight, narrow corridor. It only led in one direction, no doors or windows except for a faintly visible open archway at the very, very end. "Trying, too, but interesting."

"You have Anju, Brea, and Dr. Colbie," Han pointed out. "And that dog! You're not a bubble boy anymore."

"Right." Paxton nodded, tight on Han's heels. "But an infusion of fresh blood now and then is always welcome."

Returning to her rooms just long enough to grab her canvas and paints, Senna wandered the facility, desperate for a place to hide. A place to think.

This morning I woke up in a strange man's bed.

She could still smell the sheets and vague hints of his cologne clinging to her clothing. Whenever she caught a whiff of it, another knot tied itself into her guts. She couldn't even retrace the steps of the night before, and whenever she tried, her head gave a warning pulse, warding her off. *That way lies pain*, it seemed to say.

That's okay, she thought. *Let the pain come.*

That was what she had been running from, of course, pain. Why else would she be there? Something terrible had happened, and now she was clinging to the last concrete memories that remained. Even those were beginning to go soft, a life of vapor, constantly in danger of blowing away. That couldn't just be a side effect. If it was, wouldn't they have sedated her until this all passed? Did they want her to panic like that? Something was wrong. *Something is all wrong.*

Han and Zurri seemed just fine, so why did every step through the facility make her feel like the next could be into liquid, a plunge off the edge and then to drown? Paxton had gotten his hooks nice and deep into Han, but maybe she could persuade Zurri to leave with her. With her fame and money and power, she had to be able to just call it all off; angering her would be a PR disaster.

PR. Senna wanted to shrivel up at the thought of that ad. That wasn't her, it didn't even sound like her, that peppy, upbeat energy and cheesy grin. How could she have said those things and felt that way and not remembered it? It was utterly unethical to consider leveraging a tragedy she didn't even know about to sell this place to other people. But that was what Paxton wanted from her.

And I woke up in his bed.

She was going to be sick. Her wandering took her to the walkway above the gallery. Paxton's office doors had gone black. No sign of him or Han, or the other staff. There, on the left side of the walkway with a view down to the clinical lab door, she could wait for Zurri to come out. She would try to make her case, and see if she could convince the model to help her leave. If her schedule was clear and there were no more treatments, surely she could convalesce back on the station? Marin would probably let her move back in.

Senna crumpled onto a bench beside a rectangular plinth, a halved metal orb floating there. This place was so strange, part beauty, part confusion. How would she ever explain it to Marin? Marin . . . She closed her eyes and willed the memories to return. Marin. How was she connected to Marin? Not a blood relation, surely, but then why had she spent so much time in that woman's apartment? Islands. Every remaining memory was an island, a fogged sea of hesitation swirling between landmasses, confusing and confounding her. How she had met Marin, what the nature of their relationship was, had drowned in that awful sea, but Marin . . . Marin she remembered. And her husband, Jonathan.

Islands. Two islands nestled against each other in the dark blank of her mind.

At least she concretely remembered their faces. They would take her in; they had to. Unless that had gone sour, too. Every memory uncertain, she moaned, slamming her head against the all-black canvas in her hands, every memory booby-trapped. She hit her head harder with the canvas, as if by some miracle it would fix the jumble her mind had become.

"Who is it?" she heard a man say from around the statue pedestal. She froze, but it wasn't Paxton. "I know you're there."

Senna cried out, a surge of pressure in her head almost knocking her off the bench. The edge of the canvas dug into her forehead as she went half-blind and the ache crested and then gradually subsided. When she opened her eyes, a dark-haired man with a kind, handsome face was crouching at her side. He had the most beautiful golden eyes, and even while she shivered behind the canvas, she didn't want to look away from them.

"Hello, Senna," he said gently. "I'm Efren. It's nice to meet you again."

"Please don't tell Paxton I'm here!" she cried, squeezing her eyes shut.

"Why would I do that?" he asked laughingly.

"Because you work here, right? Or maybe . . . I'm sorry, my thoughts are so tangled up."

Efren shook his head, an inky black swoop of hair falling loose from behind his left ear. "I won't tell a soul where you are, Senna. I promise."

"Thank you. You . . . you said we've met," she murmured, her voice heavy with lethargic difficulty. It was odd; she could vividly picture the other staff, but not him. "I'm sorry, I don't remember you. But I don't remember a lot of things."

"I can see that. Please, stop apologizing, you've given no offense, not any of the times we've met." Efren stood, and looking at him, Senna felt the pain in her mind drift away. Just his presence landed like a balm. "Do you know how many days you've been here?"

Senna shook her head automatically, aware that even trying to recall that would just bring on another flash of discomfort and frustration. "No, I don't. But you've seen me before."

"Oh, yes," he said, a bit sad. "Many times. You've been here three days. That's Dome days, not the Ganymede sort. And thank Christ for that."

She managed a weak laugh. "Three days. Three days, and I can only remember this morning, and bits and pieces. Zurri and Han, the staff, Paxton . . ." She shuddered, then lowered the canvas, recalling that she had brought her paints along. Her eyes roamed to the clinical lab door, but Zurri hadn't yet emerged. She didn't want to risk going into the labs to find her. If Dr. Colbie was in there, then she might alert Paxton to Senna's whereabouts. "I'm waiting for someone, can I paint you in the meantime?"

"This is a new suit," he teased.

"Not *on* you." Senna blushed, showing him the canvas. "Would that be okay?"

"I've never been painted before," Efren replied, striking a straight-postured, rigid pose next to the statue base with the halved orb on it. "Will it hurt?"

"Only if I stick these up your nose." Opening the painting kit, she reached in and grabbed two brushes, jabbing them toward him playfully.

"I'm amazed you can make jokes at all," he replied. "You seemed distressed just now. Are you all right?"

"Not at all." Senna rested the canvas on her thighs and opened a tube of paint. Just the scent, just the feel of the brushes made her feel more herself. If she could still paint, if this skill remained, then maybe she hadn't forgotten every piece of herself. Maybe by painting she could connect those isolated islands, build bridges between them. "I want to leave, but I don't think I can do it alone." She winced. "Crap, I shouldn't have said that."

"Why not?" he asked.

She dipped her brush into a bit of ochre and began to daub, needing to gaze at him for reference less than she expected. *He exists somewhere in my mind. We've met before.* "Because you're with the staff. You must want me to stay. You'll tell Paxton what I said."

"Rather." Efren cleared his throat. "I'd like to leave, too."

Senna's brush stopped mid-stroke. "You would? But . . ."

"Keep painting and I'll explain," Efren told her calmly, and as before, it made the knots in her stomach go away. She remembered Anju, Brea, Dr. Colbie. If she couldn't remember him, then perhaps she didn't want to. Or, she thought with a grimace, someone else didn't want her to. *You're so lucky*, the unwanted voice reminded her. *Chosen.*

No, she countered. *Cursed.*

"What do you know about black holes?" Efren asked.

Senna moved her brush carefully in a small circle, noticing the black paint beneath roiling as if it had come to life, reverting from dried to wet. Her eyelids drooped, suddenly heavy. Black holes. It hadn't occurred to her until that moment that she had been the one to paint that canvas all black, and now she couldn't help but wonder what it was hiding, what she had painted over, what image a past Senna had wanted to obliterate that was hidden beneath.

28

No amount of therapy or mind alteration would keep Zurri from being nosy. She was born nosy, she would remain nosy. In the early days of her career, she got sly at checking through the other models' bags, checking for pills, cash or just juicy gossip. She learned that stealing a dollar or two never got her caught, and sometimes it was enough for one more rice ball before the money ran out and rent came due. Tokyo had almost wrung her dry so many times that she kept all her clothes neatly packed in the suitcase in the apartment she shared with six other girls.

Zurri never asked her dad or sister for cash. Point of pride. The second she did, they would pressure her to give up her career, take the L and join them on Tokyo Bliss. Dr. Iyanda, as he insisted on being called lest one be firmly reminded that he "had not put himself through ten years of school and earned three degrees to be called mister," would even pay for her passenger fee and find her a job to smooth over immigration. Wouldn't she like to work in a nice clinic as a receptionist?

Her sister, Eni (also technically holding a doctoral degree but more lenient about the usage), worked as an attorney and lived in the university district. She had been the one to teach Zurri how to frighten any man into silence with just the slightest squint of the eye and imperious tilt of the head. She also liked to send Zurri taunting pictures of her spacious flat, and all the ramen, mapo tofu and pizza she could afford now that she was angling to make partner at her firm.

When Zurri got her revenge by sending pictures of her first six-figure contract, it didn't go over so well. Now they talked only on holidays, and Zurri had stopped inviting the family to her birthday parties. They never showed up anyway.

Senna's birthday, as it turned out, was December 9, 2248. She hadn't read Senna as a Sagittarius, but then, she had only known her two days. Three days? Zurri sighed. The console screen open behind Dr. Colbie's shoulder was just visible from where Zurri stood, while the tall, untalkative doctor examined the back of her neck. With Dr. Colbie in heels, they were about the same height.

Wanting to snoop, Zurri turned just a fraction to the right, hoping to catch more of Senna's patient records displayed on the screen. Something there might explain the hair loss, at least.

"Is this position uncomfortable?" Dr. Colbie asked.

Like most doctors Zurri had met, Dr. Colbie chose not to wear perfume. That said, the woman had an almost unearthly, inhuman lack of smell. Not even a whiff of soap or hair product. Nothing on her breath, either, not toothpaste or coffee or evidence of lunch.

"Um, well, my neck hurts," Zurri replied coolly. "That *is* why I'm here."

"Yes, and as I stated before, you have a known history of alcohol and drug abuse, Zurri. It doesn't make me happy to say it, but this could all just be from a drunken accident. Try not to fidget," Dr. Colbie instructed. She carefully pressed two fingers along the ridge of Zurri's upper spine. "There is some moderate bruising present. Any tingling in your fingers? Numbness?"

"Not that I've noticed." Her fingers were cool and dry as they ghosted along Zurri's neck. The angle was no good. She couldn't read much more of Senna's file, just the header text, but the actual records and notes were too tiny to read from that vantage.

The headers, however, caught her eye. **Family History, Allergies, Prescriptions** and most tantalizing of all: **LENG Session Notes**.

"I can prescribe you a topical numbing gel," Dr. Colbie said, taking a step back.

"Hm. Any CBD?"

"Nice try," she sighed. "Stay put, I'll get the gel from storage."

Zurri painted on a placid smile, arms crossed while she waited for Dr. Colbie to disappear. The storage area was directly behind Dr. Colbie's desk, guarded by two serious-looking doors with magnetic locks. Luckily, when she went through, it was large enough to hold a maze of shelves, and the instant Dr. Colbie vanished around a corner, Zurri hopped over to take a look at Senna's records. It was even more tempting to try to find her own, but she was shit with consoles, and she doubted Colbie would be gone long.

Prescriptions actually were of interest. Zurri recognized Zolapro right away, a heavy-duty antianxiety medication she herself had tried a few months ago. It was fresh out of trials, marketed toward modern women with modern anxieties, but Zurri hated the way it made her hold water weight. It also, she saw, enlarging the text around it, in rare cases caused hair loss.

"Mystery solved," she murmured. "But why are you on this?"

Better yet, why didn't Senna *know* she was on it? With any medication that serious, a doctor would ethically have to warn about the potential side effects. But there was more, much more, as Zurri hurled a quick glance over her shoulder, listening to Colbie rummage among the shelves, before hurrying to check the LENG notes section.

"Oh my God," she breathed, counting the individual session numbers. Something hard and hot and choking gathered in her chest as she took it all in. In the just under seventy-two hours of Senna staying in the Dome, she had spent twenty of those hours over nine sessions receiving the LENG treatment. That didn't seem right. *Twenty hours?*

Behind her, in the storage room, she heard Dr. Colbie drop something and give a soft "Darn."

Of course she didn't swear. Zurri swiveled back to the notes. There would have to be an explanation for that length of treatment. Unless they were all spending that much time with the tech? Wouldn't she remember that? Could she?

Sessions 1 and 2 seemed normal enough, the notes reading:

Encouraging signs of progress adjusting connections regarding neural markers 12 to 38. Demesne DW Crash likely absorbed. Further exposure required to loosen connection between markers 38 and 41.

From Session 3 onward the notes became scattered. Erratic.

Session 3:

> Emergency exposure required after participant displayed
> acute signs of relapse. Emergency neural scan adminis-
> tered. Emergency termination of Demesne Dome Miscel-
> lany, Demesne A. Death, Demesne Recent Interpersonal
> Trauma. Six additional Demesne flagged for examination.

Session 6:

> Further relapse. Participant proving resistant to termina-
> tion of markers 67 to 89. Keep under observation. Pre-
> scribe 25 mg Zolapro to manage post-treatment reactivity.

Session 7:

> Participant displaying resistance to LENG absorption, rec-
> ommend moderate sedation throughout sessions.
> PD: Zolapro resulting in marked difference, participant
> far more compliant, in and out of LENG sessions.

A cold finger ran down Zurri's spine. *What the hell is going on here?* Trembling, she glanced over her shoulder one more time, hearing Dr. Colbie's clicking heels coming nearer. She was returning. Zurri fumbled with her VIT, managing to quick-open the camera function and snap an image of the file before throwing herself across the desk and back to her original position.

When Dr. Colbie emerged from the storage room, Zurri was forcing her hands not to shake while she pretended to examine her nails. Dr. Colbie knew about the sessions. Dr. Colbie was taking these notes. Dr. Colbie, Zurri decided with a growl, was at best complicit and at worst actively shredding Senna's mind with the technology.

One word glared in front of Zurri's eyes as she held out her palm expectantly.

Compliant.

She had a bone-deep, gut-level, feminine hatred of that word. Even when she saw it used on dry instructional pamphlets on transports, she felt her lip curl. Compliance had never been her thing. She hadn't become the most recognized face in beauty and fashion by complying with anything, and now, to see that word there, in that context, in a decidedly menacing and not-dry-pamphlet way, lit an inferno under her ass. They were drugging Senna, and, one could only assume, they were drugging her and the kid, too. Han did seem awfully content, awfully *compliant.* And it was out of character for Zurri to just accept a radical change to the rider she had submitted pre-arrival. Shit. Was *she* complying, too? Dr. Colbie placed the tube of gel in Zurri's hand, and she almost popped it open with the force of closing her fingers around it.

"Don't overuse it or it will give you a rash," Dr. Colbie instructed. "Not ideal, I'd imagine, for someone in your profession."

"Thanks bunches." Zurri pushed away from the desk, striding with new purpose toward the door, smiling with a clack, showing Dr. Colbie her teeth.

29

Han stood bathed in the eerie, pale light of LENG's source, watching it churn in place, a silver glob no bigger than his fist. Suspended in midair, two massive conductors above and below held it in place, the magnetic field containing it so loud, so powerful, that every hair on Han's arms had stood on end as he inched closer to the observation barrier.

In the old vids, kids his age would spend their summers at run-down pools in falling-down community centers. The room reminded him of that. Big and cavernous, echoing with its emptiness, and at the center of it all, in a space carved out just for its containment and existence, floated the silver orb. On the other side of it, opposite from where Han and Paxton stood, a curved disc like a lens sat outside the magnetic field, a tube no wider than Han's pinkie finger extending out from that lens and into the wall, disappearing into a hole there.

"This is the only place it could safely be removed from its

original vessel," Paxton explained, arms crossed and head tilted to the side while he watched Han watch the orb. "It had to be this place. Ganymede. We needed the magnetic core, the raw magnetic potential of the moon to part gift from wrapping."

Han could only glance at the orb in fits and starts. Even if it only appeared to be a weird glob of mercury-like substance, he knew that couldn't be it. It *pulled* on him. The moment he stepped foot into the room, he sensed a million eyes boring into him, seeing through him, the presence of a million invisible bodies, the chaos of a million barely perceptible whispers. Whenever he let himself observe the orb for too long, his eyelids began to droop. He would snap himself out of the lull, only to be drawn back again.

"D. J. Natarajan's craft picked it up on scanners before his communications went dark. It was the last comm to make it out, pinged off of the deep-space Merchantia HQ receivers." Paxton smiled as if recalling a fond memory.

"He's the one who got too close to Sagittarius A," Han murmured, hypnotized.

"No accident," Paxton replied brusquely, as if it were obvious. "He piloted right into that supermassive of his own volition."

"Why?" Han whispered. Why would anyone want to die that way? Of course, death from a black hole could only be a theory. Nobody really knew what actually went on past the point of no return.

"Because he wanted to know what would happen," said Paxton. "I would do the same. Right now, I can feel that thing willing me to look at it. Pulling on me."

"But what *is* it?"

The magnetic field, or maybe the orb itself, emitted a constant, rhythmic *wrlub-wrlub-wrlub*, a sound Han knew he would never forget, a harnessed lullaby. The silver orb shifted and rearranged itself, appearing, in Han's eyes, to be struggling against some inner, living creature, struggling and fighting to get out.

"D. J. Natarajan's last comm," Paxton sighed. "A single object resisting the pull from a supermassive black hole: this orb, contained within a metal never seen before by man. What do you think he saw? The whole of the universe stretching out in every direction, in all its infinite layers? The light of every star shining toward you, beamed into your eyes? Do you think the light bent around him in a perfect circle? Do you think he knew when he began to fall through time, or was he dead on a cellular level before he ever experienced the forever fall?"

Han tore himself away from the orb, staring up at Paxton instead. His eyes had filled with strange glitter, his mouth slack. It looked like he had fallen asleep with his eyes wide open. A single bead of blood trickled from Paxton's nostril.

"You're bleeding," Han murmured. A dark halo hung around Paxton's shoulder, then flashed, and Han clutched his stomach as if he had been punched. Another wave of déjà vu crashed over him, weightier than the last.

"Damn." Paxton brought himself out of his daze, pulling a tissue from his pocket and dabbing at his lip. "I should . . . should adjust the humidifiers."

Han squinted. "Could it be an actual black hole in there? One the size of a single particle? But how is it not distorting space and time around it? How could you even recover it from space? The density alone—"

"We don't know *what* it is," Paxton admitted with a shrug and a dry laugh. He tucked the folded tissue back into his pocket. "Black holes don't produce anything, but this thing was *right there* on the edge, just . . . just hanging out, defying all the laws of physics. When we found it, the shell and its contents weighed about a kilo. But once we measured the orb and the field and did a little math, the orb turned out to weigh nine hundred and seventy kilos. Mad, right?"

"A black hole would weigh more than that," Han said slowly. "Way, way more. At least a solar mass."

"Theoretically, yes," replied Paxton. "We had all sorts of theories, still do. Me, I mean. I do." He rubbed the back of his head and then adjusted his spectacles. "I'm sure you'd have theories, too. If you stay, you get to study this sweet baby with me. Discover all of its secrets."

Study it with him? Han brightened. "You think I could do that? You think I'm ready?"

"You will be," Paxton assured him. "I've set a few tests for you, and you've passed them all. I had to make sure you were bright enough, and ruthless enough, and I was right . . . you are. So even if you're not ready to study LENG right this minute, I'm confident you will be one day, and I'd like a protégé. It's time."

Han forced himself not to glance at the orb again, though he could feel it sucking on the edge of his vision, trying to entice him to look once more. "But you're using it, aren't you? You said this is what fuels the LENG tech."

"We know it's dense, we know it generates an incredible amount of energy, and we know that energy can be focused with the metamaterial lens." And there he pointed to the contraption set up on the other side of the orb and the tube feeding into the wall. "That force can be targeted with incredible precision." Paxton stared at him for a moment, while Han chewed the inside of his cheek, trying to decide how he felt. Sick, for one. Terrified, for another. "Han, you're the last person I expected to be

MADELEINE ROUX

squeamish about new tech capabilities. This is *the* frontier. There is no frontier farther out than this that you can reach, not even on one of my science vessels. This right here, what we're studying, is it."

"Why do you keep saying 'we'?" Han asked softly. It was the easiest question to reach for. The other questions, the scary ones, still felt too big to grasp. Paxton didn't even understand the energy source he was using to manipulate the connections between their memories. And Han would never describe himself as technologically squeamish, never, he had begged to get his VIT-optimizing implant early. Begged. Begged . . . someone. He had a mother, Paxton had told him as much; he must have begged her.

Han shivered, realizing that if he stayed, this man would be his new family.

"My partner was the one who scooped up the LENG particle in its shell," Paxton replied, irritated. He tapped his foot noisily on the floor, though it was mostly drowned out by the commotion of the magnetic field generators. "Among other things. And unlike D. J. Natarajan, he decided not to fly his ass directly across the event horizon. Nobody boldly went like Glen—he and Misato Iwasa cooked up the specs for the Mars HQ colony, for this facility—shit, he recovered Natarajan's last comm, this." He gestured to the orb floating behind him. "The original Foxfire sample recovery? First fucking contact? All him. The man was brilliant." Paxton paused, and reached into his pocket again, and Han saw his hand close around something more solid than a wad of tissue. "Brilliant but soft. Sensitive. Too sensitive for this place. For what it does to you."

The bubble boy in isolation, Han thought, taking a tiny step back. *The bubble man in isolation.*

"I'm not soft," Han squeaked. He didn't dare ask what had

happened to his partner. "I just . . . I don't know if I like that you used LENG on us when you're not even sure what it is. O-Of course I want to study it. Of course I want to know what it does. Who wouldn't?"

Paxton's posture relaxed and he blew out a blubbery breath. Then he let go of whatever was in his pocket and pushed both hands through his dark, wavy hair. "Jesus. Stay here long enough, this thing does something to you, I swear."

The dark edge surging off Paxton's shoulders remained in place as he walked toward Han. That darkness coalesced, bleeding down and out, growing a head. It stood, now apart and whole, a shadow with the size and density of a man. Han trembled and raised his hand to point, but the shadow stepped behind Paxton and gently placed its long black hands on the man's shoulders, guiding him resolutely past Han and toward the door. As they went, Han could feel the shadow's attention turn toward him, watchful and observant without eyes. It took one slender black arm and lifted it, pushing a finger to where its lips might be, warning him to be quiet.

Han opened and closed his mouth, but couldn't—wouldn't—speak. What was this thing, and what did it want from him? He shook and clenched his fists, and worried for a moment that he had peed his pants. But the shadow turned away, and focused on Paxton again, steering him toward the door.

"Who needs a vacation?" Paxton called back to him, barking with laughter. "Or a drink. Jesus."

Han hesitated, afraid to go near the shadow and afraid to be left alone with the silver orb. He stopped to see it one more time, indulging it, sensing it wanted to be seen. It couldn't be a real black hole, even an infinitesimally small one, could it? It would have to weigh more, be more, do more. But he couldn't shake the feeling that there was something trapped inside that liquid silver goo. Maybe that was why its surface seemed so strained, because it was holding so much—a puncture in the universe, the combined life and energy and matter of an entire star.

All that concentrated mass pointed at his head, angled against his thoughts, shot into his brain. And if it had taken his memories away, then somewhere inside the swirling silver mass, the image and voice and warmth of his mother might just be mingling with the anamnesis of a dead, imploded star.

30

"I don't understand." Senna finally put down her brush. The painting was nearly complete. She glanced up at Efren, and he was steadily returning her gaze. "How can a black hole take away our memories?"

Pushing back from the statue pedestal, Efren came to stand over her, scratching his chin thoughtfully as he gathered his thoughts. "Because it isn't a black hole, not exactly. Dunn doesn't know what he has. When a star collapses, it takes everything with it, planets, moons, meteors, civilizations. There is a supernova, and something is expelled. Something is always expelled. The concentration of star, moon, rock, water, life. What the supernova spits out, what's left behind, is the Vestige."

"And . . . that's what he has?" Senna's brain felt tired. She had never been one for science; art and storytelling and caretaking had always been her forte. But she tried to follow, realizing by the second that her survival depended on that understanding. Not the survival of her body, perhaps, but the survival of her heart and mind. "Paxton found the Vestige?"

"It precedes the black hole, and it is part of it, but they are not the same," Efren told her, crouching near the bench again, bringing them eye to eye. "The Vestige contains immense energy, power . . ." He swallowed with difficulty, briefly glancing at his shoes. "And danger. He does not understand it, but like all men of hubris, he would use it anyway."

Sighing, Efren stood and strode back to the statue pedestal. His hand hovered over the split container there, molding around it as if trying to memorize its shape, but without touching it. There was something sad in the movement, like a last dance, familiar and forlorn. "This place is a prison, Senna. For you and for me. You must escape it."

"If you're a prisoner, then you'll come with us," she pointed out plainly. "But you're not telling me something. I can guess, but I'm afraid to."

He smiled, laughing lightly. "There is a profound connection," he murmured, continuing to shape his hand around the broken orb. "Between the shape of space, matter and motion, just as there is a profound connection between the shape of space, matter and man. Being here, watching you all, has taught me that. There is also a connection between you, the boy and the model. It will take all three of you working together to leave this place. She intrigues him because she slighted him, you intrigue him more because he sees you as similar, two beings raised in isolation. The boy's mother is the voice of almost every machine in the universe now, and he can't stand it, it will trap him here, make him Paxton's prisoner and his protégé."

"Han looks up to Paxton," she replied. "I don't know how to convince him to leave."

Efren shrugged. "It may be easier than you think. Dunn lives in isolation for a reason, his temper cannot withstand even mild debate. As much as he thinks he is like Han, they're very different. The boy is genuinely clever, all of Paxton's brilliance is a lie. Stolen. Cleverness is not the same as ruthlessness."

"How do you know him?" she asked, standing and setting down the painting to dry where she had been sitting. "At least tell me that much."

The statue pedestal and the broken canister lay between them. Efren's golden eyes shifted away from his hand and to her, and she felt fleetingly breathless. What she saw there frightened her, but called to her, too.

"When you go into that horrid little dark room, Paxton feeds your unwanted memories to LENG, and you cannot remember the terror of it because he makes damn sure that you don't." Efren squeezed his eyes shut, breaking their strange connection. "He stops the Vestige before it can take too much from you, but there is a way for it to take everything. Dunn did not build this place alone, nor did he find and harness the Vestige alone."

The black door down on the gallery level opened. Senna jumped, rushing to the railing and waving frantically at Zurri as she emerged. The model spotted her right away, sprinting toward the ramp, a little tube clutched in her hand. When Senna turned back to tell Efren to continue, he was gone. She was standing rigid, in stunned silence, when Zurri reached her.

"We need to get the fuck out of here," Zurri said, grabbing her by the wrist.

"Yes, we do," Senna whispered, hoarse. "I . . . I don't know how."

Down below, Dr. Colbie wandered out onto the gallery, distracted by her VIT, but Senna clearly saw her glancing up at them furtively, spying.

"They're watching us," Senna hissed. "And I threw my VIT in a bush! How do we even call for help?" *It will take all three of you working together to leave this place.* "Han . . . we need to find him, get him away from Paxton. He'll know how to get a message out to the satellite to send a shuttle."

She decided against telling Zurri that a potential hallucination had just given her advice on how to escape. Just to be sure, she checked the bench, and the portrait was there, Efren's likeness perfectly captured. A tiny flash of light danced across it. So he was real, or at least real enough in her mind to faithfully render with oil paint.

"Act casual," Zurri instructed, leading her closer to the railing, in full view of Dr. Colbie. "Of course I'll tell you all about the last dance party on Ibiza, you messy gossip," she crowed theatrically, swatting Senna on the shoulder. Then in an undertone: "Smile and pretend we're bullshitting."

"You . . . um . . . you better watch out! Or I'll sell this to the drama blogs!" Senna lifted one shoulder and Zurri rolled her eyes.

"Close enough," she whispered. "Do not react when I tell you this, okay? Nod if you understand."

Senna clenched her jaw, lips hurting from her big, fake smile, but she nodded.

"These bastards are drugging you. Do you know what Zolapro is?"

Senna shook her head no.

"It's an antianxiety med, a real heavy hitter. This shit could turn a torrential downpour into a sun shower, get me? It can make your hair fall out."

She stifled a gasp, not just because of the violation of her trust, but because she remembered, vaguely, Marin tossing her wig across the room, lamenting her new medication's side effects. "Oh my God!" she let that one go, loud, channeling her frustration into it while trying to sound pleasantly scandalized and not like she was about to rip the railing out of the floor. "No way!"

"Fucking way. They've put you into that LENG room for twenty hours," she hurried on, fake smile eerily in place. "I saw your file open on her console. It's bad, Senna. Real bad. We need to get out of here before they wipe me and I lose everything I know."

"We have to work together," Senna told her softly, squeezing her arm back. There was no time to panic, no time to rage. She had to focus, plan, outsmart the smartest man in the universe, or they would be stuck there forever, Paxton's to start and restart at his leisure. If only Efren would come back and tell her more . . . "And we need Han. He's getting close with Paxton, he'll know how to get into their servers and get a message out. I think we have to play along, pretend like we don't know any of this."

Zurri nodded, her face shiny with nervous sweat. "Let me work on the kid. I'll . . . I don't know, bribe him with merch or something. Can you keep Paxton distracted?"

Bile rose in her throat, but Senna knew it was their best shot. They needed Han, she and Zurri weren't going to crack any high-tech security measures no matter how hard they tried. He didn't deserve to be left behind, even if he thought he respected Paxton. "Tell him Paxton isn't who he thinks he is. Tell him he's a fraud, that all of his big smart-guy persona is just that, a persona. He had help building all of this, he didn't do it alone."

"How did you—"

"Don't ask, just trust me. What about the rest of the staff? Do you think they're a lost cause?"

"Dr. Colbie is in on this," Zurri growled, maintaining that creepy, tight smile. "Forget them."

"Phrasing," Senna murmured, but managed a thin laugh. "Okay, we need a signal."

"Kinda tough when you don't have your VIT," Zurri chided. The double doors beneath Paxton's office swished open. "Shit. Company. If I can get Han on our side, the signal is 'all for one and one for all.'"

Senna scrunched up her nose.

"Really? You don't—*The Three Muske*—never mind, just remember it, okay? I'll explain the reference when we're a million miles away from this dump." Zurri gave a riotous, high-pitched giggle and nudged Senna out of the way with her hip, taking quick, clipped strides toward the left-side ramp near Paxton's office. Lula, who had been napping near the now fully printed dining table, got up and wagged her tail at the commotion, then went to follow her original master, Paxton.

Senna knew that was her cue. As much as it pained her, as much as she wanted to be anywhere else and with anyone else, she found her courage and painted on a smile, leaning over the railing to get Paxton's attention. It didn't take much. His eyes flew to her as soon as he entered the gallery. The slow, wide grin that spread across his face simultaneously tore a jagged hole across her heart.

Even the so-called smartest man in the universe had to have a weakness, and if she was truly *just so lucky*, then perhaps she would be his.

31

===

"You busy?" Zurri, *the* Zurri, he still couldn't quite get over it, sidled up to Han as he entered the gallery. "Got a sec?" She flashed an odd smile at Paxton's back as the man walked off. "My VIT is acting up, you're the resident whiz kid, yeah?"

Han watched Paxton and Lula trot off toward the ramp, his mouth dry, his fingers aching from clenching them into fists. The shadow had disappeared as they left the chamber housing the LENG containment field, and Paxton had seemingly not noticed a thing, bantering casually about all the avenues of study open to them. He would have forms forwarded to Han's VIT, just some formalities to make transferring custody to Paxton easier. Money would grease those wheels, of course, the foster system on Tokyo Bliss was slammed, and with no other family in the picture, Han would be clear to declare Ganymede his residency and Paxton Dunn his guardian within a month or so if all went smoothly.

Han mostly listened and didn't talk. It seemed . . . fast. Sudden. Mentorship was one thing, but being adopted? By Paxton?

Are you nuts? A week ago this would've been your ultimate fantasy. What the hell is wrong with you?

"Um, sure," Han said with a shrug. In fact, he was glad to have an excuse to get away from Paxton for a bit and clear his thoughts. He wanted to be triple sure that this was the right thing to do.

"You all right?" Zurri asked, falling into step with him. She started leading him back through the gallery, past the table and Dr. Colbie idling outside the clinical labs, toward the bright and sunny courtyard. The Dome shutters were lowered, showing the constant swirl of frosty mist beating against the barrier.

"I just have a lot on my mind," Han told her.

"Yeah? Like what?"

He snorted. "You really want to know? Like, *really*?"

"Sure, why not?"

Han detected a note of impatience in her voice, but brushed it off. First Paxton Dunn was asking to adopt him officially, and now he was getting advice from the most famous model in the galaxy. Subtly, he pinched the top of his leg, but nope, he was awake.

They crossed into the courtyard, and he noticed Zurri sped up. It was a challenge to keep up with her long, long catwalk strides but he did his best. Immediately, the humidity hit like a slap, wet and green, a totally new atmosphere. "Paxton wants me to stay on permanently. I feel like I should be stoked, you know? That's always been the dream, to work for him. But it just seems . . . I don't know, fast. Maybe it's weird here. Maybe I'm not ready. What would you do?"

"I wouldn't stay," Zurri said quickly, easily. "But that's me. I know you idolize him, kid, but you need to be careful. He's an adult, you're . . . well, you're not there yet. Adults can take advantage, and you haven't known him that long, right?"

"With all the articles and speeches and blogs, I feel like I *do* know him," Han replied. *Or I did.* "This is the chance of a lifetime. It should be an easy decision, so why is it hard?"

She smirked down at him, but it was kinder than he expected from a rich, famous woman who didn't need to give him the time of day. "Because you're afraid. You've got your whole life to be smart, it's okay right now to just be unsure."

"So what's up with your VIT?" he asked, noticing that she was leading him toward the ramp that led up and around to the overlook outside the dormitories.

"I need to send—"

As they started up the ramp, Brea appeared, dressed in a shiny white skirt and jacket, her full dark hair loose around her shoulders. In her right hand, she carried Senna's rose gold VIT.

"Have either of you seen Senna?" Brea asked pleasantly. "She dropped this."

Han, not the greatest liar around, tried to shrug coolly. "I saw her with Paxton by his office."

"Oh!" Brea brightened even more. "She is with Paxton? Lovely. Thank you both!"

Zurri paused, and waited until the woman had been swallowed up by the greenery of the courtyard before murmuring, "Dropped it, my ass."

"Yeah," Han sighed, joining her as she started to climb. "She threw it on the floor. Paxton made her film some kind of promo vid and she's furious about it."

"Han . . ." Zurri scoped out the corner around the archway leading into the dormitories behind them but they were alone.

The top of Brea's head could be seen bobbing along the mosaic path toward the gallery. "I'm gonna level with you. Senna and I need a shuttle out of here, and I think you should be on it with us."

They had reached the corridor leading down to this room, but he froze. "Is that why you told me not to stay on?"

"You're already having doubts!" Zurri replied. "Listen to them, and listen to me. Something is not right here. They're drugging Senna, and putting her in that LENG thing for twenty hours. They could be doing that to us too and we would never know it!"

"No . . ." Han shook his head, but the found himself following, slowly, tripping after her as she stomped toward his room. "Paxton wouldn't do that."

"I saw Senna's medical file," Zurri told him.

The door opened, alerted by his proximity, and they filed inside. Han rubbed his forehead, a headache brewing. Grabbing a Mega Slurp from the refrigerated drawer, he collapsed into one of the kitchen chairs. "No. He's an intense guy but I don't think he would drug us without permission."

But how to explain that vid Senna had filmed? Her anger, her hurt, couldn't be faked. She really didn't remember doing it, and using that endorsement against her will would be wrong.

"You don't have to wonder or think," Zurri told him, ripping a chair away from the table to make room for herself. She leaned over and showed him her VIT screen. There it was. The image of Senna's file, and the notes from her LENG sessions.

"Send that to me," he whispered. "I want to see it."

"Sent," she said.

"How is this . . . But there has to be an explanation," Han muttered. It was worse than he expected. What if Paxton was doing the same to him? What if he was lying about Han's family? What if there was someone out there that cared about him, that wanted him home? *Bubble boy*, he thought with a grimace. *Bubble man*.

Zurri pointed to the image, now displayed on his VIT. "Compliant. Do you like that word? Because I sure as shit do not like that word. I don't plan on being compliant, neither does Senna. How about you?"

Han felt his cheeks start to burn. It was too much to take in. He didn't want to rush to judgment, or make a call without consulting Paxton, but of course Paxton would paint a rosy picture. Han imagined the silver orb again, a sphere of mercury suspended, potentially holding an actual black hole, a tear in the fabric of the universe. How could he walk away from that? How could he walk away from his dream?

"I don't know," Han murmured, pushing his soda away and dropping his head onto the table. "He's my hero."

"He's not your hero," she replied. "You think he did all of this himself? Alone? He might not even be the brains behind it, he could just be the money."

Han's head shot up. "How did you know that?"

Zurri blinked twice, hard. "Senna . . . Senna told me."

"He had a partner," Han said slowly. "You're right, he didn't do this alone. And now that partner is nowhere to be found." He didn't need to say more, the implication, the possibility, hung there heavy and terrible between them. "There has to be a reason I've never heard of this partner, that he's taking all the credit."

"So you're in?" Zurri pressed. "You get it? You want to leave with us?"

"Say I am. How would we even go about that? Paxton controls all the communications in and out of this place. If we try to hail a shuttle, he'll notice and cancel it, the system might just auto-flag the request and deny it."

Zurri smacked her palm on the table and then paced, palms propped on the back of her hips. "You're the tech guy, yeah? If you're smart enough to get invited to stay on here, then I bet you can, I don't know, hack? Hack it? Do . . . something?" She mimed typing furiously on an invisible keyboard.

Rolling his eyes, Han slumped out of his chair and went to fetch his portable keyboard, then brought it back to the kitchen table and took a few fortifying gulps of soda. "I can try some of the scripts I brought, but I doubt they're anywhere near sophisticated enough. Usually you break into this stuff with social engineering."

"Social engineering?" Zurri went to the refrigerated drawer and grabbed a Mega Slurp for herself. He scoffed and pointed. "What? I'm thirsty."

"You can trick people out of their passwords, get them to use a fake website that logs their information, or pose as an admin. If you're convincing enough, you can get people to share all kinds of stuff," Han explained. He opened his script bank and set the text to hover above his VIT so they could both see it, then he turned on his remote keyboard and bit down on his lip, thinking.

"So social engineer," Zurri encouraged, twinkling her fingers at him. "We need this, Han. We've got to get a shuttle out of this place. So work your magic, you know, King Shit."

He huffed. A beautiful, crazy, overbearing woman was demanding he hack into what was probably one of the most airtight systems in the entire universe. No pressure. But he knew she had a point, that whatever was going on in the Dome was too strange, too unethical, too scary to make staying an option. If Paxton really respected him, he would let him come back when the timing felt better.

So where to begin?

"Right. Yeah. Easy. King Shit."

"Han is king."

They both fell silent, staring at each other as Genie's voice seemed to echo for an eternity in the little kitchenette.

"Can you repeat that?" Han finally asked.

"Han is king," Genie stated flatly. "Would you like to activate Han Is King protocols?"

"Suuuure?" Han shrugged, jutting out his lip, just as flabbergasted as Zurri, who was now sucking down her Mega Slurp like a woman dying of thirst. "Wait. Can you define 'Han Is King protocols,' please?"

"Established approximately thirty-four hours ago by user Paxton, security level: admin, accessed through device X01X23Y4XYHJ at Dome time three twenty-five p.m. Voice command: King. Would you like to activate Han Is King protocols?"

"That's the serial number of my VIT," Han breathed, his hands suddenly numb. "That means I logged in on my VIT and used Paxton's admin ID to put in . . . put in this vocal command back door. It had to be me because the serial number verifies through your VIT implant. Whoa."

Zurri's wide, wide eyes stared at him across their Mega Slurps. "Does that sound like something you would do?"

Han grinned, sheepish. "Kinda. Yeah."

"So? You social engineered! Do it. Activate it!"

"Genie? Activate Han Is King protocols, please." He had to admit, saying it made him feel good. Powerful. It also made him tremble and want to curl up on the floor. This meant his file probably looked a lot like Senna's. Han wouldn't have put in this kind of fail-safe without cause. He was worried about forgetting. And he had. None of this remained; he couldn't even remember how he had managed to crack Paxton's security in the first place.

"Protocols activated. Admin access granted to your device."

He remembered something then, something Paxton had told him while they ventured down that hall to visit the LENG particle in suspension. That Han's mother had died, that he wanted to forget her because her voice haunted him, followed him everywhere, ubiquitous and inescapable.

"I want to hear her," he murmured, not caring if Zurri saw his chin quiver. "Genie, can you revert to your default voice?"

"Yes, Han, would you like to keep these settings?"

Her voice was gentle, quizzical, feminine but still in a pleasantly low register. It was the kind of voice you would never get tired of hearing. He clapped a hand over his mouth, and knew, in the place where memories lived outside the mind, that it was his mother. Not a ghost or a haunting, but a blessing.

"Hi, Mom," he whispered. Zurri's hand touched his shoulder, and he almost crumpled. "It's so good to hear your voice."

"How can I assist you, Han?" Of course it was just Genie, but still. Still. Why had he ever wanted to run from this? Why would he want it gone?

Because it hurts. Because it hurts in places I can't even name.

"I need to get a message to the satellite." He stumbled through it, but found his way. Using his keyboard, he called up the server list, finding an absolute treasure trove of unsent notes from him, Zurri and Senna. His blood ran cold at the titles of some. GET ME OUT NOW, BEV was prominently at the top. Some were flagged for a storm warning, saved on local storage until a connection to the satellite could be reestablished, but the most recent messages just hadn't been sent. Paxton was holding them all back. "We need a shuttle here," Han added. "For three."

"Three," Zurri said with a smile. "Glad to have you on board, kid."

"Satellite comms established. Shuttle link available," his mother—Genie—informed them. Her voice, each time, was a jolt to his system. "Next available arrival time: Dome time thirteen hundred hours. Would you like to secure this flight?"

"Crap," Han muttered, shooting her a look. "That only gives us about an hour. The next shuttle isn't scheduled to arrive until tomorrow. An hour. Do you think that's enough time?"

Zurri slid her palm across her face and glanced toward the door. "It will have to be."

32

"I love this color on you." Paxton reached across the deliberate foot of space between them and tugged on the edge of her left sleeve. It was just a boxy old dress, nurses-scrub blue and faded.

"Oh!" Senna tucked her hands behind her back, worried that if she didn't, Paxton would notice her compulsively pressing her nails into her own palms, scoring them with deep half-moons. "Thank you. It's so dull next to Zurri's clothes. I wish I had her style."

"Pfft, don't say that. You don't need it," Paxton insisted, leaning against the railing, his left hip tucked against it. "You have natural beauty. No makeup. Nothing artificial. No surgery. I was into pastel punk girls for a while but it's just more of the same. I like this—you. Us bubble kids have to stick together."

Senna willed her heart to stop racing. How long would it take Zurri to convince Han to help them? What if she couldn't do it? "Bubble kids? I didn't grow up in isolation."

"Sure you did." Paxton smoothed a hand over his hair, but the dark curls sprang back. "All of you did, you're all lonely. You just came to it differently."

Is that why you picked us, she wanted to ask, *because nobody would object to us leaving our lives behind for this place? Is that why you picked me? Because you think we're the same? I'm nothing like you.*

"I'm not lonely," Senna insisted. "I have Marin and Jonathan back on the station. Zurri has her fans, her staff, nobody becomes famous on their own."

Paxton's brows went up. She held her own wrists until they ached, realizing she had blundered into a sensitive spot. That was what Efren had mentioned, that he hadn't risen to this level of power and fame and influence alone.

"Well, nobody but you," she added quickly, hating it.

That made him grin again, an easy look. The beast placated. "Why did you run from me before?"

"When?" She batted her lashes, playing dumb.

"Before. You know what I'm talking about. Why did you run?"

"All of this is so overwhelming," said Senna frankly. Maybe if she kept the lies close to the surface, he wouldn't notice her struggling. "I woke up in your bed this morning. I don't remember how I got there. That's frightening. You know that's frightening, right, for a woman? You never want to feel that way. I don't wake up in other people's beds, at least, I don't think I do."

Paxton put his hands up as if in defeat. "Whoa, whoa. Jesus! Nothing happened, Senna. If it did, trust me." He winked. "You'd remember."

She swallowed a bubble of vomit. "Sure." She tucked some hair behind her ear. "That makes sense." It didn't. "You must think I'm so naive, but I'm just . . . scattered. The treatments are disorienting." And constant. And the drugs . . . Only minutes had passed and she knew it. *How much longer, Zurri?*

"What's that?" he asked, nodding toward the bench. He had noticed the painting.

Senna blanched. "It's . . . something I was working on. It just came to me." Blinking hard, she heard a deadened voice come back to her, though the owner of it was gone, zapped away by Paxton's "miracle" tech. No warm feelings flooded her, so maybe the forgotten person was someone she truly wanted taken away. "Someone once told me I had a gift, that I dreamed even while I was awake, even if I didn't know it. 'Percolating,' that was the word they used." Pausing, she felt herself try to sink back into memories that weren't there. Even if it was deep, dark water, she wanted, just then, to sink into it. "At least I think so."

"I'm glad you're getting use out of the paints. That's a limited edition Rembrandt set. Ancient history now. Only about two hundred were made. When I saw you had applied, I did some digging, had this brought from my da's storage on the station." He pushed off from the railing, sauntering toward the bench.

"That quickly?" Senna asked.

"Things move fast when I want them to."

She went still as he leaned over the painting. His smile, an instant ago so broad and cocksure, shriveled into something twisted. A snarl. The blood drained from his face, and Senna felt gears in her head spinning in mud, stuck and useless. What was he seeing? It was Efren, but Efren could vanish. He was just a figment, she had assumed, another confusing side effect of the LENG treatments. But then he did know Paxton, didn't he? Intimately. The pieces didn't fit. It was like trying to push two north magnets together.

"How—" Paxton placed his own finger over his lips and

made a strangled *hmf* sound. His head swiveled to regard her. "What an incredible imagination you apparently have, Senna. When did this *percolate* in your little head?"

"You're angry with me," she whispered, backing against the railing.

"No," Paxton corrected, holding out his hand for her to take. She knew she had no choice. This was her assignment, to distract him, but she knew, as soon as their palms collided, that she had been handed a cruel and impossible task. "I'm fascinated. This is the most interesting thing you've ever done."

With one hand he picked up the still-tacky painting, with the other he took Senna's left hand, crushing it in his. She winced, but said nothing. He didn't drag her down the ramp to the clinical labs and the LENG room like she expected. Instead he brought her, at a bizarrely cavalier pace, to his office. The black doors there hissed open, and they nearly collided with Anju.

"Hi there." She stumbled back a step but caught herself. "Oh, Senna! Hi! Brea found your VIT, it's on Paxton's desk."

"Tell Dr. Colbie to prep LENG, please," Paxton said in passing, ignoring the rest.

Anju's big eyes slid precariously to Senna. "There are no appointments scheduled today, Pax."

"I'm aware of that. Tell her to prep it just in case."

Just in case.

Senna took a deep breath, ready to play as dumb as she needed to, but that didn't stop her heart from hammering up into her throat. She was going to choke on her own pulse, remembering that his bedroom was connected to the office. If she had to fight, she would, she decided. She would claw his fucking eyes out, if that was what was required. The doors whispered closed, shutting her inside with Paxton.

He let go of her, holding up the painting, examining it in the full light projected from the bright, marbled mass of color along the back wall of his office.

"Fascinating," Paxton said again. He laughed, harshly, and Senna put distance between them, going to the desk and picking up her VIT. There was hardly a scratch on it. "Of course it would make a difference. I should have known it would make a difference. Glen, you bastard. Is this your idea of revenge?"

Senna held the VIT to her chest, eyes on the door, trying to imagine a way out. Maybe the little wrist device was heavy enough to whack him over the head. There was also a small bust of his own head on his desk and—

Paxton dropped the painting, the wet surface leaving smudges on the floor. He was on her in the next second, long legs chewing up the ground until he was against her, over her, hand locked around her throat. The VIT fell out of her hands, clattering to the floor. Her vision blurred, her chest pins and needles as he forced the back of her head down onto the desk. With his free hand he reached for one of the digital frames, snatching it before smashing it against her face. Senna screamed, thrashing, too weak to slip out of his grasp.

"Is this your revenge, mate? Weak. You can do better. So can I."

He relaxed his grip on her throat, but only a little. The frame moved back enough for her to make out the image—two men, arms around each other, goofy, boyish smiles. Paxton looked younger, no glasses, and beside him, rucked up tight to his side, was Efren.

"You're seeing this man?" Paxton demanded. "How? How do you know about Glen? I wiped him from the news, deleted him utterly from history, from memory. How?"

"You're hurting me!" Senna wheezed.

Paxton reared back, then threw her roughly to the ground. She scrambled on hands and knees away from him, but Paxton put his shoe to her back and pressed, hard, flattening her to the cold tiles.

"Glen Ferne is a dead man," Paxton spat. "A soft, sad corpse. He was the best of us, smarter even than me. Brilliant. But he didn't like LENG, wouldn't use it. *Hated* it. We cracked open the vessel holding it and we both saw its potential. It *spoke* to us. This will heal people, I told him." He pushed harder; Senna flailed. "He only thought it would hurt people. 'It's already hurt you.' Risked his life flying to the edge of a black hole to recover the thing and he wanted to *take it back*. Can you imagine? Paxton Dunn does not stare the innovation of a lifetime in the face and turn away."

So Efren was a ghost, or . . . or . . . Senna's nails scratched in futile squeaks against the tiles. Her VIT lay at arm's length. Desperate, she lunged for it. Maybe she could send a message, or at least turn on the vid chat for someone to see what Paxton was trying to do to her. She managed to just flick the edge of it, the VIT spinning across the floor, landing just inches from her face. The screen lit up, the pain surging through her back.

ONE NEW MESSAGE: ALL FOR ONE AND ONE FOR ALL, BITCH.

Senna sobbed. So close.

"Give me that," Paxton grunted, his foot letting up long enough for him to bend down and scoop up the VIT. As soon as he was upright again, Senna rolled onto her back, just in time to see a strange, concentrated light flash across Paxton's eyes, like the reflection of water, hot and white. He winced and batted at it, temporarily blinded.

"What the hell? Shit, it burns." He hissed and stumbled.

Senna forced herself to breathe, even though it stung. Gulping for air, she pulled herself up by the legs on Paxton's desk, finding the stone bust of Paxton's head and hurling herself toward him. Her arms shook with shock and fatigue, but she managed to give him one good thump on the forehead. He moaned and crumpled onto his side.

The light bouncing across Paxton's eyes grew and grew, first a pale shadow of a man, sparkling and bright, then resolving into a fully formed figure with human features. "Oh God," she said, falling to her knees, clutching her legs and shaking with relief.

"So he showed you the picture."

Senna gasped, sliding onto her back to find Efren there, standing just at the edge of Paxton's shoes.

"Is he dead?"

"I don't think so, no." Efren—Glen—shook his head. "Are you all right? Can you stand? Can you run?"

"I don't know." Senna touched her chest, coughing. "Why didn't you tell me?"

"I was about to," he said. "This is all a horrible mess. I'm sorry. I'm so sorry."

"What are you?" Senna demanded. Beside her, Paxton gave a spasm, a stream of hissing air releasing from between his lips. Not dead, then. She didn't know what to feel, whether to be thankful or just more afraid. "What do I call you? Are you his partner? Glen Ferne?"

"Efren," he replied softly, kneeling. "Efren Leng. Glen Ferne. The Vestige. Whatever you like to call me you can, you've more than earned that. Glen tried to stop Paxton from using the Vestige, but he wouldn't listen. He never really listened. Paxton fed him to LENG, gave over his entire mind, all of his thoughts, his memories, his very essence. Clearly, it did not have the intended effect. It didn't erase Glen the way he wanted it to."

"We need to get away from him. Zurri called the shuttle," Senna whispered, every word a strain. "Han must have come around."

"Then we need to get you ready to depart, don't we?" He frowned and shook his head. "I wanted to protect you from all of this. What I am, parts of me are all of you, and Glen, and the shattered fragments of the civilizations pulverized by that imploding star. A crucible of pain and love and memory. If you want your memories restored, all of them, I can give that to you. The Vestige takes, LENG takes, but it also preserves."

Senna sobbed again. "That's possible?"

Efren (she decided that fit this strange amalgamation best) peered at her with his soft golden eyes and nodded. "We're sitting on top of miles and miles of ice and oceans. Ice on top of oceans on top of ice on top of oceans. Anything is possible. It's going to be difficult, Senna. It's going to hurt."

"I want it back," she assured him, hot, needling tears spilling down her cheeks. "The good and the bad. Don't leave anything out. I want to know what happened to me. I want to know what was taken away."

"If you bring me to your friends, I can restore them, too," he said.

"Then that's what I'll do."

Senna watched his hands reach toward her.

"Close your eyes." She did, and felt the light pressure of his thumbs resting on her eyelids. "Don't forget to breathe, Senna. I'm sorry."

Her mind had been quelled, even with just her vague, fractured memories of the compound; she sensed that all her life she had been quelled. But then everything was coming back, and hard. Merciless. There was an uprising, a swell, and the intensity of it startled her. Pins and needles over every inch of her body, a sensation like lightning across the skin.

The compound. The brood. The sea of faces flooded back into her, a tide of lost friendship and possibility. All those lives snatched away. And Preece, he returned, too, not gray around the edges and dull as she remembered him a moment ago, but Technicolor violence, the teacher, mentor, doctor, tyrant, murderer in all his complicated, tangled reality. She remembered Mina, her pretty oval face and narrow eyes, how they sometimes held hands at night when the lights went out, the touch hidden beneath their blankets, away from Preece's prying eyes.

And the crash. There it was, around her, with her. That was what she had come to forget, the death of her old life, her unbearable birth into the new one.

"You can't leave me," she had whispered to Mina. They were holding hands when she woke up to her dead friends on the *Dohring-Waugh*. Mina was cold, and the numbness of it passed into her briefly. *No, no, feel all of it. Be inside of it. This is what you came here to forget, but you own every moment of it.*

Preece came to find her, and when she remembered it now, he was smiling.

"Senna," she heard him say. "I didn't know you were awake."

"You killed them. You killed them. How could you . . . All of them. All of us! Why couldn't you kill me, too?" She had screamed, hysterical, stumbling across the bodies, tripping over them, until she could beat him on the chest with both fists. Carefully, Preece held both of her wrists, his white beard haggard and thin as he looked down into her eyes.

"We're going, too," he explained, calm and fatherly as ever. "We can hold hands," he told her, "at the end."

Senna tore her hands away from him, and fought. Her shoulder rammed hard into his chest, forcing him into the wall. He was old and frail, and somehow she had decided she wanted to live. In the evac pod, she wrung out her hands, the cool, dead flesh of Mina's fingers lingering against her palms while she sped to safety, and the *Dohring-Waugh* made its doomed descent into the surface of Mars, killing Han's mother and hundreds of others.

"He taught me everything." Senna didn't realize she could speak while Efren restored her memories. "He taught me how to read, how to paint, how to count. How to sing, how to cook. He taught me history, science and art. He taught me how to give of myself, how to be selfless."

Efren didn't respond, but Senna could tell he was holding his breath. Waiting. Was there more to say?

"He taught me everything," she concluded. Maybe that wasn't so, in the end she had fought back, and he never taught her that. So he hadn't taught her everything and tainted everything, just most of what she knew. Some of it had hemmed her in, caged her. "Sometimes I feel like I was grown in the lab of his ideas. Maybe he taught me good things, but . . ."

Still, Efren said nothing. The memories flowed in; his hands grew warmer as they rested on her face.

Senna thought about what she had felt the first time Mina had held her hand in the compound. They weren't supposed to do those things unless Preece said they could start to court, but Mina broke rules occasionally and Senna clamped down on all her good girl impulses to avoid tattling. When Mina held her hand, she felt like she expanded past the bars of her cage. She had felt it again, that expansion, then, as the grief poured into her through Efren's hands.

"He didn't teach me how to be ravenous, or wild," Senna told him, her voice growing stronger. "Why would he? That would make me free. And rebellious."

"And how do you feel now?" Efren asked. The stream of pain was relentless, but clarifying.

"Wild," she said. "Dangerous."

"There's more," Efren warned. And there was. She saw her arrival on Ganymede, and her terror at seeing the shadow. She remembered the shadow, and how the lights and sirens of the storm lockdown sent her into a panic. She met Han and Zurri; she met them four times. She watched LENG, the shadow, reach its fingers into her eyes and take, and take.

In a darkened hall, Senna saw Anju slam into the Dome barrier and then tear away into the wind and mist. Paxton must have reprinted her, her first chassis still spinning across the ice.

"Fuck. This complicates things." Paxton fucked a headless woman, or an idea of a woman, and Senna looked on in horror. A Servitor body skinned to be so real, so lifelike . . . They were doing that now, Marin had warned her; those undisguisable Servitors were coming. On Ganymede, they had already arrived. Paxton truly was isolated, then, surrounding himself not with real employees but with simulacra he could control. She didn't allow herself to wonder if they were once real women, or entire figments, fictions created to scratch some fantasy itch in Paxton's dark mind.

More and more returned. She watched her mind torn apart until Paxton was satisfied with its emptiness. She felt the drugs dull her to the confusion. She watched the memory of Efren go, and return, and go, and return again. She heard his warnings, and wished they could've stuck.

Last, she watched Paxton carry her, limp and brain-dead, from the LENG room to his office, then to his bedroom, where he put her under the covers and crawled in beside her. A moment's hesitation crossed his features, a grimace, a smile, then sobering blankness, and he turned onto his side, calling out to Genie to cut the lights.

It was done. Senna rested her hands over Efren's wrists.

"You have a physical form," she said, his thumbs shifting away from her eyes.

"Stardust and density from the black hole collapse, memories, dreams and everything Paxton asked the Vestige to take from Glen, and from you all," he said, holding her hands in his before placing them in her lap. She opened her eyes, and he stared back. Her breaths came in ragged and went out just the same. There was no telling when the tears would stop.

"It's given me—us—form. Me, the shadow . . . When that star imploded, it took everything with it," Efren said, standing and offering her his hand. "The good and the evil. The shadow is that evil, and I am, or try to be, the lightness and the good."

"Where's Glen's body?" she asked. "If LENG destroyed his mind, his body must be somewhere."

"Lost," Efren replied, detached from the answer. "Scattered into a trillion shards across the ice fields."

"God. Why did you sacrifice Anju that way?" Senna asked, trembling but finding her strength as Efren hoisted her to her feet. His hand felt real enough, smooth and kind, warm with life.

"I wanted to wake you all up," Efren sighed, glancing away, perhaps embarrassed. "I didn't know if you would believe me if

I just came out and told you what I was. She's not living, so the cost seemed bearable. He uses algorithms to control how compliant the female Servitors are, but Glen devised that technology, and now it's in me. I changed her protocols, and made her walk out the hatch."

"Bearable," she repeated, huffing, and staring down at Paxton. He wasn't dead, not even close, and he had begun to swim in agony against the tiles.

"Are you all right?" Efren asked, touching her elbow.

"No, not nearly. But I will be someday." Maybe, she thought. Or maybe not; the pain was better than whatever the empty life Paxton planned for her would be.

"What will you do with him?"

Senna's eyes traveled from Paxton's limp body to the door. "I have a few ideas."

The doors slid open, two silhouettes stamped against the bright light of day streaming in from outside the office. It wasn't the duo she hoped to see. Anju and Dr. Colbie. Before Senna could beg them to wait and reconsider, the Taser dart sank into her shoulder.

33

"She's not coming."

Han opened a single eye, wishing he could just go back to stew-ing with anxiety. Zurri climbed to her feet, tossing her Mega Slurp into the bin and rousing Han. He was slipping into a sugar coma on the table while they waited for Senna to show up. The signal had gone out, but there was no reply and no sign of her. They had given it twenty minutes, the agreed-upon time limit, and now they had to hurry. Genie was no help; Senna wasn't wearing her VIT, al-though it appeared to still be in Paxton's office.

"Let's go."

"How are we going to get her away from Paxton?" Han asked, close on her heels as they left his room.

"Any damn way we have to, kid. That shuttle is landing in forty minutes and we are going to be on it."

"I don't think he's going to just let us walk out of here."

"I know, Han." Zurri fell back to walk beside him and ruffled his hair. "But we've got your brains and my beauty, we'll figure something out. We have to. Besides, we've got Genie on our side now, too, right?"

"Not entirely," Han muttered, swishing his lips to the side. They left the dormitories, swinging left and down the ramp, dipping into the courtyard and its enveloping humidity. Han couldn't help but think he would miss the courtyard specifically. It was beautiful, a marvel, but there were trees on the station, too; he'd just have to leave his room once in a while to see them. "I'm not sure how many fail-safes are hidden in Paxton's code. Pretty much anything could trigger a hard reboot."

"Crossing bridges, et cetera," Zurri replied, leading him confidently through the mosaic path toward the gallery.

"There you are!" Brea ducked out from behind a tree. Han and Zurri shared a quick glance. Her being there didn't seem quite casual, or at least, he couldn't figure out a reason for her just planting herself in the bushes unless she was trying to ambush them. The shuttle hail. The system could have sent out a wider alert. Han surreptitiously checked his VIT. The landing was still scheduled; the shuttle would break atmo in fifteen minutes.

"It is just about time for lunch," Brea said, studying Zurri's face intently. "I hope you are both hungry. Sixteen has truly outdone itself today."

"Sorry." Zurri shrugged. "We ate in Han's room. Not hungry. I'm sure Tin Head will get over it."

Brea forced a laugh, throwing her head back. "I insist. We can film a brief segment for the promo going out this week. Paxton is eager to show everyone back on the station your progress!"

Han could feel his will to live vacating his body as the seconds ticked by. They didn't have time to argue with her.

"Have you seen Senna?" he asked.

"I believe she is with Paxton in his office," Brea told them, gesturing for them to follow her along the path that led to the gallery. "She will be joining us later, after lunch."

"Why after lunch?" Zurri pressed, nudging him when Brea looked away. "Don't you want her to be part of your big glossy segment?"

"So many questions!"

"Sure, now go ahead and answer them." Zurri refused to move another step, parking herself in the middle of the path. But Brea did the same, equally tall, squaring up to Zurri, her face calm and steady.

"You do not want to pick this fight, Zurri," Brea told her. Her slight accent, Spanish, Han had always thought, wavered. "This is not you."

"Nah, pretty sure I'm an argumentative bitch, and I'm even more sure that I protect my fellow ladies from creepity creeps who can't help but creep, can't brainwash that out of me."

Brea grinned, her accent vanishing altogether. "We can try."

Her hand moved too quickly for Han to even track it. Lashing out, she took Zurri's wrist and spun, pinning her arm up behind her back, Brea's face hovering over her shoulder while she glared at Han and Zurri screamed in pain.

"You are not brave, human. You are a pile of meat. Your weakness is in the body *and* the mind. A man on fire brought you to your knees. You cannot save Senna, just as you could not save yourself. You could set fire to me, my flesh coating could burn to cinders, and still I would be standing." Brea took Zurri by the throat with her other hand, eyes latched onto Han's as she started to squeeze. "Comply," she told Han.

"Don't comply!" Zurri gurgled, eyes beginning to bug. "Never fucking comply!"

Han couldn't leave her, so he darted forward, clawing at Brea's hands and arms, kicking at her, but nothing made a dent. She was Servitor Sixteen's body covered in flesh, sturdier and stronger than any human ever could be. He fell back, her laugh ringing in his ears, twining with Zurri's fading yelps for air.

"M-Mom!" he heard himself shriek.

"Calling for your mother," Brea snickered. "How like a human. I am, however, amazed you can even remember her."

"Genie! Stop this! Override . . . you have to. There has to be a way!" He threw himself at Brea, tangling his hands in hers, trying to at least lever her wrist away from Zurri's neck. Zurri's cold sweat soaked into her shirt, her chin pressed to his forehead as he grunted and gritted his teeth and pulled.

"Genie! Override! Make her stop!" He lost his grip, his hands too slick, and he tumbled back, skidding to the floor. Brea lifted Zurri, the model's toes dangling off the floor. He slapped at his VIT screen, waking it up. Typing, typing, searching . . . If he had admin access, then the commands and scripts for Brea were somewhere on the server. But which one? Servitors. They were Servitors! He couldn't believe it. There were so many damn servers—which one held her code? Server Alpha? Bravo? Charlie?

Alpha. Bravo. Charlie. They were bots. AI. Paxton had designed, printed, skinned and programmed them. The amount of data it would take to run such a complex Servitor would take up an entire server. Anju. Brea. Dr. Colbie. He selected the Bravo server, and knew he had guessed right. Highlighting the scripts folder, he slammed DELETE.

"What are you doing?" Brea's voice was all wrong. It dipped and swung back up. Her hands went loose and Zurri slid to the ground, coughing, hacking, scratching at her reddened throat but alive. "What . . . what . . ." She froze, eyes wide and unblinking. An automated, default voice took over, playing through the slack slit of her lips, though they had ceased moving. "Debug mode. Core function not detected."

"Holy . . . holy . . ." Zurri flopped onto her back, wiping at her mouth with the back of her hand. "She was a robot?!"

"Yes!"

"I knew it. I knew it . . . Christ, this hurts." She reached for her neck, touching it carefully. "Am I dead?"

"No!" Han let out a whoop of laughter. It had worked. It had actually worked! "We have to get you up, come on. We have to find Senna."

"Whatever you take from me," Senna whispered, "it won't be gone forever. I can get it back."

Paxton held a blue, curved ice pack to his forehead, leaning against the star field as it projected itself across his bloodied face and shirt. When he grinned, his front left incisor was chipped. Anju and Dr. Colbie held her tight to the chair. There was no use arguing with them, or struggling, the effects of the stun gun were only just beginning to wear off.

"That's where you're wrong," Paxton told her, his speech slightly slurred. "This time, we're giving you the full Glen. Since you two are besties now, it's only right. I'm going to make LENG give you the hard reboot. You won't remember your own name when we're through here. And then I'll do it to your friends. Brea is out there collecting them as we speak."

Senna swallowed and it tasted like blood. "You don't want to take all my memories, Paxton."

He rolled his eyes. "Because at heart I'm really a good person?"

"No," she sighed. "You're not."

Dr. Colbie shifted to take the syringe and jab it into her arm, but Paxton waved her off. "There's no need, nothing to repair this time."

"You don't want to do this," Senna repeated, breathing in through her nose. She wanted to believe LENG wouldn't hurt her, not after she and Efren had talked. But there was no guarantee. They were light and dark, good and evil, according to Efren, and that might mean the shadow, LENG, could not be controlled by anyone.

"It's warmed up?" Paxton leaned away from the wall, moving the ice pack down to his jaw before strolling across the center of the room, pausing by her chair. The heavy door remained ajar, letting in a thin sliver of light.

"We're ready, Pax," Anju told him.

"Hold her," Paxton instructed. "There's nothing in your minds to wipe anyway."

He gave Senna a wink, and in the loudest voice she could muster, she said, "I know what LENG is."

"Bullshit."

"I know what it is," Senna countered. It at least got him to pause. "Efren told me."

"Efren," Paxton spat. "His name was Glen, not that garbled nonsense. I don't care what you think you remember, Senna, you don't know what LENG is any more than I do. I've studied it for years, if it won't relinquish its secrets to me, it won't give them up to anybody, certainly not you."

"You can't see him because you've never used the technology on yourself," replied Senna. Returning her memories had weakened Efren. All the memories of hers Paxton had fed to LENG had bolstered him, made him more creature than just silhouette of light. With his physical form fading, they were no match for

Paxton's Servitor servants. Anju and Dr. Colbie overwhelmed her easily, and Efren vanished. It hurt to see him go, but Senna knew he was somewhere, waiting to return Zurri and Han's memories. She just had to survive.

"You think that's going to work on me?" Paxton slumped over to her, touching his icy fingers to her chin, forcing her to look up at him. "I'm not getting in that chair. I don't belong there. I've lived a perfect life. You're the mess."

"I'm the mess," Senna agreed. "But I still know what LENG is. Aren't you curious?"

"Shut up."

"Wipe my memories and you'll never know," she whispered. "Efren—Glen—will never tell you."

Paxton regarded her for a long moment, pinching her chin and jaw until it ached. His eyes, already beginning to bruise in the corners from the blow she had landed with the bust, unfocused. Then he shrugged. "I don't know that I care."

"What?"

"I know what it can do," he said, pushing her head back hard against the chair. "You're too much like Glen. Knowledge isn't everything. Utility is."

"And clever isn't the same as ruthless," she hissed.

Paxton's eyes refocused, and grew huge, and then he swung and slapped her across the face, her teeth slicing into her cheek. "You know Glen said that to me the day he died. His words in your bitch mouth, what a truly abysmal combination. Let's go, ladies. Start it up." He pointed at the ceiling and made a whirling motion with his forefinger. "I don't want a single ridge left on her brain at the end of this."

Senna closed her eyes, bracing. Anju and Dr. Colbie's hands bit into her arms. She could feel the hum and churn of the machine, sense the pressure building, the shift in atmosphere before LENG and the shadow arrived. The door eased shut, plunging them into darkness and trapping her inside.

She stared into the star field and waited for the shadow to appear. It was harder now, worse, knowing how it would all go, remembering every hour of torment she had spent in that chair. There was scratching at the door, then a thump and a yelp. Lula. Senna closed her eyes, afraid, knowing it would be Han and Zurri next, and they would spend the rest of their lives as mindless dolls for Paxton to pose and laugh at in his little bubble world.

"Please," she whispered to the darkness. "Don't let him take everything."

The whole room contracted, the star field narrowing to a pinpoint on the wall across from her. LENG was coming.

She heard another sound at the door, louder, a commotion as something weighty rocked against it. Then the hands holding her eased and went slack, and when Senna snapped her head up to look, she found Anju and Dr. Colbie standing perfectly still, their heads angled downward, dead eyes trained on the floor. The shriek and scream of the lock turning on the door came, and then light, and faces. Two silhouettes. This time it was the pair she hoped to see.

The hum of the machine grew softer, fainter, until there was just the sound of Lula's panting as she burst into the room. Senna levered herself out of the chair and limped toward the door, desperate for the light. On the other side of the door, she found Paxton in a heap, out cold, Servitor Sixteen looming over his body. The Servitor gave Paxton a swift kick in the ribs.

"You enjoy," it chirped.

"Are you *you*?" Zurri asked, pulling Senna away from the door and the LENG room. "I mean, do you remember us?"

"Yes!" Senna gasped, leaning into Zurri's side as the woman wrapped her arm around her shoulders. "The shuttle . . . is it still coming?"

"Ten minutes to arrival," Han announced. He held his VIT aloft, typing on it constantly. "We need to get to the LZ and call the rover."

"What do we do with him?" Zurri asked, joining Sixteen in kicking Paxton's unconscious body.

"Take his VIT," Senna said, glaring down at him. "And put him in that room. Lock the door."

"Oh, I like where this is going!" Zurri nodded toward Han. "Make that robot thing do it, he's way too heavy for me to drag. I don't know how to spin up that machine, the Servitor forced Paxton to kill it before he thumped him."

"Don't use LENG on him." Senna shook her head. "Just let him think things over. We can decide what he deserves later. Or the station agents can. I just want to get out of this horrible place."

"Fair enough," Han agreed, typing away again. The clanking, shining Servitor seemed to jump to his every command, stooping over Paxton and easily gathering him up, dumping him inside the room with the chair and stars before shouldering the door closed and spinning the bar of the lock. Han held up Paxton's chrome VIT. "I'm keeping this, though."

"Good," Senna said. "It's evidence."

"Come on," Zurri said, hobbling with her, shoulder to shoulder down the clinical lab corridor and toward the black door leading out to the gallery. "We're going to a weeklong spa after this, Senna. God better raise Ibiza back out of the sea just so we can go party there."

"Wait." Senna detached from Zurri at the door, shielding her eyes from the sudden flood of light shining in from the gallery ceiling. Her eyes slid from the chandelier to the walkway over-looking where they stood. "There's one more thing."

"We don't have time, Senna—" Han tumbled out of the black door, Servitor Sixteen at his side like a bodyguard.

"Tell the shuttle to wait, there's one more prisoner here we need to free."

34

Paxton grew hungry before he grew thirsty, but then the thirst got bad. His throat felt like sandpaper. Someone would come eventually. Nobody forgot the smartest man in the universe. He could just imagine Glen gloating over this moment, or his first wife, Sandi. Then again, Glen and Sandi hadn't been gloaters. Still, he imagined them chuckling at his demise. No, not demise, inconvenience.

Someone would come. Someone would save him.

Nobody just forgot the smartest man in the universe.

He didn't like the dark. Hated it as a kid, hated it just as much as an adult. At least he had the star field, although he was pretty sure he had made out where the clip looped. Annoying. He kept compulsively reaching for his VIT, but there was just an itchy wrist, a bit skinnier than the other one from a life of wearing that thing on his arm.

Every item in the room had been thrown at the door, but it

was solid. Glen had been the one to make sure it was that intense. Maybe that soft fucker had been right to worry about LENG. It had all gone to shit, but Paxton would recover. He always did. What he really didn't like was that Glen might be right, and that Glen might win. Worse, a couple of total idiots had outplayed him. Paxton would give the win to Glen, because if Senna was telling the truth, then it was his irritating soul stuck in the tech making all this go to hell. The altruistic weren't known for getting revenge, but then, maybe once LENG sucked Glen's entire mind away, it had changed the man's soul somehow, and the darkness of that machine had melded with Glen's goodness, and this was the result—the kind of odd poetry his old partner had always enjoyed.

I didn't know it would kill him, did I? Maybe I hoped it would. A gun firing its own bullets, I didn't even go near the trigger.

What a sad end. What a sad, stupid end. But poetic, at least.

No, this wasn't the end, nobody just forgot the smartest man in the world. Someone would come for him, even in total isolation, there had to be a way. This was his Eden. God didn't die in Eden.

He knew the thing had come before it appeared. The second they had opened that weird metal orb and pried the LENG sphere out of it, he sensed a change in the Dome. There was a presence. There was always a presence. That idiot Scooby gang should have fired up LENG and roasted his brain until it was a shriveled, charred peanut, but they chose dumb, pointless mercy over the killing blow.

Clever isn't the same as ruthless.

Something ruthless had come. He couldn't hear the machine, the bassy, chest-rumbling churn of LENG when it was all warmed up and ready to sizzle. But somehow, the thing had come for him. In a way, it felt inevitable. There was comfort in that, maybe.

There was comfort in it until it arrived.

I am LENG, it warned him. *I am the Vestige. A billion lives and a dozen planets are in me, and now I will consume one more being.*

The machine isn't on, Paxton insisted to himself, huddling against the wall across from the star field. *I'm hallucinating.*

The shadow grew itself from the floor, stark and black and vaguely human as it absorbed the light of the star field. Nothing reflected across it; the light, in fact, seemed repelled by its presence. As it neared, its fingers grew longer and longer, lengthening and sharpening in anticipation of the feast.

I am the Vestige, it told him. *And I have come to take.*

EPILOGUE

Someone had left a bouquet of white silk flowers on the floor near Tony's grave. Zurri couldn't decide why she had come, or whether she wanted to spit or cry. She had done both when, on the shuttle rocketing away from Ganymede and the Dome, Senna had handed her an odd, engraved metal orb. A moment later, a man appeared to her, handsome and kind, with dark hair and golden eyes, and the most inviting smile. He pressed his thumbs against her closed eyes, and everything Paxton had taken from her came flooding back.

It hurt. It burned. God, it burned.

She saw the halo of fire bursting around Tony's head. She saw him leering over her bed. She saw the Servitors that careened into her condo, initially mistaking her for the perpetrator, him the victim. They hit them both with sedation darts. SecDiv settled the lawsuit with her, but she still eviscerated them in the press. She saw the headline again, of Tony making bail, of his hideously early release. Of his slap on the wrist. She saw him burst into flames, smelled his burning flesh, and the urge to cry and spit rose in her once again.

In the end, she didn't regret taking it all back into her mind; now she just had to figure out what to do with it. Tony's family could only afford a modest plot on the station, a warehouse-like building in Sector 5, where people were cremated and then put into drawers. They would shoot you into deep space as a solid rock, but that cost money.

No words were said. She found her mind strangely, comfortingly empty as she left the Sector 5 Public Cremation and Cemetery Services building. Empty, that was what she had wanted from Paxton, from the drugs, from the jam-packed schedule that never let her so much as peek at her past or her thoughts. She was finding empty a different way now. It only worked some of the time, but that was all right. Outside, beneath a glittering pink holographic tree, Senna and Han waited for her. Han wanted to go see real trees in the university district, so that was their next stop.

"Ready to go?" Senna asked. She was in her same shapeless sack dress, this one candy red. No matter how Zurri pushed, the girl never seemed to outgrow the sartorial finesse of a circus clown. It was hard to rib her too hard when she carried around the probable fragment of a black hole in her tote bag. They hadn't yet figured out what to do with the Vestige, but they were working on it. Zurri had a feeling it would be hard, very hard, for Senna to let it go. Without it, without Glen or Efren or the Vestige or whatever one wanted to call it, they would have wound up trapped on Ganymede forever. It had set them free, but only after it had taken from them.

Zurri didn't see it as the benevolent force Senna did. She didn't like the way her mind seemed always to bend toward it.

"I'm ready," Zurri said. "Trees next?"

"Hell yeah, trees!" Han shouted, handing her the Mega Slurp he had been holding on to for her. He fell back into whatever game he was playing on his VIT as soon as custody of the almighty Slurp was relinquished. A little AR corgi, shabby and blinking constantly in and out of existence, trotted along beside him. A gift from Han's brother. It glitched just as Zurri glanced at it.

Senna fell into step with her, silent for a while. Perfect, virtual cherry blossoms drifted through the air, fizzling out, an AR trick, as Zurri reached up to catch one. They fell like a gentle pink snow, collecting in drifts that scattered and disappeared whenever someone happened by. More would come, and more would be scattered, and for a little while it made a very pretty picture.

"Are you all right?" Senna asked, clutching the tote bag with the Vestige close to her hip.

"No," Zurri said, smiling faintly. "But I will be."

ACKNOWLEDGMENTS

I would first and foremost like to thank Anne Sowards for pushing me hard on this project, even when it was a tough ask. I'd also like to acknowledge her patience and generosity throughout the process of realizing *Reclaimed*. To my agent, Kate McKean, thank you for remaining my rock during one of the toughest years of my publishing and personal life. I must also acknowledge the research and work of Priyamvada Natarajan, whose work on supermassive black holes inspired many aspects of this book. Thanks to Marcella Waugh and Alex Cautley for their consulting and research assistance. And finally, I want to acknowledge the hard work and dedication of the entire team at Ace—without their support, guidance, and artistry, this piece would not have been possible.

Photo by Colin O

Madeleine Roux is the *New York Times* bestselling author of the Asylum series, which has sold in eleven countries worldwide, and whose first book was named a Kids' Indie Next List pick. She is also the author of the House of Furies series and has made contributions to Star Wars, World of Warcraft and Dungeons & Dragons. A graduate of the Beloit College writing program, Madeleine now lives with her beloved dogs in Seattle, Washington.

CONNECT ONLINE

Madeleine-Roux.com
🐦 Authoroux

Ready to find
your next great read?

Let us help.

Visit prh.com/nextread

Penguin
Random
House